"Relatable and inspiring. A perfect rea[...] of life's 'what's next?' moments."

—ROBYN HARDING, author of *Chronicles of a Midlife Crisis*

KELLY MILLS JOHNSON IS A 39-YEAR-OLD WIFE AND MOTHER STUCK in the rut of her suburban life. A happy but routine relationship with her lawyer husband, two uber-successful businesswomen for best friends to envy, and an all-around predictable existence as a mom of two who's lost her passion collide—motivating Kelly to devise an ambitious and oftentimes humorous midlife makeover plan. Is Kelly brave enough to take the painful but necessary steps toward her own reinvention before it's too late?

With hilarity, endearing gusto, and charm, Kelly begins diving into new projects (armed with Post-it notes and a Things to Change list), revisiting old memories and rediscovering passions. Whether she is taking care of the anorexic teenager dumped on her doorstep, making amends with an old high school friend, or trying to avoid the boozy advances of her divorced neighbor, Kelly's insistence and panache at moving her life in a new direction and finding the perfect blend of home and career is both inspiring and entertaining.

As the realities of her midlife crisis come crashing down, Kelly works to repair the damages she's inflicted; realizes how deeply her husband, Patrick, truly understands and loves her; and ultimately grows into a woman empowered by her own reinvention.

Readers of *Here, Home, Hope* will be rooting for Kelly and ready to transition into something new in their own lives.

PRAISE FOR *HERE, HOME, HOPE*

"Reading Kaira Rouda is like getting together with one of your best friends—fun, fast, and full of great advice! *Here, Home, Hope* sparkles with humor and heart."

—CLAIRE COOK, bestselling author of *Must Love Dogs* and *Best Staged Plans*

"I loved Kaira Rouda's book. I love its irony and its courage and humor. . . . It's the real thing."

—JACQUELYN MITCHARD, bestselling author of *Still Summer* and *The Deep End of the Ocean*

"Endearingly honest, consistently upbeat, *Here, Home, Hope* is an inspiring read that left me feeling genuinely hopeful."

—JENNA BLUM, *New York Times* bestselling author of *Those Who Save Us* and *The Stormchasers* and one of Oprah's Thirty Favorite Women Writers

"Witty and uplifting, *Here, Home, Hope* is a charming debut that explores the courage it takes to reshape life and how to do it with a dash of panache."

—BETH HOFFMAN, *New York Times* bestselling author of *Saving CeeCee Honeycutt*

"If you've ever felt your own life contained a list of Things to Change (and whose hasn't?), then you will fall in love with Kelly Johnson. This funny, moving novel is a model of inspiration and reinvention for anyone seeking to find what's next in life."

—KATRINA KITTLE, author of *The Blessings of the Animals* and *The Kindness of Strangers*

"A warm, witty, and engaging debut that had me laughing out loud. Rouda has created a lovable and perceptive heroine who navigates her struggles with honesty and awe-inspiring determination to succeed. A fun and totally satisfying read."

—AMY HATVANY, author of *Best Kept Secret*

"A wonderfully warm read about finding happiness in yourself, Kaira Rouda's debut novel skillfully portrays the triumph of self-belief over society's threatening elements."

—TALLI ROLAND, author of *The Hating Game*

"A must read for anyone who's had their own midlife crisis, *Here, Home, Hope* reminds us that it's never too late to reinvent ourselves."

—LIZ FENTON, author of *I'll Have Who She's Having* and creator of *Chick Lit Is* Not *Dead*

"Things to Change (T2C): Make more time to read—starting with Kaira Rouda's *Here, Home, Hope*, a story about how women can have it all if we own it all."

—KELLY MEYER, mom, philanthropist, and one of O Magazine's Power List personalities

"I found Kaira Rouda's debut novel . . . inspiring, empowering, and fun to read. You'll want to share it with the women you care about in your life."

—ROMA DOWNEY, actress/producer

"An engaging read with something to offer every woman—married, single, widowed, or divorced. I couldn't put it down."

—JACKLYN ZEMAN, actress, nurse Bobbie on *General Hospital*

"Delightful, insightful, and spot-on inspiring! Immensely enjoyable read!"

—MARLA PENNINGTON, actress

"Kaira Rouda's voice is . . . full of humor, angst, and vitality. She does a wonderful job capturing the emotional journey that marriage and motherhood thrust upon us and encourages us all to find ways to enjoy the ride with grace and humility. *Here, Home, Hope* is full of hilarity and crackling insights into our modern culture. A must read for all women!"

—LAURA ZAHN ROSENTHAL, PH.D., Mayor Pro Tem, Malibu, California

"Inspiring and challenging, *Here, Home, Hope* is the story of Kelly, a suburban mom drowning in middle-age angst. Her struggles and ultimate success inspire us to step out of our comfort zone and live like there's no tomorrow."

—ANDREA CAMBERN, News Anchor, WBNS-TV

HERE, HOME, HOPE

HERE, HOME, HOPE

A NOVEL

KAIRA ROUDA

BOOK GROUP PRESS

Published by Greenleaf Book Group Press
Austin, Texas
www.gbgpress.com

Distributed by Greenleaf Book Group LLC
For ordering information or special discounts for bulk purchases, please contact Greenleaf Book Group LLC at PO Box 91869, Austin, TX 78709, 512.891.6100.

Design and composition by Greenleaf Book Group LLC and Alex Head
Cover design by Greenleaf Book Group LLC

Publisher's Cataloging-In-Publication Data
(Prepared by The Donohue Group, Inc.)
Rouda, Kaira Sturdivant, 1963-
    Here, home, hope : a novel / Kaira Rouda.—1st ed.
    p. ; cm.
    ISBN: 978-1-60832-091-2
    1. Middle-aged women—United States—Fiction. 2. Conduct of life—Fiction. 3. Self-realization—Fiction. I. Title.
PS3618.O8694 H47 2011
813/.6   2010940189

4619 3610 6/11

Part of the Tree Neutral® program, which offsets the number of trees consumed in the production and printing of this book by taking proactive steps, such as planting trees in direct proportion to the number of trees used: www.treeneutral.com

TreeNeutral

Printed in the United States of America on acid-free paper
11 12 13 14 10 9 8 7 6 5 4 3 2 1

First Edition

To Harley
For everything

PART 1: HERE

1

HERE'S HOW I KNEW SOMETHING ABOUT MY LIFE HAD to change.

I was sitting in the dentist's chair, waiting for the topical numbing goo to take effect on my gum so the dentist could jab a needle into the same spot. My only choice for entertainment was to stare at the light blue walls surrounding me or flip through the channels available on the television suspended on the sea of blue. I chose the latter and discovered an infomercial: Learn to preach in Spanish. The sincere narrator promised to tell me how many souls needed saving, and what an impact I could have, after I took their course, of course.

Maybe this was the answer to the problem I couldn't name, the cause of the sadness I felt just under the surface of my life? I could become a successful Spanish missionary. I stared at the screen transfixed until Dr. Bane appeared to administer the shot of Novocain.

Unfortunately, I missed the rest of the infomercial as my tooth's issues took center stage.

I was at my dentist's office because, overachiever that I

am—even when it comes to grinding my teeth—I had ground down through a thick plastic mouth guard and cracked a tooth. This, I knew, was not healthy, but it was simply a fact of my life. Or was, up until that moment when I knew something had to change. Which, as I said, was just a moment ago.

At age thirty-nine, just, and dreading forty, I have one gray eyebrow hair that angrily grows back when tweezed, two adorable boys—a teen named David and a tween named Sean—and a husband named Patrick. I also have two loyal and trusty steeds: my dog, Oreo, and my car, Doug. I am in the middle of life. In a suburb in the middle of America. And I cracked a tooth because I am too busy being restless in my subconscious—"chewing things over," as Dr. Bane put it. And whatever that busy subconscious had been doing at night, during the day it was drawn to infomercials about preaching in Spanish even though I'm not particularly religious and I don't speak Spanish. I'm a mess, actually, but I have to say, especially compared to some of my neighbors, I'm lucky.

On the misery scale, far beyond tooth-grinding people like me were the people who were unhappy. And then there were the truly miserable like my neighbors the Thompsons. Heidi Thompson departed yesterday to I don't know where, the tires of her black Lexus sedan screeching as she reversed out of her driveway. She fell in line behind the three moving vans that had showed up at her house as I was taking a shower and left fully loaded before I headed out to run errands. Heidi's kids seem not to have made it either on any of the vans or in her car, though it appears that the family dog did make the cut. Heidi's husband—well, soon to be ex-husband—Bob was sitting alone on the front lawn of his empty, furniture-less house this afternoon when I left for the dentist. That was miserable.

So at least I know I'm not Thompson miserable. I am just in

the middle. Middling. Muddling. I've looked ahead and thought, wow, there are so many things I want to do. I've looked behind and felt proud of what I've accomplished, especially how my kids have turned out so far. After Patrick and I married and I got pregnant with baby boy number one, I gladly gave up my job as an account executive at a public relations firm. Sure, I had loved my friends at work and the creativity at the office, but I knew I wanted to be a stay-at-home mom. And Patrick's career path at the law firm has been remarkably smooth. It's worked out as planned, and he's a partner now.

We have a wonderful standard of living based on Patrick's success, my sons are reasonably independent these days, and everyone is healthy. We're doing well. So what's the problem? I feel stuck between what I've done and what I want to do. There was a time when every moment of my day revolved around my kids and their needs, but not anymore. And that's the question I need to wrestle with, the cause of the restlessness: What's next?

The thought of reentry into the PR field is daunting. Regardless of how much progress women have made—and we've come a long way, baby—stepping back into that world after a long hiatus would mean, if I were lucky, a job behind the receptionist—literally behind her, filing. Actually, interns hold those jobs, not somebody like me. And maybe there isn't even filing anymore? It could all be digital, paperless. So obviously, that field isn't it.

I'd once dreamed, in my most private of dreams, of being a television reporter. I think it's time to finally cross that one off. That whole high-definition television isn't flattering, even to the twelve-year-olds who anchor the local news every night.

Other women found answers. A friend of mine started her successful restaurant while raising four kids after her divorce.

Another friend of a friend makes healthy meals and delivers them to busy working moms' houses in time for heating and serving. Who am I kidding? I get overwhelmed cooking for just the four of us.

I attended a luncheon last week featuring jewelry made by women in Kenya. The beautiful woman in charge of the program spoke passionately about how our purchases will make a difference in these burgeoning jewelry designer's lives. How was I going to make a difference, though, aside from buying jewelry made by a woman in Kenya? In fact I am, at this moment, wearing a gold ring with an elephant carved into the center. The artisan who made it did so with care. Looking at it now, I could almost cry because of its simplicity and beauty. I hope I helped the artist's life in a small way; but what can I do to help mine?

I can't feel my chin. That's disturbing in and of itself, but what's most disturbing is the fact that my two sons will arrive home from camp at the end of the summer and ask me what I've been doing. They're busy sailing, shooting things, fishing, climbing mountains, swimming, building campfires, and eating really unhealthy food. Me? I've been stewing, thinking, pondering, grinding my teeth, and supporting other people's passions, as well as eating really unhealthy food. Patrick says I'm using carbs and my summertime spending sprees—elephant ring included—to replace the comfort of kissing the boys good night, driving them to practice, and basically caring for them.

After seventeen years of marriage, I'm not about to admit he might be right.

Each summer David and Sean are gone, I manage to pack on at least six pounds, not an insignificant amount of weight on a 5'5" frame. I also tend to indulge in shopping sprees that fill my closet with assorted clothes and accessories I don't need. A check of my closet right now would already reveal a few hangtags. I rationalize that if I keep the tags on, I can always take the clothes back.

The weight is harder to return, though. This summer I've already gained two pounds, and we have another six weeks to go before I get my babies back. They—whoever "they" are—say that once you hit the big 4-0, you gain up to ten pounds a decade just doing what you've always been doing. At that rate, plus the annual camp pounds, I'm headed for obesity land, or maybe just the Deep South. Today's paper claimed that Mississippi, Alabama, and Louisiana have the highest rates of obesity in the states. Perhaps I'll find my future there?

Drool just made its way to the crease below my chin. Maybe it's a crease between my double chins? Here's the thing: too much time on my hands is making me care about small things and lose sight of the big ones. Ever since I opened that seemingly innocuous letter on December 15 last year, I've been torn between trying to be happy in the moment and focusing on my future. I guess that's what happens when you get a wake-up call.

Mine came in the form of a letter from my doctor instructing me I needed a diagnostic mammogram. And that I should schedule it right away. Two things I've learned since: Don't have your screening mammogram right before Christmas. Waiting for results during the holiday season was hell. And the second? I am so lucky. After a double needle biopsy; after stitches for the one site that wouldn't close, just below my nipple; after waiting for four days including the weekend before Christmas; after Googling and finding everything tragic and horrible about ductal cancer; after crying on my couch and trying to be brave; and after the call came telling me that all was benign, I was fine.

I know I need to do something for me that's outside my comfort zone, just like my boys are doing while they're at camp. Sean, for instance, left for camp sure he'd conquer waterskiing this year, and that was his biggest fear. What's mine? What am I going to tackle? A friend of mine just climbed Mt. Everest, for the fourth time. But that's not my dream: I hate heights—and cold weather.

My New Year's resolution was to seize my year. I'd been given a gift: a cancer-free breast. But here I sit, six months into the year, with drool working its way under the blue paper shield around my neck and tracing a line down between my breasts. Maybe I could invent a better dental drape?

Maybe I need a nap.

I never sleep well during my boys' summer absence. Last night was no exception and I'd had a horrible dream. Not only had my one gray eyebrow hair turned into two gray bristly hedges above my eyes, my face was covered in wrinkles. Not just crow's feet, not just laugh lines, but full-out, you-didn't-wear-sunscreen (I hadn't) and you-used-mirrors-to-tan (I had) weathered lines that looked like crevasses.

It was a sign. I need to take charge of my life, take advantage of the sense of urgency I'd felt when I thought I'd had breast cancer. While I want to grow old gracefully and happily, and I want to be a grandmother and enjoy slow walks on the beach, between now and then I need to get moving. Seize my year.

Fortunately I've just invested in the latest sonic skin scrubber—like an electric toothbrush for your face—and it's guaranteed to keep those wrinkles at bay. At least I think that's what the saleswoman at Sephora promised. Or did she say it simply helps the lotion sink into the wrinkles better?

I'm a salesperson's dream. Even a suggestive selling novice can make me buy. Just ask the Sephora saleswoman. She'd even talked me into buying the latest blush, called Orgasm. Everybody had one, she said. I bought two.

Hey, maybe I could work retail. I could talk women into Orgasms. I could convince other women like me that the key to happiness was the next wrinkle filler, scrubber, zapper, blush. I could wear a black apron and learn how to paint on makeup in just the right way to make it appear as if you weren't wearing any makeup at all. And, since the new look is "dewy" instead of matte—according to my sonic scrubber saleslady—I would tell women to toss their old facial products and start all over. I could do that!

No I couldn't. I'd have to work for someone else and pretend to care deeply about makeup. I'd have to go to the mall, thereby being in close proximity to all the things I didn't need but would buy if given the right push. "We'll need to give you two bags!" the Sephora Siren had gushed with a big smile while tossing in a couple of free samples and my shiny new frequent buyer membership card.

"Okay, Kelly, that's all for today. We'll need a follow up in two weeks, and the bottom guard will be ready then too," said the perky dental assistant.

My head was back and my eyes were closed. Maybe she was talking so loudly to try to wake me up. A quick image flashes across my mind: I envision myself climbing into bed each evening, top and bottom teeth covered in plastic. Patrick gives up even trying to kiss me good night. I just clack my guards together as a sign of affection, like a seal slapping her front flippers. At least my face will be smooth and sonically scrubbed.

As the dental assistant elevated me back to a sitting position, I tried to feel my lips. Nope. Chin? Nope. Could I learn to preach in Spanish? Nope. Could I start a restaurant? Could I go back to the PR firm? Could I move to Kenya? Could I sell sonic face scrubbers? Nope. Nope. Nope. And nope. I headed toward the door and friendly, helpful Susie sitting at Dr. Bane's front desk asked when I would be free to come back.

"Really, I'm free anytime," I slurred, sounding and feeling pathetic.

"I'll call you when the appliance arrives," Susie chirped back happily.

You'd think I'd ordered a new refrigerator; that's how happy she sounded.

2

I CROSSED THE PARKING LOT, MY NUMB LIPS AND CHEEKS JIG-gling with each step, and started to relax once I'd settled inside the safety of my SUV. He's named Doug after his license plate, DUG847. I know it's an odd habit, but I don't particularly like cars; I view them as sort of a necessary suburban evil. Personifying the steel box helps me form a bond with it. Before Doug, I had Q. I still miss him a bit.

I pushed the button to crank up the air conditioning and took a moment to look at my droopy mouth in the rearview mirror. Suddenly someone tapped on my window and I jumped, causing drool to escape from both corners of my mouth. It was Rachel White, my omnipresent nemesis. My very own personal Gladys Kravitz. I wished I could twitch my nose and make her disappear like Samantha could in *Bewitched*. In terms of elementary school mom-to-mom combat, she was the general. No matter what task I, or anyone else for that matter, volunteered for, she would double-check, redo, or simply do it better herself. Rachel had one daughter: Amy, poor child. Amy and Sean seemed to always land in the same class each year, much to my dismay.

"Mrs. White is here more than the teachers," Sean once remarked. "She needs to get a life." Of course I scolded my observant, brilliant little boy. But really, she was out of control. Not only did Rachel volunteer for every committee, field trip and party, she also micromanaged Amy's homework and projects. One of my personal favorites was when Sean and Amy were in third grade. It was biography month. Each child selected a person to study, then at the end of the month, dressed as the person and did a presentation for the class and assembled parents. Sean picked astronaut John Glenn. This was a brilliant selection, I decided, not least because David had trick-or-treated as a milkman, so we had the white get-up already. For his "visual," Sean made a rocket ship out of Legos. We were set.

On presentation day, all the moms (and a smattering of dads) attended Third Grade Biography Day. When I arrived twenty minutes early, the front three rows were already taken. In Grandville, we parents modeled overachievement for our tykes starting at an early age. Little Amy had selected Priscilla Presley, and wore disturbingly provocative low-rise bell-bottom jeans, a midriff-baring yellow polyester shirt, and dangling hoop earrings. Her project was an amazing to-scale replica of Graceland, plus peanut butter and banana sandwiches for all. The audience murmured in appreciation for the child-bride re-creation. Sean told me later that all the kids knew Amy didn't make her project and that she didn't even know who Priscilla Presley was. Rachel sat beaming in the front row, projecting her love for her daughter—and Elvis—for all to see.

"How are you?" Rachel asked, looking into my eyes. She herself wore wire frame glasses with lenses so thick she appeared to be able to see into your soul. She also resembled an owl—an odd, meddling owl—as she poked her head inside my car. "You Ain't Nothing but a Hound Dog" played in my head as Rachel continued.

"Are the boys at camp already? How hard it must be for you to be all alone all summer. I just love my little girl too much to send her away."

"Yes, the boys are at camp. Great to see you, too, Rachel," I slurred. "Gosh, look at the time. I have to run." I reached down and popped Doug into reverse, but when I looked back up, Rachel hadn't moved.

"Did you hear about Heidi? Scandalous, huh? Just up and left. So much for the Thompsons' summer. We're going to the beach, of course, and then, well, I'm just spending every second with Amy. I can't believe we'll be sending the kids to middle school, can you? No more elementary school. I'm really going to miss that place."

She seemed genuinely hoping to engage me in a conversation. It wouldn't work. I willed myself to find an ounce of kindness, of sympathy. After all, I was finished with elementary school, too. Maybe I should be misty, reminiscing? Maybe I should feel sorry for Rachel, realizing how much time she would have on her hands now?

"I really do have to go," I said, wiping the drool from my chin on the sleeve of my white blouse and waving as I backed out of the parking space. I looked in the rearview mirror and she had turned toward the door to Dr. Bane's office.

3

TEARS HAD FORMED AT THE CORNERS OF MY EYES. SURE, I couldn't feel most of my mouth, and Dr. Bane was charging me an arm and a leg to fix a tooth and add another retainer. Yes, I missed the boys, and Rachel's insensitive statements about camp stung. But why did I feel sorry for myself? I was blessed. I had an opportunity to create my future. Starting this fall, both boys would be in middle school, enjoying a mostly mom-free zone. I'd have nothing but time. Tears began working their way down my cheeks, clinging to the frame of my sunglasses. I shook my head, blinking quickly, willing them to dry up.

Think happy thoughts, I told myself. Maybe there was a reality show I could sign up for; one that helped middle-aged women figure out what was next? I could go on *America's Got Talent*. Sharon Osbourne would smile, knowing we were reinvention kindred spirits. But what talent would I perform before someone pressed the big X and kicked me off the stage? I could grind through plastic mouth guards? I could make a great vegetarian lasagna? Aside from tooth grinding and my mom's lasagna recipe, there really wasn't anything I'd perfected in quite a while.

I could be the car whisperer, I thought, patting Doug's dashboard. Especially in big cities like L.A. or Atlanta where people sit in their cars for hours a day, wouldn't it be nice if people could learn to have a special connection with their cars? I would bring Doug onstage and demonstrate our teamwork. We could make YouTube videos about the secret life of cars. Maybe we wouldn't get millions of hits like Susan Boyle, but we could still wow them with our act. I'd buy a gold sequin dress to match Doug's paint job.

At the stop sign, I pulled off my latest pair of drugstore sunglasses and dried the rims on my pant leg. I was drooling, but my blue eyes weren't even red from my mini-breakdown. Heck, not even a mascara smudge. I had stemmed the flow soon enough. My wavy blonde hair was comforting in its humidity-filled predictability.

Ever since the biopsy, I've been misty. The other day I even welled up at a cereal commercial when the mom and son hugged over a heaping bowl of cornflakes. I can't seem to shake an underlying—something. Maybe I just need a Reese's Peanut Butter Cup. Even a miniature will do.

"No," I said out loud to myself and Doug. Somebody honked behind me, so I stepped on the gas, causing all of the random items nestled on the dashboard to fly into my lap, including my nighttime driving glasses, the shiny penny David gave me for good luck just before he left for camp, and a business card the radiologist handed me after the needle biopsy procedure.

The card is for a shrink. "Well," the radiologist equivocated, "Dr. Weiskopf is a counselor," but we both knew what he'd meant. I suppose he had sensed my tension and panic before I'd even started to lie down on the table—probably because I'd hyperventilated and they'd had to give me a brown lunch bag to breathe into.

That was before we knew it was nothing. Still, it had turned out to be nothing, so why would I call the shrink now?

I placed the lucky penny, my prescription glasses for driving at night, and Dr. Weiskopf's business card back on Doug's dashboard, popped my sunglasses back on, and decided my best course of action was to focus on someone else's misery. Bob Thompson came to mind. A little investigating might be in order. If Heidi really had departed for good, what would her family do? A drive-by reconnaissance might provide answers. To appear as if driving by the Thompsons' house was on my way, I had to circle back and approach my house from the opposite direction. Being directionally challenged even after living in Grandville my entire life, it took me five extra minutes to get to the bottom of the curved road leading up the hill first to the Thompsons' house on the right and then a bit farther up the street to mine, on the left.

My friend and neighbor Charlotte was pushing a For Sale sign into the grass in the exact spot where I'd seen Bob Thompson sitting just a few hours earlier. I waved at her and tried to smile through my still-deadened lips. I pulled into the opening of my driveway, parked Doug haphazardly, and headed straight over for the scoop.

4

"YOU LOOK AWFUL!" CHARLOTTE SCREECHED AS I CROSSED the street. The high-pitched cheerleader voice of her youth was endearing at normal octaves, but it became nails on a chalkboard when thrown across the street at me.

"Thanks," I slurred, and then reluctantly acknowledged for the gazillionth time what everyone does: my friend Charlotte is a beautiful woman. So beautiful, to be exact, that the city, state, and nation have made it official: Miss Grandville, Miss Ohio, and fourth runner-up in the Miss America pageant. Kind of made you sick. She could perform on *America's Got Talent*, no doubt about it. Somehow, she was able to switch her screech-like voice into a thing of beauty when singing Whitney Houston's "Saving All My Love for You" during pageants. She'd had the judges mesmerized during swimsuit competitions. Howie Mandel would be putty in her hands.

"I didn't mean that how it sounded," she said giving me a quick hug before turning back to the For Sale sign she was shoving into the ground. "Gotta make sure I don't hit the sprinkler system line. That's always a bad omen. But really, what is wrong with your face?"

"Dentist. I hate dentists. All of them."

"Thank God. I thought maybe you'd had a stroke," Charlotte said, handing me a hammer. "I'm sure you'll be better in a few hours." She was obviously unaware that I was about to hit her with the hammer.

Charlotte is only three years younger than me, but from her looks it could be fifteen years. Why did I befriend this perky brunette in the first place? Oh, right, she's my sister's friend, and I adopted her when Sally moved away. It was a moment of weakness that has turned into a friendship for life.

Charlotte was one of those girls who, upon entering high school, was automatically the "it" girl. Her status never faded. In fact, when I'd heard some of my friends discussing the new freshman class and "that girl" I knew they were talking about Charlotte. Her life seemed, to me and all of us closely watching her from afar, to be a dream. She wore the right clothes, had the perfect hair, smiled and laughed at the right times. Somehow, Charlotte even did the *Flashdance* trend well. She, of course, dated only the most popular seniors until she became one herself. By then, I was at Ohio State University, but I'd spot Sally and Charlotte down on High Street, barhopping with fake IDs, flirting with the cutest undergraduate guys. Invading my school, my space. I'd ignore them or talk my friends into leaving and going to a different bar.

It seems that in the end, though, I could run but I couldn't hide. Charlotte eventually won me over with her charming personality and loyal friendship. Although, just as my relationship with Sally has its ups and downs, mine with Charlotte does, too. I mean, as much as I try to squelch it, that green envy monster still pops up, especially during neighborhood get-togethers when she makes her entrance. All the men on the block stop whatever it is they are doing and ignore whoever it is they are talking to whenever Charlotte walks into a room. Even Patrick gets sucked into her vortex, although I've kicked, pinched, and glared at him on numerous occasions. Once he even told me Charlotte was "a force of nature" and he was "powerless in her wake." That one comment escalated into a fight and got him a night in the guest room. I mean, how couldn't it?

But as I thought about his remark that night and since, I realized it isn't Charlotte's fault. I can't hate her because she's beautiful, as the line goes, but I can control how she makes me feel about myself. Or, I can try harder. It seems to me the culture of the suburbs is to put down anybody who appears to have more than you do: more money, more looks, more talent—more whatever. Not that everybody participates, but it's an underlying pulse of the community. I've been trying to rise above it and ignore the snarks. But—well, it's hard. Especially when your chins are encrusted in dried drool.

And now, despite the real estate slump, Charlotte even has a listing. Some real estate agents who have been in the business for decades don't have a single yard sign up around town. I thought Charlotte was just dabbling in real estate as a part-time hobby. I tried to think happy thoughts as I growled under my breath.

"There, it's official," Charlotte said, stepping back to admire her handiwork. The gleaming Coldwell Banker sign featured her name right below the familiar blue and white logo. "Hold on, I've got to get the rider for the top of the sign!"

There I stood, holding a hammer in front of the Thompsons' suddenly empty house as Charlotte's twin daughters—Abigail and

Alexandra—bounded around the corner of the garage. Each girl had her mom's spunky attitude and good looks boiled down to third-grade size.

"Aunt Kelly!" they squealed simultaneously as I quickly dropped my weapon and bent down for the warm onslaught of the girls. They smelled like chlorine and sweet suburban grass, and their skin had the warm Mediterranean glow of their mother's.

"We've been playing on the zip line in back! It's sooo fun!" Alexandra informed me. "Your mouth looks funny!"

Charlotte returned with the sign rider reading "Make an Offer."

"Okay, I've been patient, but you've got to give me the scoop," I said while keeping an eye on the twins, who were showing off their latest gymnastics routine on the front lawn.

"Great!" I yelled to the girls through my now-tingling cheeks.

"Well, as you probably know, Heidi had one of her usual fits. She threatened for the two-hundredth time to leave him, and Bob told her to go. So she did. Bob called me and said he feels better than he has in years and that he was ready to move on. And move. That's it. I got the listing!"

"Wow!" I yelled to the twins. "What do you mean 'that's it'?" I said to Charlotte.

"You're right; there is more to the story, but I am really not at liberty to discuss that, Kelly," she said, all businesslike. Then she smiled and leaned in closer. "Okay, well, according to the gossip—and you should know all of this better than me since you live across the street—Bob was having an affair. But really, do you blame him? Heidi wasn't really nice to anyone, even at the school. Her youngest is just a year older than the twins, and she would never even smile at me." Right on cue, we both turned and clapped for the twins' synchronized cartwheels.

"I hardly think not smiling at someone she doesn't know is a sign of meanness," I slurred. I was hot and starting to get a headache; Charlotte hadn't broken a sweat. Had I put on sunscreen under my new, dewy makeup? Did my Orgasm have sunscreen? If not, last year's thousand bucks' worth of Obagi treatments were down the tubes faster than you could say sunspots. And as for Bob's affair? I was sure rumors would fly that Charlotte was the other woman. That was inevitable with her sign in the yard.

"Kelly, it's against code. Everyone smiles and says hi to the other moms at school. That's the way it's done," Charlotte said, leaning her perfect frame against the sign. If she stayed in that position too long, someone would definitely make an offer, though not on the house.

I've often wondered, given her natural ability to draw people—especially men—to her, why Charlotte had married Jim. Jim Joseph was a nice guy, but really, the only thing remarkable about him that I could ascertain was that he had two alliterative first names as his moniker. They'd met when Charlotte was a freshman and Jim was a senior in high school. But as soon as Jim left for Ohio State, Charlotte's attention was drawn elsewhere. When my sister and Charlotte departed for college three years later—both on lacrosse scholarships to Duke—naturally I figured they would each marry a southern gentleman and be sipping mint juleps somewhere on a plantation or the modern equivalent for the rest of their lives. That was how Sally's future played out, but Charlotte had come back home to Grandville, and back home, eventually, to Jim.

"Let's go over to my house," I said, changing the subject. "The girls can play with Oreo—who is probably crossing his legs about now, since I haven't let him out for awhile—and we can cool off. Are you finished here?"

"Yep, this is all I need to do right now, but I'm coming back later and doing a little digging in the garden. Burying a St. Christopher statue in the yard is the traditional real estate good luck strategy. I decided to take it a step further. I Googled patron saints and came up with a pair. St. Barbara protects against fires, explosions, lightning, storms, impenitence, and death by artillery. She's the saint of architects, builders, and carpenters," Charlotte said. "I'm putting her and Christopher in the garden over there. They can work as a team. He can handle the floods, hailstorms, lightning, sudden death, bad dreams, epilepsy, and toothache."

Maybe I could bury a St. Christopher in my garden to protect my teeth?

"It's hard enough to sell perfectly beautiful homes in this market," Charlotte explained. "It's going to be even tougher to sell this house without furniture, but I'm going to try. And with Heidi's scandalous departure hanging over the place, it is sort of a stigmatized property. Of course, not as bad as a murder or ghosts or anything."

"Well, yes, that's looking on the positive side."

"You know me, I've always loved a challenge," Charlotte said. "Girls, let's go to Aunt Kelly's!"

5

"YOU KNOW, KELLY, YOU REALLY DO HAVE EXQUISITE taste," Charlotte remarked as she walked through my kitchen door, acting as if she hadn't been here a million times before this moment. Perhaps compared to the empty house for sale across the street where a family was being ripped apart, any house would look exquisite. It was still a home, after all.

A home in Grandville to be exact: a beautiful community of twenty thousand people otherwise known satirically as Uppityville or Upper Wonderful because most of the town sits on a hill. Mature trees, winding streets with sidewalks, good schools, and European revival style homes were everywhere. We're all lucky here, at least in terms of lifestyle—the fortunate few. Yet holding onto this position, this luck, causes restless nights and many arguments behind closed doors. Some of us are drawn to misfortune like moths to a flame: one of my neighbors calls herself a disaster whore. If something bad happens—a car accident, a robbery—she is the first on the scene, the first in the know. In our suburban collective subconscious, others' misfortune makes our fortune feel more secure. That's why I was so interested in Bob and Heidi's implosion, I suppose.

"Maybe you should become an interior decorator?" Charlotte suggested as she walked around my kitchen and the adjoining great room. She picked up a picture frame holding a portrait of the four of us taken a couple years ago in our backyard. I'd forced all the males in the family to wear emerald green shirts; even Oreo had a green collar on for the occasion. It wasn't a good choice, considering the grassy backdrop. We looked like we'd fallen into Oz. "You could do it, you know!"

Patrick and I had lived in a series of houses since we married seventeen years ago. I was in charge of the decorating and the life inside the home. Patrick, as an attorney and business guy, was in charge of the finances, the mortgage, and the like. Truly, we were a 1950s couple in that respect, although my lack of financial savvy sometimes bothered me.

I still had our community college's fall semester catalog open on my desk in the kitchen, as a matter of fact. I'd marked a class called "Becoming Your Family's CFO." I would make it a goal to understand finances better and then take over for Patrick. It sounded like a good idea at the time, but I hadn't signed up yet. Maybe I'd call as soon as Charlotte and the girls left.

"Thanks for the compliment, Charlotte, but that still doesn't make up for the stroke comment." I pulled the cork out of a semi-classy bottle of chardonnay. "Actually, I have been thinking about going back to work in some way. I know I couldn't break back into the public relations world after sitting out these past fifteen years, but something part-time could be just what I need. Or maybe I'll take a class?"

"That's how I got into real estate," Charlotte said. "I just sort of decided to do it. I went to real estate school and really liked it. My timing could have been a little better, though. I got my license right before the housing bubble burst."

Charlotte had decided to go for it, to try something new. And she was becoming successful. Maybe I'd been over-thinking, over-chewing things for too long. Maybe I needed to do something. I would start a list of things to change. It would be the first step on the road to self-fulfillment, or at least to doing instead of just thinking. Number One on my list: capitalize on decorating prowess. Number Two: minimize visits to the dentist. Number Three: buy a Suze Orman book/take a class at community college to understand more about our finances and worry less. Change was in the air for me; maybe I did have talent. I was feeling energized, and the feeling was coming back in my mouth. All in all, the day was ending much better than it started.

We decided to celebrate Charlotte's new listing outside on my porch, my favorite place in the house. I was in charge of carrying the wine and the two glasses. I needed some pain relief now that the Novocain had worn off. It was five o'clock somewhere, as the saying went. As we headed through the living room and outside, Charlotte yelled up to the twins who were playing upstairs with my beloved, unconditional love-filled mutt, Oreo, whom I still call my puppy even though he turned nine in February.

"Are you sure the girls are OKAY up there?" Charlotte asked. "They won't mess up any of the boys' game settings or anything, will they?" It was a good point. The boys guarded their video games and the levels achieved like buried treasure.

"Well, if anything happens, I'll play innocent. It will give them something to work on when they're home from camp and bored," I said leading Charlotte to my favorite couch, made of wicker and sporting thick cushions for comfort. Here we could sit and over-look my little slice of paradise. I was proud of my flower garden this year, especially my periwinkle-blue hydrangeas in full bloom.

"So, how much are you working, Charlotte? It seems like the real estate gig is more than just a part-time deal for you these days."

"It's more than part-time, that's for sure. This listing—the Thompsons' house—was just lucky. Bob and I have known each other for a while, and he used to play tennis with Jim once a week. It's my highest priced listing. I have a couple others on the fruit streets," Charlotte said, referring to the traditional starter home streets in Grandville that all have names like Peach, Pear, and Cherry. "This is my first in the uppity, most wonderful side of town," she added, winking at me.

"Please. You live a block away," I said.

"Yes, I do consider my house part of the uppity," she laughed. "It keeps me calmer as I've watched our real estate values plummet in the last couple of years."

"Is that why your sign says, 'Make an Offer'?"

"Yes, well, Bob needs money quick. He's hoping to settle with Heidi and move on. He knows he'll take a bath, but the way he's looking at it, he can grab another house at a fraction of what it would've sold for a couple of years ago. It's a wash that way," Charlotte said, filling up our wine glasses.

I looked across the yard, noticed the sun was drooping a little, and realized this was the first time I'd stopped and watched the sunset since June 12, Drop-Off Day at camp in Maine. After helping our sons unpack their trunks and move into their lodges, and after much hugging, Patrick and I had climbed back into the rental car, me with tears in my eyes and Patrick looking away so I wouldn't see the tears in his. Every year, the night of Drop-Off Day, we stayed at a rustic lodge just down a winding dirt road from them. The lodge overlooks Webb Lake, the same lake the camp borders. On the balcony where we sat, we could hear the dinner bell ringing, the sound of laughter, and the campers yelling to each other. Beyond the lake, the mountains were beginning to turn purple and magenta at the start of another spectacular sunset, marking the start of another camp season for them and another long summer for me. Looking out over my backyard, I smiled, thinking of my boys and how much fun they were having.

"What about Bob's kids?" I asked.

"He's keeping them, for now. Actually, they're staying at Bob's mom's house."

"Oh, my. That's a handful," I said, and Charlotte nodded. Both of Bob's teenage boys had what can only be described as a bad reputation, complete with suburban rap sheets for underage drinking, pot smoking, pranks, and more.

"What're ya gonna do?" Charlotte asked, and I suddenly noticed she'd taken over the slurring duty and I could actually feel my top lip as I took a sip.

"Let me go get us a snack and some water," I said. Wine on an empty stomach was never a good idea. Given Charlotte's birdlike frame, she might topple over if she drank any more. Come to think about it, I hadn't had much to eat today either. "When was the last time you ate, Charlotte? Last week? You're a toothpick—well, comparatively speaking."

"Food sounds great. Yeah, I don't eat when I'm stressed. Always been that way."

I remembered that, and wondered what was going on. I hoped she wasn't on the path to her too-thin phase again.

"What's up? Do you need to talk?" I stood up and put my hand on her shoulder. Our relationship was close, but we'd always kept a little distance. I guess it's because she was my sister's friend first. And even though Charlotte and Sally don't talk much anymore, I'm still a bit guarded. I don't want Sally knowing anything about me that I haven't told her myself. Ergo, Charlotte probably doesn't share all with me, either. Maybe she was having trouble with Jim?

"No, I'm fine. Great, actually," Charlotte answered, gazing out at my yard instead of making eye contact with me. "How are the boys, by the way? Don't you just miss them to death? I could never send my girls away. You're brave."

I felt the tears well up, and I shook my head to push them down as I hurried inside. The telephone started to ring. My home phone never rings unless it's someone selling something. I almost didn't answer, but then I recognized a few digits of the number. I used my gruff, salesperson-hating voice as a precaution, though, just in case.

"Kelly! Oh my gosh, so glad I got you," said a woman in a rushed, shaky voice.

"Kathryn? What's up? Are you okay?" No fooling my friend Kathryn with my fake telesalesperson off-putting voice; we'd known each other since Ohio State. Back then she was a fun-loving, although driven, small-town girl with dimples and long, auburn hair. Now she was a stunningly glamorous, high-powered businesswoman. Not to mention being the mother of a stunning daughter and the wife of a stunning man. And usually too busy to talk to me unless it's a dinner we plan in order to get caught up.

"Everything is fine, but, well . . ."

"Kathryn, talk to me," I said, knowing she was crying. I looked down at my cell phone. I'd left it on the kitchen counter, and I saw three missed calls. I checked. All Kathryn. "Where are you?"

"In your driveway," she wailed. I dropped the phone on the counter and rushed outside.

6

"THIS IS SO EMBARRASSING," KATHRYN SOBBED, SITTING IN THE front seat of her car. I'd walked around and slipped into the passenger side. Her BMW smelled like new car and had so many electronic gadgets I felt like I was in a private jet. She could fly us out of here, right? Maybe that's what we both needed. I'd whisper that to her car, later.

"What's embarrassing? Crying? No, that's healthy. I just did it on the way home from the dentist," I said, not mentioning that I'd almost started to cry again just before she'd called.

"I wondered what was wrong with your face but didn't want to say anything." Kathryn blew her nose into a tissue she pulled from some secret compartment. Clearly, even in moments of distress, my friends and enemies alike noticed the puffy left cheek where the tooth repair had occurred. I am a lopsided chipmunk, I thought. I hate dentists.

"How about coming inside for a glass of wine, to relax and talk?" I ignored her face comment; she was my friend, after all. I made a mental note to get her back later.

Kathryn and I had clicked instantly as newly minted Kappa

Alpha Theta sisters. Standing together on the front yard of the sorority, we'd both chugged the obligatory shot of tequila. Then, much to the horror of many of the other new pledges, we each had another. Not that our friendship required alcohol, but it certainly cemented it back in those days.

"Is anyone else around? I don't want Patrick to see me like this," Kathryn said, sliding her oversized, bejeweled Bulgari sunglasses down her nose to look in the mirror of the driver's-side visor. "Argh."

"Patrick's golfing, and he'll be hitting the stag bar at the country club after that, so it's just me and Charlotte. Come on in."

"Charlotte??"

I knew what she was thinking. It's hard to be around Charlotte even when looking your best. After a crying jag or dental procedures, it was a true ego setback. It was akin to my experience at an exclusive spa where Patrick had taken me in March. He knew I'd needed a break and surprised me with the weekend trip. While receiving our couple's massage, my masseuse leaned forward and asked if she could ask a personal question. "Sure," I whispered.

"Are you pregnant?" she murmured.

"No," I said, my relaxed mood instantly replaced by angered tension.

"Oh, you looked like it in your robe," she said.

Grrrr. I'd almost bounded up and out of there, but Patrick appeared to be enjoying his massage so much, I just stuck my face back into the headrest and tuned her out.

"Look, I handled Charlotte with my mouth looking like this. You can do it. Besides, you look beautiful in that dress—Prada, right? It shows off your figure. So what if your eyes are red and puffy? Just keep your sunglasses on."

Just then it struck me that I should practice what I'd just preached. This mini-lecture should go on my life-change list. Number Four: don't compare yourself to others. I wasn't convinced I could hold myself to this one, though, so I was reluctant to assign it a number.

As we walked in the back door, Charlotte was busy arranging a great-looking cheese plate and making some macaroni and cheese from a box for Abigail and Alexandra. It looked like dinner would be at my house tonight, and that idea made me smile. I didn't realize how lonely I'd been. When did I forget about the literal care and feeding of friends? Somewhere between driving to soccer and football practice, overseeing homework, and sitting through guitar lessons, I suppose. Life-change list Number Five: Don't forget the care and feeding of friends. I needed to start writing these down.

"We have another guest for our cocktail party," I announced in a chipper voice as Charlotte looked up and smiled at Kathryn.

"Hi there," Charlotte said, intent on cutting the cheese—literally, not figuratively. "It's been so long; you're like, never in the burb, are you?"

At that, Kathryn choked up again and hightailed it for the powder room, walking impressively well in three-inch Manolos. I can spot 'em, but I can't walk in them.

Charlotte and I stood in my kitchen looking at each other while the macaroni water boiled over on my stove, leaving that signature white film over everything.

"Oops, let me get that," Charlotte said, and wiped up the mess. She served up two plastic bowls for the girls and then headed upstairs. I took the moment to locate a pack of yellow Post-it notes. My life-change list would materialize here and now. "Things to Change," I wrote at the top. Too long. "T2C," I wrote on the second note, and smiled when I realized my boys would be proud of me; this was like my own special text message code. I hurried and wrote numbers one through three and number five, each on its own T2C Post-it. (I couldn't quite commit to writing Number Four just yet.) I hid them under the community college catalog. I wasn't ready to advertise my change.

Next, I rummaged in my non-kid-friendly refrigerator for something other than cheese and chocolate to feed my friends. I guess it wasn't really an adult-friendly refrigerator either. With the boys at camp, I didn't grocery shop. Two reasons: avoidance of the judging acquaintances who would ask if the boys were away again for the entire summer, and the misplaced hope that without a stocked pantry and refrigerator, I'd manage to not gain the yearly six camp pounds. It never worked, neither the avoidance of judging folks—they were everywhere—nor the food plan. Food was everywhere too.

After managing to retrieve a chorizo and a summer sausage from my cold vegetable drawer and checking their impossibly far-into-the-future expiration dates, I set forth to complement the cheese plate with salted and cured meat. Whenever I feel bad, bacon calls me. Well, actually, bacon calls me when I'm happy, too, but I knew Kathryn needed some feel-good meat.

"I'm a mess," Kathryn said, walking slowly back into my kitchen right on cue, her shoes dangling from her left hand.

"Come here," I said, draping an arm around the shoulder of my suddenly three-inch shorter friend. "Let's go out on the porch. It's relaxing and I've made a plate of our favorite comfort foods."

"Thanks, Kelly. I'm a wreck. And now, along with everything else, I'm really worried about Melanie." Kathryn settled into a chair on the porch and looked at my hydrangeas. "She's stopped eating. The school counselor called me to report that Melanie has been kicked off the volleyball team because she showed up too weak to practice. I just don't understand what is happening. She's always been my perfect girl, my little star."

"Is Melanie anorexic? I haven't seen her in so long. She's fifteen now, right?"

"Right. Fifteen and weighs about a hundred pounds. If she doesn't start eating again we're going to need to admit her to an in-patient facility. At least that's what the pediatrician says. I just don't know what to do. We've been to family counseling, she's been to counseling. Nothing is working. She's killing herself." Kathryn took a sip of her chardonnay and then released a huge sob.

My image of Melanie was the happy kid I'd always known. Since she'd begun high school last year, I hadn't seen much of her—or her mom. I missed them both.

"Bruce is no help," Kathryn said. "He's gone most every week, all week. You'd think with the growth of his company, he could send the people who work for him on location, but no, he always goes. He likes to be away. And I think I like it that he's away. Actually, we aren't doing well." Kathryn sobbed, drank more chardonnay, and ate some cured meat.

I grabbed a big piece of the summer sausage, chewing it slowly so I couldn't say anything. I agreed that it would be better for everyone if Bruce stayed away. I hadn't liked him from the moment Kathryn brought him to our sorority house the night of their first date, and the feeling has stayed with me no matter how hard I've tried to shake it. Even while I was standing up as maid of honor in their wedding, I kept expecting him to run from the altar in some dramatic, last-minute escape and thus prove himself to be the fraud he was. It didn't happen then, but maybe it had now.

"I hate to even tell you anything about Bruce, since you never liked him," Kathryn said. Drink. Sob. Meat. Cheese.

I tried not to flinch at having my mind read. "That is not true," I mumbled. "I just love you and want to keep him on his toes. Heck, he's your husband and you're a treasured friend." But he was probably cheating on her, I thought.

Bruce was as close as we got to celebrity in Grandville. His television production company started as a one-man operation and had grown into the largest one in the Midwest, with divisions handling trade shows, TV, and even movie production across North America and even in Europe. He always made sure to name-drop upon returning from one of his shoots, thus earning spots at important dinner parties and photo ops with mayors and chamber of commerce folks. Grandville, the heart of sophistication and your connection to the stars . . . as long as Bruce Majors was in the room. Yes, he even had a cheesy celebrity name. I'd never been sure his name was real, either.

"Maybe if I hadn't been a working mother, this wouldn't be happening," she said. "I don't know. I'm just not sure what to do." Sob. Cheese. Wine. Meat.

"Wait a minute, Kathryn. You're my hero. Trailblazer. Woman in business who's made it to the top. And you've been a great mom. It's the quality time, not the quantity; you always told me that and you're right. Your job is your passion and you're great at it. You're a great role model for Mel. You're a great role model for me," I said, taking another piece of sausage to comfort myself at the news that Kathryn was doubting herself, her choices.

Kathryn's spectacular career was at least as impressive as Bruce's. She'd started after college as a regional manager for the fastest growing chain of women's clothing stores in the country. The chain kept growing and Kathryn kept being promoted. Described in the *New York Times* Style section as "one of the brightest, most fashion-forward creative directors of a major chain" when she was in her late twenties, Kathryn was the chain's first female vice president by age thirty-five. Six months ago, when we'd had dinner, she shared her expectation that she'd make president by the fall. She hadn't mentioned any trouble at home back then.

I marveled about our collective ability as women to keep all the pain hidden, just below the surface. In Grandville, and I suspected many places just like it, real emotions were locked behind closed doors. They weren't on display at the country club, never on the tennis court or at bridge or bunko. They weren't revealed during book club and especially never at PTA meetings. The façade of everything being fine, just fine, was as thick and hard to crack as the shiny white veneers covering our teeth. But it shouldn't be this way with a person's closest friends.

Why didn't I know Kathryn was distraught? For that matter, why haven't I been aware that Charlotte's business was booming? My self-absorption seems to have reached dangerously high levels since the Christmas cancer scare. Just last month, for example, the city magazine's lead feature story had an unoriginal headline declaring Kathryn Majors "a major force to be reckoned with." She was a fashion industry rock star, but I hadn't found the time to call and congratulate her on the story. Perhaps jealousy kept me from doing so, but I think more likely it was pure self-centeredness. Between making sure the kids and Patrick are happy and that I'm there for them, putting on my supermom cape whenever necessary, I haven't really been available for my friends. I guess I'm lucky to still have them. I could fix the situation, too. If I could figure out what was bothering me, I could be a better friend to both of them. And maybe I can open up to them about what I've been dealing with.

"Hey ladies, sorry to interrupt," Charlotte said coming out onto the porch with the twins in tow. Oreo jumped onto my lap in a clear sign of his superiority and my lack of discipline. He made a small whining sound and pointed his nose in the direction of the sausage. "The girls and I have to hit the road. I got a call to show the listing already. Someone read my name and number on the sign. It's really amazing. Signs are the number one way to get a home sold. Well, that and the Internet, but around here, signs are key. People drive around and look for deals! Bye, Kathryn, good to see you. I'm sorry we didn't get to catch up. Come on, girls!"

I got up to walk them out and each of the twins gave me a squeeze. "Are you alright, Charlotte?" I said, when I was sure we were out of Kathryn's hearing.

She seemed nervous, and once again she wouldn't make eye contact with me. "Kathryn needs both of us," I said.

"No, she needs you right now." She gave me a guilty glance, then looked away quickly. "Okay, maybe I stretched the truth a little bit just now. I do have a showing, but it's for tomorrow. But . . . I need to get the girls home and showered and in bed. And I haven't even celebrated the good news with the man in my life." She began hustling the twins across the yard toward her car.

"Tell Jim I said hi," I called after them, but she didn't seem to hear me.

7

BACK ON THE PORCH, KATHRYN SEEMED CALMER. BEFORE, SHE had been alternating between desperate and suicidal. Now she was settling for just miserable. She blew her nose. It sounded as loud as a foghorn.

"Let's start with Melanie. How can I help?" I asked.

"Maybe you could talk to her. The only other friends I have are women who work for me, and I can't let them know what's going on. Bruce is no help at all. I don't know who else to turn to. The problem is, Melanie won't talk to me. I make her all her favorite foods and she'll say she doesn't want any. She hates the counselor I found her." She pinched the corner off a piece of cheese and began rolling it into a tiny ball. "I spoke to an eating disorder clinic in Southern California and they had space, but I don't want to admit her to some program across the country. Maybe she'll open up to you."

Yeah, sure, I thought. Your middle-aged, slightly overweight college roommate seems like just the person a struggling teen would open up to! Well, I could give it a shot. Clearly this was more up my alley than, say, learning Spanish or selling cosmetics.

"Why me? Kathryn, I'm happy to do whatever I can, but—"

"Kelly, even though we haven't spent a lot of time together in the last few years, I still consider you my best friend in the world. My maid of honor, my other half of the hot dog bun." She smiled.

I smiled too. With another friend of ours, we'd dressed up as a hot dog for a college Halloween party. I ask you: how could anyone who could create a three-person hot dog costume not have a future in the fashion business?

"I don't have anyone else to turn to," she said. "I've made a career of being in charge, in control. That's how I've lived my life. But that comes with a big cost. My life seems glamorous, and it is at times, but often it's very lonely."

I reached out and put my hand on her arm. "I'll do everything I can to try to help. Just keep reminding yourself that Melanie doesn't hate you. She's a teenager. Maybe she's more troubled than some, but remember, we were there too. I could've killed my mom at times. It's hormones and pressure and, well, life."

"With her, it's more intense, though, especially recently," Kathryn said.

I just couldn't believe it. Kathryn and Melanie had always been so adorable together: dressing in matching mother-daughter clothes when Mel was young; vacationing in Chicago to shop at the American Girl store; flying to New York to see plays on Broadway. I always longed for a girl of my own when I'd hear their stories or see photos from their trips.

"How about I drop by tomorrow and visit her? Assuming she's home alone while you're at work. I need to head to Target and gather stuff to put together some care packages for the boys. Maybe she could help me out? What's she doing during the day? Would she be up for a run to Target?"

"Basically, she mopes all day. Now that she can't practice with the volleyball team, she just sits in her room and wastes time on her computer. She won't go to the pool; she won't call a friend. She does see her boyfriend, but I think that's because I don't like him. Oh, this is a mess," Kathryn said.

Feeling almost certain this should be on my Things to Change list—do not offer to care for a wayward teenager—I chose instead to say, "Look. I'm lonely. Bored. All I have to look forward to until I pick up the boys is the fitting of my lower bite plate. Let's give it a shot. Do you think Melanie would help me with the care packages? Maybe I can figure out some other things we could do together during the day. Camp Kelly will open its doors if you give the word. And, it'll give you the break you need. Deal?"

"Okay, it's worth a try," Kathryn said. She smiled at me. "What would I do without you?"

"You don't need to worry about that because I'm here—always will be."

"Thanks Kelly." She took a breath and seemed to relax. "But what should I do about Bruce?"

Tread lightly, I reminded myself. Anything you say about a best friend's spouse or boyfriend can and will be used against you should they stop fighting and profess undying love for one another once again. This is a fact on my Life Lesson list, which is an altogether different list from my T2C list. Life lessons are truths sometimes learned the hard way. "Let's not deal with him for the moment. Let's worry about Melanie and you. We'll focus on getting the Majors girls settled and then we'll figure out what Mr. Majors is up to."

And with that we went inside and called Melanie to tell her the exciting news that she and I would be spending some quality time together. We put the phone on speaker, and I thought I heard her perk up at the notion of my coming over. Or maybe it was the trek to Target. Or I could've been imagining it. Whatever it was, however, Kathryn was thankful. Perhaps Melanie's summer at Camp Kelly would be just fine after all.

As I watched Kathryn's car's retreating taillights, it struck me that I had just volunteered to help my best friend's troubled teenage girl. What was I thinking? Okay, I'd had two-and-a-half glasses of chardonnay, so I thought I was a superwoman with the answers to all life's problems. Yes, my friend was in need. But really, what did I know? I'm the mom of two boys, and they are entirely different animals.

8

PATRICK, UPON RETURNING FROM HIS DAY OF GOLF AND evening of cards, was too frisky and happy for me to tell him a teenage girl would be hanging around the house for awhile. So instead of spilling the beans, I took out my mouth guard and we had very sweet, married-with-children-who-aren't-home sex.

After he'd gone to sleep, I stayed up, trying to get back into the novel I'd been reading before he'd come home. Problem was, I wasn't paying attention to the words on the page. I was more focused on the fact that neither Charlotte nor Kathryn had asked how I was doing. How did I feel lately? What was going on with me? And, really, I guess I'd acted fine in front of them. But shouldn't they have asked? The care and feeding of friends is reciprocal, isn't it? Mutual asking, mutual sharing.

If someone had decided to ask me—with Patrick snoring loudly beside me—how I was doing, I would have burst into sobs. In fact, thinking about the subject brought tears to my eyes, so I turned out my light and closed them tight.

✻

The next morning, as Patrick poured his second cup of tar—he makes high-octane, coal-black coffee every morning and then drains almost the entire pot before I come down for a mug of my own—I announced the news.

"So, hey, before you leave, I just wanted to mention that Kathryn's daughter Melanie will be hanging around here for a few days. That's okay with you, right? I mean, last night was crazy, what with Charlotte actually having a real estate listing across the street and pounding her sign in where Bob had been sitting looking miserable, and then even though her real estate career is booming she looks really thin, so I think something is bothering her, but before I could find out, Kathryn just shows up and she's sobbing and I sliced some comfort meats and, well, she's still married to Bruce and I'm all that she's got, really, and she asked me to help so what else could I do, you know?"

I batted my eyelashes. Patrick didn't seem to be falling under my spell. Maybe I needed Latisse?

"Kelly, I'm not really sure what all that means," he said, not smiling.

"Well, okay. Kathryn needs our help. Her daughter, Melanie—"

"I remember Melanie," Patrick said, plopping his briefcase down in the middle of the island in my exquisitely decorated kitchen. "But I don't remember you having any sort of expertise in counseling a teenage girl. Besides, aren't you excited about the precious time we have together when our twelve- and fourteen-year-olds are away? I feel like we are being sucked into a drama, here, like *Law & Order: Suburbs*."

"Very funny. Do not bring my obsession into this discussion." So what if I'd watch *Law & Order* 24/7 if I could? Actually, come to think of it, with cable and my DVR, I could . . . Note to self for the Things to Change list. Number Six: Curtail time spent watching *Law & Order*. "Kathryn asked for my help. She is desperate. Melanie is sick; she's anorexic. This is what friends do. This is what we do. Thank you."

He is right, of course. I may have acted a bit impulsively, offering to hang out with a teenage girl who doesn't know or trust me. What have I gotten myself into? I only thought about helping Kathryn; I didn't think I'd be honking off Patrick in the process. I knew Patrick would come around, but maybe I hadn't handled things perfectly.

My jaw clenched, I circled the island, and walked into the hug he was heading my way to give me. Patrick smelled like coffeetar and his favorite aftershave, a bottle of something we'd picked up in St. Kitts on yet another one of his partners' awards trips. I couldn't wait for this fall's trip to Italy. For the last few years the annual trips had been to the Caribbean. They were taking it up a notch this year. We always had a great time together. Patrick still made my heart sing, and I knew he'd see the light about Melanie. It seemed impossible for him to sustain anger. At least, toward me.

"Honey, if it's this important to you, give it a try. I'm just pointing out that, as far as I know, you and I have zero experience with a troubled teenage girl, and we pray every night we won't have troubled teenage boys. But if we can help, we should," Patrick said.

His blue eyes sparkled as he looked down at me. At almost six feet tall, he is my knight in shining armor, the perfect fit for me. He was wearing my favorite shirt and tie combo: blue shirt with a blue-, white-, and yellow-striped tie. All in all, he's as good as it gets. My jaw relaxed.

"You are the best," I said. "Thanks for being a sport. For all I know, Melanie might refuse to see me, but I'd like to invite her over here to spend time on sort of a neutral ground in her life. I'm good with exchange students, you know. This is similar, like rent-a-teenager. I would be sad if I didn't even try."

"At least this one speaks English. Hey, this is reminding me of the Chilean exchange student I didn't know about and, oh, yeah, the French exchange student before that. They were great, just a little extra work around here." He chuckled. "I gotta go, Kelly. Good luck!"

Fortunately, he didn't mention the Chinese exchange student we almost hosted. Turned out that the program was during the summer, when the boys would be away at camp and thus not enriched. Truth be told, I love having kids around; I love a busy home. Pets and people—especially kids and teens—even if they're from foreign lands and I don't speak their language. I can always smile and make them feel welcome.

When Mathieu came from France, he spoke not a word of English except "Hello," and we all managed a mean "Bonjour!" which sounded exactly how Americans who don't know French pronounce it: Ban jer. Embarrassing. But the kid was a trooper, and smart too. Eric from Chile was shy, but very kind and always smiled. He laughed every time I tried to say good morning. But both were great for the boys to get to know. It was like having older brothers.

But . . . an anorexic American from a few blocks away . . . not so much. But still, maybe I am good with teenagers. Even if, or maybe especially if, I don't speak their language. Perhaps I could be an exchange student coordinator. Were there jobs like that? I'd add it to my Things to Change list. Number Seven: Consider employment with an exchange student organization.

With Patrick on his way to work, I turned to the fount of all knowledge: Google. What do I do with a teen who is anorexic? Why is she broken? How do I fix her? Judging by the 3,698,201 results located in my Google search, there was a lot to sort through.

Anorexia can be caused by family dysfunction and almost always affects females: one out of a hundred, and mostly those from higher socioeconomic backgrounds. Hello Grandville. Many anorexic girls come from high-achieving, high-pressure families. Or they are involved in sports or activities—modeling, for example—that require thinness. Many of these circumstances seem to fit Melanie's. Bruce and Kathryn aren't getting along, and that's dysfunctional. Both parents are high-performing overachievers who, consciously or not, have modeled that behavior for their daughter, and probably expect it from her. They're a wealthy family, and when I last saw her, Melanie had been fixated on *America's Next Top Model*.

After getting ready for my day, which included stressing over a neutral, cool outfit to wear and realizing I had none, I climbed into Doug, ready to head over to Kathryn's. Before I started the car, I spotted Dr. Weiskopf's card, which seemed to be glaring at me. "Oh, alright, it's now or never," I said out loud, thinking I could ask the good doctor about Mel. And then, before I could chicken out, I picked up the card and dialed the number.

Dr. Weiskopf could see me today, the helpful man who answered the phone explained. Well, this doctor was obviously no Dr. Phil if he had appointments available on such short notice, but I made an appointment anyway, for 2:00 pm, which would give me plenty of time to craft some amazing care packages with Melanie to ship to David and Sean.

Kathryn had called earlier and confirmed that Melanie would

still love to go to Target with me. I doubted the love part, but as I pulled up in their driveway and before I could even open Doug's door, Melanie had sprung out through the front door of her house.

Maybe she was excited to spend time with me, or maybe, like any other fifteen-year-old who couldn't drive, she was simply excited to go somewhere, anywhere without her parents.

I got out of the car just as she reached for the handle, and we awkwardly waved across Doug's roof. Once inside the car again, I smiled at the beautiful young woman Melanie had become. Not knowing whether to attempt to hug her, I patted her hand instead. She was thin, no doubt about it, and her dark brown eyes were framed by dark brown hair like her mom's. She smiled at me.

Next thing I knew, she'd popped in a pair of earbuds and was fiddling with her cell phone. I backed Doug out of the driveway and turned toward Target, clueless as to how to start a conversation. So I didn't, until we turned into the parking lot.

"So, the boys really like getting cases of Coke in their care packages," I said, loudly.

"Okay," she answered, giving me a weird look as if to say I shouldn't be screaming at her.

"Do you babysit? Do you have any other ideas what the boys might like? David and Sean are fourteen and twelve now. You haven't seen them in a couple years, but David is really almost your age, so you'll know what he might like," I said, trying not to yell, but she still had the darn plugs in her ears.

"I don't babysit, and I'm almost sixteen," she said.

This was going to be one long trip to Target, I thought.

❋

But actually, it wasn't. I pulled out a cart, and so did Melanie. She smiled and then took a sharp right down the first aisle. I stood frozen by the cart corral, watching Melanie walk away—that is, until an irate woman with a screaming toddler barked "excuse me."

Yes, exactly. Excuse me. I zipped forward and caught up to Mel as she turned into the toothbrush/toothpaste aisle.

"Hey," I said, and clearly I'd surprised her. Good, I thought. Ditching me wasn't going to be that easy. "Glad you're in this aisle. I should send each of the boys a new toothbrush. David loves these battery-powered automatic ones, and I swear his teeth are the whitest in the family. Maybe I should get one myself." Why not, I thought? I could sonic my face and my teeth.

"Aunt Kelly, do you need me for anything?" Melanie asked, giving me a hand-on-hip attitude like nobody's business.

"As a matter of fact, I do," I said, shooting attitude back at her, while noticing a faint burning in my eye. Oh nuts. No tears. I shook my head and said, "Yes, I need you to help me pick out things for the boys. For camp. Can you help?"

"Yeah, just give me a sec, okay? Where are you going to be? I'll be right over."

"Electronics," I said, feeling banished to Siberia by the tiny teen. "Hurry," I added, clearly asserting my superiority.

"Whatever," she mumbled as I rolled away.

She did join me, though, and gave me her opinion on different gift ideas: lame, lame, sick (good?), lame, fine. We hit the camping aisle where there were always new gadgets and gizmos to send to the boys. My favorite so far this season had been a tiny clip-on camping lantern. David had requested a new sleeping bag, and Melanie picked one out that I assumed she deemed not lame.

After a swing down the various food aisles—picking up Coke, candy, beef jerky—we were ready to head out.

"So, how about you come over to my house and we can pack all of this up?" I asked in my most friendly Kelly Johnson/Carol Brady voice.

"I really need to get back," Melanie said in her best imitation of a bored and hostile teenager. Well, actually, I think she was a bored and hostile teenager.

"Okay, I just figured since both of us were kinda hanging around the house, we could hang out together. That's all," I said.

"Yeah, I know that's what you and my mom think. I'll just hang out with you and life will be all better. It's not gonna work that way," she said. We'd rolled up to checkout lane 14. It reminded me of one of my most miserable summer jobs: checkout for Gold Circle, a much less glamorous, low-end version of Target. I wore a red polyester apron. It was long before scanners, so we had to key in each SKU. Big fun. Maybe that's what Mel needed. A job. That could teach her how boring things could really be.

"So, maybe you could get a job. I saw that the library is hiring. That would be fun. Or Graeter's? I know they hire a lot of teens for the summer. Scooping ice cream would rock—ah, be great," I said. David told me to promise never to say anything rocked; I was too old.

Melanie looked at me like she wanted to punch me and said, "Maybe you should get a job."

We rode back to her house in silence. She had her earphones in, but I wasn't sure who or what she was listening to. I kept my grip tight on Doug's steering wheel, repeating to myself, "I will not cry." I didn't. Not in front of Melanie, at least. I saved my angry tears until later.

9

LATER, ACTUALLY, WAS ALMOST AS SOON AS DR. WEISKOPF SAT down and asked me how I was doing. I'd been relieved to discover that the doctor was a woman, and I was charmed that she had a male assistant who answered the phones. Her office was in a discreet location: a small townhome tucked into the back of a commercial office complex. I could park right in front of her door and dash in. Nobody in Grandville would be the wiser.

"More tissues?" she asked, patiently, smiling a half smile and looking quite motherly. She was wearing a long purple flowing dress and sensible clog-like shoes. She'd wrapped a multicolored scarf around her neck, and her hair was an inch long all over, and completely gray. She was my new idol. T2C #4, about not comparing myself to others, flashed through my mind. Maybe she was who I wanted to be later? There, that was better.

I nodded yes, and she handed me the tissue box.

"Kelly, why don't we talk a little bit about why you decided to come see me?"

I told her about getting her card during the biopsy. I told her everything was fine then, as well as at my three-month follow-up.

And then I told her how even the smallest things were making me cry.

"And, the strangest part is that I can't even talk about the big things. Not with anyone. Not that they ask," I said. What I didn't add, however, was that if they did ask I wouldn't know what to say.

"Kelly, it's very common to start to reexamine your life purpose after a scare like you've had. It brings up all types of questions about why you are here, your time on earth, what you still long to do, unfulfilled dreams and the like," she said. "The key, and I believe you already know this and that's why you're here, is not to push these things down. Not to hide from the fact that these questions are coming to the surface for you. Moreover, it's quite common to feel depressed. Have you ever suffered from depression?"

"I . . . I'm not sure." There had been a time in my life when I had felt this lost. Just after college graduation, before starting my job, starting my life, I had felt alone. It was before Patrick and I married, and, well, I was sad. "Maybe."

"For women who've had previous depressive episodes, it's quite common for depression to show up again at major life incidents. Your cancer scare and turning an age that you tell me is a milestone to you, are major life incidents," she explained.

"So what do I do?"

"What you are doing. I think it's wonderful that you are making a Things to Change list. And reaching out to help your friend's daughter is a great gesture. We always help ourselves when we give to others. Coming to see me was a big step forward, and I'm so glad you had the courage to take it.

"I'm also going to give you a prescription for an antidepressant. It will take a couple of weeks to build up in your system. It will help even out your mood swings, and hopefully dry up those tears, until you don't need it any longer.

"I like to explain depression like this. Imagine your brain as a bathtub, and it's usually filled all the way to the top with endorphins. In a depressed person, the brain alone can fill the bathtub only halfway. With medicine, the brain is then able to fill the bathtub all the way to the top. The medicine will help you continuously fill the tub back up until you can do it yourself."

"Okay, I think I understand, but what do I do with myself?" I asked.

"I'd like you to see me again in two weeks. And I'd like you to keep making your T2C list. It's a great idea. And remember, Kelly, it's not just a fun list to make. These are all items you will need to put into practice, to act upon, in order to achieve results and truly change your life. It's quite common for a death scare to cause a thoughtful woman to reevaluate her life and the people in it. You want to have a bigger purpose, to feel more real. You need to be sure you get beyond thinking about things, however, and actually make some change. That's the key." And then our time was up.

I felt better. I'd talked to someone who didn't know me, or anything about me, for the first time in my life, and I felt better. Maybe I wouldn't need the pills, I thought, but maybe I would. I'd fill the prescription anyway. Back home, I decided to call Kathryn's work number.

"Thank you so much," she said, the instant her assistant put the call through.

"Ah, for what?"

"Melanie had a great time with you and can't wait to hang out again tomorrow!"

Maybe I had picked up the wrong child? No, I knew Kathryn's house. I'd had the right girl.

"Hmm, well, alright. Maybe we could go to the library or something. I noticed that they're hiring teens for some part-time summer hours. Do you think Mel would enjoy getting a job?"

"Oh no. I work enough for both of us. I just want her to relax, to enjoy her summer, to get to know you better, and to get well."

Alrighty then. "Okay, I'll pick her up again at ten o'clock tomorrow. We'll do something fun."

"Thanks so much, Kelly. You can't imagine how much this means to me," she said, and hung up.

I'd decided Melanie could not out-snark or outwit me. Heck, I'd been a teenage girl at one point; I could do this. I was prepared for battle. We'd go grocery shopping, come back to my house, cook a big pan of lasagna, and deliver it to the homeless shelter downtown.

"Cute necklace," I said to Melanie as she climbed into Doug. She had been ready and waiting for me on the front steps. It was as if she was eager to see me, but then as soon as she did, she'd clam up and retreat.

"Thanks. Got it at Target," she said and then gave me a look. We both knew she hadn't bought anything at Target the day before. I'd specifically asked if she had needed anything, and she'd demurred. Her cart had remained empty the entire trip. "Last week," she added quickly.

I didn't believe her, but I didn't press. Not now. "So, we're going to go get some groceries and then make a casserole to take down to the shelter. Sound okay?"

"Sure," she said, and popped in her earbuds.

"Ah, Melanie, could you talk to me, you know, instead of putting those in? Please?" I asked in my sweetest Kelly Mills Johnson/ Shirley Jones Partridge voice.

She pulled them out and stared straight ahead. I made a mental note to take my first happy pill when I got back home. "Come on, Get Happy," the Partridge Family sang in my head.

"So, your mom says you have a boyfriend."

"Uh-huh."

"What's his name?"

"Gavin."

"How long have you been going out? Is it serious?"

"Um, I don't know?"

"I'm not your mom, you can tell me," I said. We were stopped at a traffic light and I was staring at my lucky penny. "I can't wait until David has his first girlfriend."

She looked at me for a few seconds. "Actually, he's great. He's the only person who gets me."

Well, that was something. Every woman (and man, for that matter) needed somebody to get her. Him. I wondered if Patrick still got me. He had me, but did he get me? Of course he did. Right? Focus on the teen, I reminded myself and said, "That's great. I'd love to meet him."

"Uh-huh." Melanie plugged the earphones back into her head.

Day by day, we were making progress—slow progress—Melanie and I. We actually had walked together through the grocery store.

I had been afraid she'd grab her own shopping cart again. Back home, when we made the casserole, she'd been a big help in the kitchen. We discovered that we both loved Starbucks—me, a soy latte, and her, the roast coffee of the day, black—and that we both hated our hair. Melanie's wouldn't hold a curl; mine wouldn't stay straight. We were bonding. Well, sort of. She was still text messaging like crazy, but she was no longer putting her headphones in to totally tune me out. Progress.

Tonight, after Patrick and I had grilled our meal and cleaned up together, the telephone rang. It was Kathryn. She thanked me again for the time I'd spent with Melanie, who reported she was having a great time with me. Kathryn had to make a business trip and she'd feel better if Melanie was not home alone. She'd convinced Bruce to agree to allow her to come stay with me since he'd be out of town a lot, too. I'd readily agreed. Why not? It was like having an exchange student from the country of Thin. Perhaps I could learn from her and show her some of the customs of the country of Fat.

We could do this, Melanie and I. I hoped Patrick would agree. I decided to wait until the morning to tell him. He was, after all, a morning person. I was feeling better after talking with Dr. Weiskopf. And I was taking my pills and making my lists. I'd be a new, improved Kelly in no time.

Telling Patrick I wanted to read for a little while downstairs, I headed to my desk in the kitchen, fired up my computer, and did some more research on anorexia. I found out that it leads to severe depressive disorders, or may be caused by them. Maybe Mel needed antidepressants too. And then I thought again about the outwardly perfect Majors family. That's the thing: you just never know what goes on behind closed doors. One out of eight households suffer from domestic violence—our society's code word for abuse and murder when the victim happens to be related to you—so as I looked out my window at the houses illuminated by the streetlights, I was looking into the windows of someone suffering in silence. Who knew how many anorexic girls and women populated the town of Grandville?

T2C #8: Remember all of my blessings. In fact, along that remembering line, I decided to make sure I'd written all of my ideas on Post-it notes and found out that so far I was caught up. I'd even written down #4: Don't compare yourself to others. Now I decided I needed to stick them around my kitchen and upstairs in my bedroom too. That way I was holding myself to them.

I'd put T2C #4 on Doug's dashboard (he shouldn't compare himself to others either) because out in the world was where the others I tended to compare myself to were most likely to appear.

10

IN THE MORNING, BEFORE ENJOYING MY FIRST CUP OF TAR OR mentioning to Patrick we would have another exchange student (sort of), I had a slight crisis. The gray stripe that appeared every three weeks or so had arrived on the top of my head and had marched, seemingly overnight, three inches down either side of my part. The hair at my temples was glistening with gray. Handling a perfectionist teenage anorexic with a gray stripe on my head would not be good. After all, I needed all the self-confidence I could muster.

I immediately called Thomas on his private line and told him an emergency blonding was required. He agreed to work me in at 9:30. That catastrophe avoided, I got ready and hoped Patrick would be out the door by the time I made it to the kitchen. He wasn't. But I decided instead of jumping into the "Melanie moving in" discussion, I'd keep it light for now. I had hair problems to deal with first.

"Don't forget the call with the boys today," I said sweetly.

"Of course not! It's the highlight of the week." He poured me a cup of tar. "I've got to run, honey, but I'll talk to you with the boys later."

Today, being a Wednesday, was camp telephone day. The boys would call at 2:10 and 2:20 respectively. This also meant that I would neurotically check my watch all day in the desperate need to know I wouldn't miss hearing their angelic voices.

Time to start thinking of witty questions for them. "What did you have for dinner?" wasn't good. "Camp food stinks," Sean would say. Then I'd ask, "What's your favorite activity this week?" "All of them," David would answer. And then, silence. Nope. Must maximize the conversation. Of course, Patrick would be on the call, too, helping to bring in some manly bantering. "Did you kill anything with your bare hands?" Then they'd all laugh. Men. Boys.

Doug and I, both committed to T2C #4, pulled into the salon parking lot at 9:25 am sharp. My cell phone rang. I grabbed it and dashed in the door, answering the call. The NO CELL PHONES sign on the front door glared at me just before the receptionist did.

"I can't talk now," I whispered to Charlotte, covering the phone and my mouth with my left hand and walking back outside. "I'll call you back. I'm having emergency gray stripe repair. Thomas, God love him, worked me in."

"Okay, but you have to call me back the minute you're through! I need your help and it could be really fun!" Charlotte chirped.

Sounded suspicious, I thought, as I changed into the plastic smock that would protect me from the hair chemicals I probably shouldn't be allowing on my scalp.

I had turned almost completely gray just after Sean was born, twelve years ago. I thought I'd just give in to nature and go gray then, thus saving a fortune on hair coloring and, perhaps, warding off brain cancer. But Patrick and Thomas both thought I was crazy, that I'd look old—so here I am.

Someday, I'll go gray. Perhaps I should say I am gray and I'll let it show. Someday. At this rate, however, that's not going to be until I'm about seventy-five. I have no guts; I must be a born follower. That was going to change, right now. Things to Change list Number Nine: Take charge of my hair. I was sick of being in here so often, even though I loved Thomas and his humor. I wanted to grow my hair out, and I wanted to lighten it up so the gray didn't show the next day. Then I could work my way slowly into Linda Evans hair. Ah, just the thought of her hair on *Dynasty* made me swoon—minus the poofiness, of course. Patrick will love Linda Evans hair; he just doesn't realize it.

"Thomas, let's go blonder, and no cut today," I said assertively. He gave me a look as though I were speaking the French I didn't learn from our exchange student.

"Not the Linda Evans thing again?" he said as he rolled his eyes.

"Yes, and since it's my hair and my gray, we're going to try it," I said. We were having a standoff, both of us staring at each other through the mirror. Even though Thomas stood behind me, he had pumped up my chair so we were almost at eye level.

"Fine. I guess I'll just have to fix it when you decide it's a molto tremendo mistake," he said and hustled to the back of the salon to mix my new color. I smiled. Change happens one step at a time. I was taking charge of my hair and that felt good.

As Thomas began to apply the poisonous lighter-blonde-to-be

goo to my scalp, and after he had asked about Patrick and the boys, I shifted the conversation.

"So, hey, do you know anybody who was or is anorexic?" I asked in my most innocent, off-the-cuff, confiding—though definitely not subtle—Kelly Johnson/Oprah Winfrey voice.

"What? Why? What a weird question. Do you need coffee?"

"No. I'm asking because a friend of mine has a daughter who's suffering from it and she's going to live with me—us—for awhile. I just thought maybe finding a woman who's been through it would be good. Clearly, I've never come close to starving to death." Instantly I made a mental note. T2C Number Ten: Keep self-deprecation to self, at night, while wearing both mouth guards.

"Hello? Beth, your friend? You referred her to me. She told me she had been anorexic. In high school, right?"

I should've thought of that myself. "Yes! Beth! You're right! How is she? I haven't seen her for years."

"She's healthy; her second marriage is a joke—he's gay, but she doesn't know it. I used to see him out at all the bars. But anyway, she's doing well. You should call her. You'll love what I've done with her hair."

"How can you not tell her that her husband is gay?" I asked, shocked. Equally shocking, which I admitted solely to myself, was how I could possibly call Beth and ask her to help me with Melanie after what I'd done to Beth in high school.

"Because, mio amore, some things people just need to figure out for themselves," Thomas said. "Oh, and since I let you pick the color, I'm going to demand that we try a little flat iron today. You know, Kelly, you're probably going to want a straightening treatment. It's costly, but so worth it. It'll tame this Midwestern frizz action subito."

I knew Thomas would have to assert himself after I did. That was okay. My bigger problem was getting up the nerve to call Beth, a friend I'd abandoned in her own time of need. I'd need to genuinely make amends before there was any hope of having her in my life again.

11

THREE HOURS AND $275 LATER, I HAD A NEW LOOK: LIGHTER
blonde, shoulder length, straight instead of my usual waves, and
a few bangs that hadn't graced my forehead since eighth grade.
Thomas said they would take six years off my face; I told him
they'd better because it would take six years to grow them back
out. As I pulled Doug out into the midday Grandville traffic, I
nodded to T2C #4 attached to the dash, smiled at my lucky penny,
and remembered to call Charlotte. I also remembered I now had
a reason to shop. I pointed my trusty steed in the direction of my
favorite boutique, Clothes the Loop.

My friend Jennifer, another of the female entrepreneurs I
knew, had created the business based on her great eye for fashion
and the strength of her personality. Even Kathryn admired the
shop's unique, high-end lines. Then Jennifer received a devastating
diagnosis of breast cancer, and an unfortunately too-familiar story
of courage unfolded.

Sitting there in my car, I shuddered as I thought about Jennifer's battle with the disease. My scare had been nothing in
comparison, and yet, I knew the black hole of fear that the mere

thought of receiving the diagnosis opened up in me. A hole I was still climbing out of, judging by my easy tears and lack of connection with my friends since Christmas.

But, I was getting better, while Jennifer was still fighting for her life.

I am so blessed. T2C #8—Remember my blessings—rang in my mind as I made my way toward the boutique. All of us in Grandville tried to shop here as often as we could afford to. Plus, selfishly, I had been working hard all week, entertaining an ultra-thin teenager and trying to staunch my tear ducts, so I deserved a little retail therapy.

I punched in Charlotte's number and wondered, again, why it was legal to dial and drive. It should not be for me.

"Thanks for finally calling me back! That was a long hair appointment," she said accusingly. "Look, here's the situation. I have six houses listed, no assistant, and I'm running myself ragged. I wondered if you would consider helping me. I'd pay you, of course, and we can talk about what you think is fair. Hold on—Stop it girls, or I'll take away TV rights for tonight. Sorry, Kelly. You know, maybe summer camp is a good idea. Anyway, the first project is Bob Thompson's house. I just can't show it the way it is. Okay?"

A paid job! Working with a friend. Perhaps this could be the answer to my life-changes list. I could earn money, thus become financially savvy (T2C #3); I would have a purpose during the day while the kids were at school, thereby having something to talk about when asked (#3); and I could tap into my design skills (#1). I'd never thought about the real estate arena, but many others had. Some, like Charlotte, had found great success. What would it feel like to have a paycheck again? The last paycheck I cashed was the day I took maternity leave and never went back.

"What, exactly, would you want me to do?" I asked as my heart thumped with excitement.

"It's called staging. I need you to make the house warm and inviting. Staging is like interior decorating, but the point is to get a home sold as quickly as possible. You could do this in your sleep!"

Maybe I could do it in my sleep, thereby saving my teeth from the incessant grinding and minimizing visits to dentist (T2C #2). "Let me think about it, Charlotte. I'm so flattered you asked, but I'm sort of worried about whether I'm truly qualified, as well as the whole working with a friend thing."

"No, it wouldn't be like that. You'll do your thing, I'll do mine. You bill me your hours. A piece of cake. Besides, it's so lonely being in business by myself," Charlotte said. "I work at an office filled with real estate agents, but each one of us is our own business, and there's really no team spirit at all. It's brutal competition, even if we're supposedly on the same side."

"That sounds tough," I agreed, pulling into a parking spot in front of Clothes the Loop. Charlotte's office—the one she was complaining about—was just down the street, but I didn't tell her I was nearby. Having my own money to shop with could be a very life-changing event. Guilt-free buying could be fabulous.

"It's brutal. Worse now, with the market the way it is. People are leaving the business and going into other fields. It's time for me to go for it, and then when the market comes back again, well, it'll be great. Jim just got laid off from his new job. All the more reason why the girls and I need to be able to take care of ourselves."

"I'm sorry, Charlotte. That's got to be tough on Jim," I said. Maybe that was what was bothering her, the topic she hadn't gotten around to telling me about the other evening.

"Yeah, it's tough on all of us. So, help me?"

"Okay, I'll think about it."

"Think fast. I have a really important showing in two days at the Thompsons' house. Out-of-town buyer. Thanks so much! You're the best!"

Did I just take a job? Jeez. All I did was decide my life had to change, and now it was, faster than I could've imagined. I'm a believer in tossing thoughts out into the universe; I just didn't know the answer would be tossed back so quickly, via cell phone. I needed a new dress.

Inside Clothes the Loop were the same saleswomen Jennifer hired when she was creating the store, a fiercely loyal group who had stayed on to support her business partner, Jacob, who now ran the boutique. He spotted me and started to head my way. I needed to put up my best anti–sales pressure front. Problem was, I didn't have one. The smallest suggestion and I would impulse-buy. I must've got it from my maternal grandma. My mom could with-stand all types of sales pressure, but I was a sitting duck.

"Kelly, darling, you haven't been here in ages," Jacob gushed, kissing me on both cheeks while giving me a big hug. "We have some of your favorite designers, just in for the summer."

Quack. Quack. "So good to see you," I said. "And how's Jennifer doing?"

"Not much change there, unfortunately," Jacob said quietly.

I was sure he was accustomed to the question, and that he wished he had something better to report.

"I'll tell her you were in and send your love. What can I help you find today?"

"Okay, here's what I need. An outfit or two to impress a fif-teen-year-old girl. I'm tragically unhip. Oh, and I may be going back to work, so something semi-professional looking." I looked at the beautiful and abundant clothing surrounding me. "Two outfits. Really. Don't let me get anymore than that or Patrick will kill me."

"He never has, never will. What exactly will you be doing in the working world?"

"You know, I was a great PR person in my day, but now I'm leaning toward something in the interior design arena. We'll see."

"Lots of competition in that field, but you do have great taste," Jacob said. "Head on up to the dressing room and I will pick out some—ah, two—outfits to show the teen you're a force to be reckoned with!" Jacob turned his attention to the racks while I worked my way through the small store and up the stairs, thinking yes, I do have exquisite taste.

At the top of the stairs stood Rachel White. I need to add her to my list, somehow. Ignore Rachel White. That's not very empowering, though, and I really don't want her name on my wall.

"Hi Rachel," I said, trying to get past her to the dressing room.

"Oh Kelly, so glad to run into you again so soon! Your mouth looks better," she said, putting her hand on my arm to trap me. "I've been meaning to call you. I know you're busy and all, but we really need to do a baby shower for Mrs. Faller this summer, and since you were the room parent in third grade, you should head it up."

Rachel's enormous wedding ring blinded me for a moment, the light reflecting off her owl eyeglasses. Some sort of primal force made me want to smack her.

"Unless you're too busy?" she said. "I suppose I could gather up some other folks to do it. Where are you going this fall, by the way? You know we all live vicariously through you, all of us stuck here in the bubble just taking care of our kids while you gallivant all over the globe."

Would it be bad form to punch her right here, in an upscale

boutique? If she bled, would she ruin the Oriental rug? Deep down, I decided, I am too nice to throw a punch, and besides, it would hurt. Me. I would indirectly add Rachel to my list after all. Number Eleven: Take self-defense classes. And remember Number Eight. Count my blessings. Here's one: I am blessed to not be Rachel White.

Instead of hitting Rachel, I simply glared and said, "Mrs. Faller's friends should give her a baby shower, not the parents of her third grade class from two years ago, don't you think?" Open-ended, yet firm.

My stomach was churning; I was starting to get an acidic taste in my mouth. I needed to eat lunch. It took a lot out of me to stand up to a militia mom. Especially the general. Maybe I was developing an ulcer? Was that the next step in depression and anxiety after grinding all my teeth away? Did ground teeth cause stomach ulcers—all that fluoride powder down the hatch?

Rachel tilted her head; the store's canned light danced off her Botox-perfected forehead and glinted off her glasses. "You don't have time and that's fine. It was quite obvious from the way you ran the Halloween party that these sorts of things aren't your forté. What a fiasco! A piñata? Really? Anyway, I'll handle the shower. I guess you're busy doing something since the boys are away? I mean, I would just miss Amy too much to ever do that to her."

Okay. It was getting brutal. If I knew an effective Brazilian capoeira move I'd throw one at her, but I hadn't even mastered the Brazilian Blowout. Under suburban attacks of this nature, I tended to slink into submission. Trapped just outside the dressing room, face to face with the enemy, I was a wimp. (Note to self: Really need T2C #11.)

"Of course I miss the kids while they're gone, but it gives

Patrick and me a chance to reconnect," I said, sharing far too much information and knowing it could be spun into a hundred stories of bad mothering and selfishness. What would Patrick say, I wondered, and then smiled. "Actually, Rachel, it's given us a chance to have some amazing sex. I brought the latest issue of Cosmopolitan to bed with us last night, and well, let me just say—"

"Oh my God," Rachel interrupted, as aghast as I hoped she'd be. "Really, Kelly? Sharing intimate details of your marriage?"

"My favorite article was all about more than one climax in a single sack session." It seems unbelievable that in the enlightened twenty-first century women still judge each other's choices and mock them, just like mean girls on the playground. When would it end? Not with Rachel, ever. She just brings out the worst in me, and I guess I bring out the venom in her.

"Aren't we both lucky to have solid marriages?" she said, her manicured hand resting on her chin. I hadn't shaken her with my sex talk, at least not for long. "Did you know Matt and Wendy are getting a divorce? He's been having an affair for years with his secretary. Wendy just found out. Isn't that sad?" Rachel tried to lean in and air-kiss my right cheek. "Don't worry, Kelly. I'll cover the shower somehow!"

I watched her perfect, Spanx-clad backside retreating as Jacob waved her good-bye and shoved me into the dressing room with a pile of clothes to try. Behind the curtain, finally alone, I pondered my question once again. Did we all simply have too much time on our hands, we Grandville stay-at-home moms? What about the other six million women who stay at home full time? Did all of us use our time to judge one another and feel fortunate, superior even, that we were the chosen ones, able to quit our jobs and be there for our kids? Of course, from the reactions I get, sending them to camp breaks the "being there" rule, at least according to many of the chosen ones. I wondered what the 74 million moms who work outside the home would think about these petty salvos. It was then that I knew I would take the job Charlotte offered. I would join the ranks of women some of my stay-at-home colleagues derogatorily called "weekend moms."

"Knock, knock," Jacob said as he threw open the curtain. His arms were bursting with more items on hangers.

"That is waaay more than two outfits, buster," I said.

"We want you to look great, Kelly. Take a deep breath. You know," he said, nodding in the direction Rachel had gone, "she never buys a thing. She just drops in, upsets people, and leaves. I'm not kidding. It happens at least three times a week."

"Ban her," I said, and pulled the curtain shut. I heard him chuckle, but knew he would do no such thing. Rachel was a potential customer, after all, who might buy something someday—maybe. And in this economy, maybe was good enough. I looked at the new items Jacob had brought me, loved four outfits, looked down at my watch, saw it was fifteen minutes to camp call time, and did what I always do: grabbed more than I needed and headed for the cash register. I'd look good, but I'd also feel guilty until Patrick got the bill. Then I'd just be in trouble. Working and making my own money was beginning to sound like a really good idea.

It was odd that I'd ended up this way: a vintage housewife living in a modern world. My mom had been a stay-at-home mom, a model of domestic perfection. Perfect house, perfect kids, perfect meals. And then poof! My dad ran off with a neighbor. We thought he spent so much time there because he liked her pool. And the next thing you know, Mom was falling apart. She'd been totally dependent on their relationship. And where had she ended up? At age forty-five she'd found herself looking for a job, with no applicable workforce skills and little alimony.

So why had I allowed myself to follow in her footsteps? I trust Patrick, of course, but what if he starts thinking his legal assistant is hot? What if his assistant is hot? Who is his assistant right now? Oh my God . . .

"Kelly, you didn't even show me one outfit. I bet the camel-colored dress looked divine," Jacob said, interrupting my mental frenzy but not my worry as he started to ring me up. I needed a paycheck, I needed a savings account. What if Patrick cut off my credit cards today?

"Kelly?"

"Oh, yes, I'll take the blue shirt and the white jeans, too, and well, I've got to get going," I said. I hadn't tried anything on, and I'd come bursting out of the dressing room like a crazy woman. I knew I looked flustered, but I had a job to start, a husband who may be in love with his assistant, and boys to talk to in Maine. And I would now have more items hanging in my closet with tags still dangling from them, but that couldn't be helped right now.

I needed to talk to Patrick, really talk to him. About the fact Melanie was moving in this evening and he didn't even know it yet. And when was I going to tell him about Charlotte's job offer? About Dr. Weiskopf? I wondered if that was my private business. Is it better to hide my insecurities from my husband? He knows I'm not superwoman; heck, he's seen my Post-its all over the place. But I want him to think I have things together. That I'm okay, that I don't need drugs to stop crying all the time.

I wonder why I want to keep my seeing Dr. Weiskopf private, to keep my antidepressant prescription private? I'll need to ask the doctor. Until then, I decided, I wouldn't say anything. Patrick had a whole life outside of our house that I knew very little about. I didn't even know his assistant's name, although I knew he'd hired a new one. His law firm was one world. His golf games and time spent in the stag room were another. And me, I just had the world inside our home. It was the world I'd chosen, a world I cherished. But now, with the kids spending less time at the house, it was time for me to, as well.

I had decided, like Michael Jackson sang in "Man in the Mirror," I was going to make that change.

I was back at home just in time for the highlight of my week.

"Mom, this is so cool!" Sean's voice—a bit squeaky, a lot loveable—said into the phone. "Guess what? Okay, so a guy in my cabin told me if I put my iPod earplugs in my nose and turned up the volume really loud, the song would come out my mouth when I opened it! And it worked. Close—no music. Open—rock concert!"

"Wow, that's great! I think. You always learn so much at camp."

"Aw, Mom, that's not all I'm learning. That was just during rest time. I'm also learning some bad jokes and—"

"Sean."

"Just kidding, Mom. Really. This traveling band came to camp and they let all the kids try an instrument and sing with them, and then we started our own group, and I was the lead singer and the lead guitar. It was cool!"

"That's great, champ," Patrick said, joining the call from his office downtown.

"Hi Dad! Guess what? I got sailor of the week, too!"

Sean's list of accomplishments would fill the ten-minute call. I don't know why I worried so much about having something to say. The most important thing was the listening. I pictured my youngest, scrawny still (his brother called him Twiglet), but so full of life and energy his presence filled the room. My heart ached to hold him.

"So, are you missing us?" I asked, needy person that I am.

"Yeah, of course, Mom, but don't try to talk me into leaving early. Oh, and can you send another care package? Please. I'm out of Skittles and Pringles."

"Such good health we're promoting by sending you that junk," Patrick said. "But I'm sure your mom would send a big care package your way in exchange for a letter home."

"Yeah, sure! I'll send you a copy of the poem I wrote, too!" Sean said.

"Wow, a poem, too. I might even throw in some Cow Tales! By the way, a care package is already on the way," I said.

"Thanks! Gotta go, guys! Love you!" And then, he was gone.

After failing to receive a call from our oldest child at the pre-arranged 2:20 pm, and waiting an excruciating ten minutes more, we called the camp. The receptionist said David was on a nature hike and asked if he could reschedule. So much for our place on David's list of priorities; we fell somewhere after nature hike and before—well, I'm not sure. Patrick tried to cheer me up before hanging up to head to a meeting. I forgot to ask about his assistant. Jeanne was her name, I suddenly remembered, but I had no idea what she looked like. I'd Google her pronto.

But first I went out to the garage, unloading my new clothes from Doug's trunk, and hurried upstairs to incorporate them into my closet in the summer-extra-weight section, tucking and hiding hangtags as I shoved the new clothes into place. I pushed the plastic garment bags and the decorative shopping bags into the bottom of their respective recycling bins. Patrick would never notice.

A quick glance at my closet satisfied me. It appeared as if the new clothes had been at home here all along.

PART 2: HOME

12

THAT EVENING, WHEN THE DOORBELL RANG, OREO AND I were ready. He was wearing his usual black fur coat, and he carried his favorite squeaky toy, the one shaped like a red fish and called "The Lucky Carp." I was adorned in one of my new ensembles from Clothes the Loop: white jeans ("a must have for the summer" according to Jacob and *People* magazine), Tory Burch silver ballet flats, a silver peace sign pendant around my neck and a Velvet blue cotton tee ("$89 for a tee shirt?"). Together, Oreo and I were chic and ready for a fifteen-year-old to join us.

The fifteen-year-old in question appeared to be pouting.

"Melanie, welcome back," I said. I hugged her, pulling her inside at the same time, and felt bones. This was the first time I'd touched her aside from a pat on her hand.

"Kelly, thanks so much for taking care of Melanie," Kathryn said, walking inside my house while somehow propelling Melanie and her suitcases forward. Kathryn was dressed in black, like Oreo, but hers, again, was Prada. Melanie was in a tee shirt with a tie-dye peace sign on the front and torn jeans. I had the peace sign right, at least.

Kathryn continued, "I'm so sorry this was such a last-minute trip, particularly with Bruce gone. Melanie wants to be home by herself, but I just knew, what with your boys out of town and all, that you two would have a fabulous time keeping each other company. You've already had so much fun this week!"

"Yep, we'll do our best. I really am lonely, Melanie, so it's great to have you here. I know it probably seems like you'd have more fun by yourself, but let me tell you, it's not all it's cracked up to be. Plus, I can drive and we'll go places. Can you stay a little while, Kathryn?" I knew I was rambling so I tried to stop.

I saw my friend flinch, and she averted her big brown eyes. I knew she was hiding a lot more than just her daughter's eating disorder. She put her sunglasses back on, covering any insight I could gain.

"No, I really have to go home and pack. Melanie, I love you; and Kelly, thank you." She turned quickly and then dashed to her BMW, idling in my driveway.

"Bye," I said, closing the door behind her, and then Melanie, Oreo, and I were alone.

"Well, come on, let's go see your room!" I said in an overly enthusiastic voice. Melanie seemed to be ignoring me, even without her earphones in. She sat down on the floor, and I was about to try again to start a conversation when she said, in a small, childlike voice, "I wish I had a dog."

I watched as Oreo climbed into her narrow lap. Folded up, Melanie looked like a wooden marionette. Even when at her normal body weight, she could only be described as long and lean. Kathryn told me Melanie was almost 5'9".

"Except my parents would probably pay more attention to the dog than me," she said quietly to Oreo. "Well, actually, they're pretty good at ignoring anything but themselves. So I guess it would be my dog, after all."

I sat down next to her and put my arm around her shoulders. She tensed. I plunged in. "So, kiddo, it's great to see you again. I really do enjoy hanging out with you, you know. Maybe we could make another meal for the homeless or go volunteer at the YWCA? There are a lot of girls who need tutoring there. One of my friends has talked me into getting involved in their work to empower women. And well—"

"I know you're trying to help, Aunt Kelly, but you're kinda . . ."

"Sounding desperate?"

"Uh, yeah. I'm used to doing my own thing. I really don't need a babysitter, especially one of my mom's old friends."

"Hey, watch the 'old' comment! I'm working on my midlife crisis here," I said, chuckling, but neither Oreo nor Melanie laughed. "I'm serious, though, Mel. Life is complicated. I know. I'm trying to figure out how to get mine right, and I'm almost forty. It's okay to be confused at fifteen."

"I'm not the one who's confused, Aunt Kelly," Melanie said, reaching into her pocket and, in one swift move, putting her shoulder-length hair up into her signature ponytail. "Is it okay if I have a friend over later tonight?" She'd also pulled out her cell phone and was texting someone.

"Sure," I answered, pondering her first answer and tuning out the question. "Let's go get you unpacked."

"Do you have wireless Internet?" Melanie asked, as we hauled her suitcases—two, Louis Vuitton—up the stairs.

"Of course, Mel. My Internet is your Internet."

When we reached the guest room, at the top of the stairs, she saw the Lucky Carp I had hung from the doorknob (a backup in case Oreo lost the original). "What's with the fish?" she asked.

"It's Oreo's. If you squeak it, he'll come running. Also, since this door doesn't lock, you can leave it on your doorknob as a sort of 'Do not disturb' sign." I hoped she'd take it down, keep her door open, and welcome me with a smile every time I climbed the stairs. Okay, I knew I was dreaming.

"Well, thanks, I can handle it from here," she said, pushing the second suitcase into the room and closing the door, fish swinging from the doorknob behind her.

Oreo and I looked at each other and then headed back downstairs.

Fortunately, I'd asked Patrick to bring home dinner—I'd been too busy being fashionable and worrying to cook—and he delivered just what I'd ordered from our favorite Italian market, Figlio's: whole wheat fettucine with pine nuts and sundried tomatoes, house arugula salad, and a whole loaf of fresh Tuscan bread. Heaven.

I opened a bottle of Chianti Classico, lit a candle for the center of the table, and waited patiently for my husband. I was nervous and felt guilty, since I'd not yet had a chance to tell Patrick about our newest exchange student—Mel—who'd already moved in. I hoped it was a good bottle of wine. I'd break it to him after he'd had a glass. Then, over dinner, he'd have a chance to get to know his new houseguest. With my fabulous new hairstyle and hip clothing, I just knew everything would go smoothly.

Oreo barked when he heard Patrick's car pull in, so I was ready.

"Hi, babe. How was your day?" I asked as he walked into the kitchen. I swooped around the island and brought him a glass of Chianti and a big kiss. I grabbed the carryout bag from him, placed it on the island, and smiled. I unloaded the aromatic food and displayed it on our Italian dinnerware. "Follow me, my love," I said, leading him to the table.

"What's going on, Kelly?"

Apparently, he had noticed the third place setting. Very observant.

"What's the special occasion?"

Hmm. He sounded suspicious. Smart man.

"Well, um, Melanie, Kathryn's daughter, is going to stay with us for a little while. Sounds good, huh?"

"Kelly, really, don't you think we should talk about things like this? You can't just unilaterally make decisions that affect both of us, you know?" Patrick put his wine glass down and loosened his tie. He looked tired. I probably should've let him relax a little bit before dropping this on him.

"Let's eat, alright?" he said.

"Sure. I'm sorry." I called up the stairs for Mel.

No answer.

I tried the intercom.

No answer.

I got worried. Was Mel okay? Was she listless, lifeless? Did I fail already? It'd been only half an hour since I'd taken her to the guest bedroom.

She was fine; I was being overdramatic. Or maybe she wasn't fine, I thought, as I rushed up the stairs. Life-change thought Number Twelve: Cardio exercise would be good to avoid dying on missions to find houseguests. I stopped at the top of the stairs just before crashing into her door.

"Mel?" I yelled, knocking on the door, clearly marked "Do not disturb" by the hanging, now-swinging, fish. I couldn't take it, and burst through the door.

Melanie was lying facedown on the bed, cell phone in her ears, laptop in front of her nose. Fine. She minimized the screen when she felt my presence in the room, and rolled over on to her back to address me. I was used to that trick. My boys did it to me all the time.

"Oh," she said. "What's up? Why are you panting?"

"Just doing a little aerobic workout before dinner," I answered, willing my pulse to slow. My bangs were sticking to my forehead. "So, hey, Patrick is home and he's brought dinner from Figlio's. Come on down!"

"I ate a huge lunch with my mom, late, just before we came over, so you guys go ahead. I'll come down in a little to say hi to Patrick," she said before plugging the earbuds into her ear sockets and rolling back over to face her computer.

Blown off, I walked slowly downstairs. Patrick didn't seem surprised when I entered the kitchen solo and dejected.

"Come on over here and sit down, Kelly," Patrick said. "I know you mean well, I do. You're going to help her, for as long as she's here. But you're not going to be able to change her, fix her. Don't put too much pressure on yourself. Your teeth can't take it."

Times like these I felt a resurgence of first-love emotions: of slow walks together; of talking about all of life's possibilities. I'd shared my dreams, my fears, the creation and birth of my kids with this man. I was so glad we were still together, still holding on. He knew me so well and loved me no matter what.

"Thanks, I needed that. Cheers!" I said. "And I need you, so much. What would I do without you?" I realized I had echoed Kathryn's words to me, and felt blessed—T2C #8—that Patrick was my best friend. I smiled. I gazed into Patrick's sparkling blue eyes, now bracketed by laugh lines, and enjoyed the reflection of candlelight flickering there. I reached over and squeezed his left hand with mine. Our wedding rings bumped into each other.

"Nice outfit. I saw the Clothes the Loop bags in the trash, by the way. Good try," he said, shaking his head.

I never could get away with anything.

"Ah, well, I needed to look hip for our teenage girl boarder," I said, smiling. Sweetly. I'm an angel my smile said. An expensive angel, but an angel nonetheless.

"Right," Patrick said, twirling pasta on his fork. "Just remember, things are tight. The economy is in the dumps, so we need to be cautious."

"Are you telling me you're being laid off? Jim Joseph was just laid off. Oh my God!"

"What? No, I'm a partner, a rainmaker. I won't lay myself off, but the firm may not do the trip to Italy as planned. Didn't know how to tell you earlier, Kelly. I'm sorry."

"No, it's fine, really. You know how I hate to leave the boys in September anyway," I said, trying to look on the bright side as I ripped off a big chunk of bread, dipped it into the dish of extra-virgin olive oil, and kissed my dreams of the Amalfi coast goodbye. Okay, call me selfish, but I have one trip a year, and boy, do I look forward to it. T2C Number Thirteen: Make own vacation plans (not during back-to-school month) so rug cannot be pulled out from under you. Refer to life-change list item Number Fourteen: Get a job to pay for trip and other essentials.

In an effort to change the subject before I could show my disappointment and to broach the subject of Patrick's fidelity, I asked as nonchalantly as I could, "So, um, Jeanne, your assistant . . . How old is she?"

"What? I don't know. She's been with the firm for twelve years. When Ralph retired last year, she was transferred to me. She's amazing. Why? You've never asked before."

"Is she cute?" Since Doug was in the garage, I didn't have T2C #4 handy; technically, though, I wasn't making a direct comparison.

"No, Kelly, she's not cute. She's efficient, talented, and married with two kids. I'm not sure why we're having this discussion."

"That's fine, I'm finished," I said, and took a deep breath. Now I just needed to mention the little thing about getting a job. At least I wouldn't be in Italy when my new business needed me; that was something.

The doorbell rang.

"I wonder who that could be? I'll get it," Patrick said, and leaned over to kiss my cheek as he walked past. "And I truly am sorry about having to cancel the trip, Kelly."

As I followed him to the front door, I smiled. Here Patrick was, feeling bad about the trip to Italy being called off, and here I'd been, worried about his reaction to Melanie. Everything would be fine.

1 3

MELANIE BEAT US TO THE DOOR AND STOOD BEAMING AS HER "friend" stepped inside. He had the all-American boy look. He was polite, shook hands, made eye contact. He wore the prerequisite high school uniform: Abercrombie/Pac-Sun/American-Eagle/Hollisterish getup consisting of collared shirt, layered tee shirt, khaki shorts, Vans. He smelled of Axe and his name was Gavin. He had tousled brown hair and he was tall, maybe 6'3". Suddenly Patrick and I looked like midgets in our own foyer.

After our brief introductions, Gavin and Melanie headed outside to my beloved porch, Diet Cokes in hand, while Patrick and I returned to our meal.

"Now what?" I asked Patrick.

"Well, I'm assuming they make out and we go to sleep."

"Maybe she should go to sleep and we could make out?"

"Now you're talking. What did Kathryn say about Melanie's curfew and boyfriends? About going out, drinking, and stuff like that?"

Oh no. "Well, she didn't really specify anything. I thought my job was to plump me—I mean, her—up."

"Oh jeez. Teenage girls are much more complicated than that. I had three sisters, Kelly, and you have one. Heck, you were one!"

"As I said, now what?"

"I guess we tell her how to turn out the lights downstairs when she comes in," Patrick said, getting up to clear our plates. We cleaned up the kitchen and tucked Melanie's meal in the refrigerator. I put a pink Post-it note—not one of my yellow life-changing T2C Post-its—on the takeout container, with a heart and "Mel" written on it.

Patrick and I walked out to the porch, but Melanie and Gavin weren't there. A glance into the yard revealed the two of them nestled in the hammock in the dark (and I had to admit, romantic) corner of the yard.

We both stopped and stared.

Now what? I thought.

"Now what?" Patrick asked.

"Well, I could call Kathryn and find out what to do."

"Lame."

"Sean said nobody says 'lame' anymore, remember?"

Patrick chuckled, wrapped an arm around my shoulder, and started leading me over to the couch on the porch. "I guess we could sit out here and enjoy the evening. Draw a little inspiration from the teenagers."

"Except then we'd be geeky voyeurs or losers or something. Besides, I just got a mosquito bite. How about we leave them out here tonight, and I'll get some boundaries established tomorrow?" I took Patrick's hand and led him inside. I glanced over my shoulder, and as far as I could tell, there was indeed what we called making out going on in that hammock. I don't know what it's called now, but it looked like fun.

I'm not sure what time Gavin left; I fell asleep as soon as my head hit the pillow.

Patrick left for work early, and I, too, was up and at 'em.

Google browser loaded, I started researching my new job opportunity. I hadn't told Patrick about Charlotte's offer because I wasn't sure that what I loved to do could be something I could get paid to do. Sure, I'd thought about the interior decorating business angle, but there were almost as many decorators in Grandville as there were real estate agents, lawyers, and doctors. Home staging, however, could be in my future.

And, I could start with a project across the street.

But then I felt guilty; I should be researching anorexia. Not knowing what time a teenager who stayed up late making out in my backyard would wake up, I knew I had to play it safe and research a little more before she caught me.

From all I had read, it seemed that the best treatments were therapy with a specialist in eating disorders, antidepressants (if Melanie was depressed), and eating under the guidance of a nutritionist and doctor. I needed to broach the subject today. I knew Kathryn said they'd tried therapy, but I didn't know if she'd found an eating disorder specialist. I didn't know if they'd tried any medications or had simply focused on forcing Melanie to eat. Did that work? Nope. It said right here on my screen that forcing an anorexic to eat could create a problem with bulimia.

Okay. I needed to call my long-lost friend Beth. We had met in sixth grade when both of us were plopped into the "gifted" classes. She and I had shared cans of Tab together and made cootie catchers to predict our futures. In the summer, we rode our bikes to the pool every day, and later, in high school, we got into mild trouble together. We'd had the best sleepovers, crashing in beanbag chairs as we listened to my favorite Air Supply album. Beth was the only one who would let me play "I'm All Out of Love" without cringing.

She'd been my best friend until I'd pulled away. Now, all these years later, I sat practicing in my head what I'd say to her on the phone—for half an hour. I finally dialed Beth's home phone number and got her answering machine.

"Hi Beth, it's Kelly Mills—well, now Johnson. Well, Kelly Mills Johnson. Anyway, I know we haven't talked since our tenth high school reunion, and that was only a quick hello, and phew, that was, well, years ago, but I wondered if we could catch up. I've always felt bad about how the group treated you when your parents divorced, and well, about your health, and that I wasn't there for you. I have a young woman, she's the daughter of a friend, and she's staying with me. She's going through—at least she appears to be going through—what you went through, although I don't really know what you went through because I let Megan talk me into not being there for you, but I could, she could—the teenager staying with me, that is—use your help. I wondered if you could call me back. And I'm sorry I sound like such a dork, which is so not a cool word according to my twelve-year-old. Okay, gotta go, sorry for rambling."

I hung up. Not only did I make a fool of myself, I forgot to leave my phone number. My face was flushed and my palms were sweaty.

When I called back to leave my number in a second voice message, however, Beth answered.

"Hello Kelly."

Oh nuts, I thought, not prepared to speak to the person herself. "Um, hi Beth, how are you?"

"Fine."

Ouch. Work with me here, I thought, but then realized, nope, it was up to me. "Listen, Beth, I don't know if you heard my rambling message, but I really am so sorry for abandoning you all those years ago. It was so wrong."

"Yes, it was. That was a time when I needed my friends the most. And suddenly, you weren't there."

"If it makes you feel any better, I know exactly how you feel now, since my parents got divorced too, although that happened while I was in college, so I guess that's different, and really, I didn't get anorexia. Unfortunately, I got the freshman fifteen, though, and . . ." I finally stopped my second round of nerve-induced idiotic rambling. A lot of good my practice did me.

"I appreciate the apology, Kelly. Even though your parents divorced, no two people handle that situation the same, as you know. But you and I did have some great times, you know, in the early years." There seemed to be a little smile in her voice.

"How about when we both tried our very first cigarettes together? I can't even recall where or who we got them from, but we tried those Virginia Slims sitting in your Camaro, remember? You instantly threw up and I instantly got addicted, unfortunately. It took me a long time, too long, to quit smoking. And it all started that night, with you."

Now I had her laughing. "Don't blame me for that! Remember I called you egghead? That was something I did start," Beth said.

"Yeah, you were hilarious, buying me egg books, egg cards . . .

why was that, by the way?" I asked, realizing I was actually getting mad.

"Well, you have a long, oval face. You know, like an egg. I always thought you'd look good in bangs, incidentally. Do you have those now?"

As of this week, I thought, but said, "Yes, I do, as a matter of fact."

"We do have so many shared memories," Beth said. "It's really nice that you called, and I could try to help. It's actually what I do now, or rather, what I want to be doing. I have my master's degree in social work, and I want to specialize in eating disorders. At the hospital where I work, I have to be a jack-of-all-trades, dealing with people with all types of emotional problems, issues, and addictions. But my passion is helping young women with eating disorders."

Jackpot! "Well, as long as you promise not to call me egghead in front of Melanie, I'd say you two are a perfect match. She's so skinny, Beth. She reminds me of how you looked during our senior year in high school. I'm so sorry for the pain you went through back them."

"It's okay, Kelly. The past is past. I got help and made some great friends in college."

Probably loyal friends, unlike the one I had been. Also unlike me, Beth had spread her wings, leaving the bubble for Vanderbilt University. I wondered why she came back to Grandville.

"We have too many happy memories to let one bad year and an influential, mean girl ruin that any longer," she said.

"I miss you, Beth. Thanks for picking up the phone just now rather than ignoring me. Thanks for forgiving me. Can we get together in person sometime soon?"

"The baby and I are free pretty much all day every day. I'm still on maternity leave from the hospital," she said, and after realizing she'd just given birth, I was even more amazed. I couldn't wait to meet the baby, and I wouldn't have to wait long. She agreed to come over for lunch the next day.

Right after I hung up I wrote down this amazing realization. T2C Number Fifteen: Reconnect with old friends. Reconnecting with Beth could lead me to helping a troubled fifteen-year-old and thereby helping said teenager's mom, another friend. And maybe this was partly the way to help myself out of a funk and on to my new future. A triple whammy! With those happy thoughts and a loose, clench-free jaw, I typed "home staging careers" into my browser.

14

WELL, ACCORDING TO THE WEBSITE OF ONE OF THE SELF-proclaimed experts in the business, home stagers aren't decorators, interior designers, or fluffers. That was a relief. Instead, stagers focus on the details, on decluttering and depersonalizing homes. The key is to make sure the next owner of the house can see herself living in it without all of the current owner's stuff getting in the way.

Hmm. This sounded great. Heck, I could depersonalize without fluffing and I could declutter without designing; I've been doing that with Patrick's parents for years.

Of the profoundly messed up family of his origin, we didn't speak. How Patrick made it out alive and relatively healthy was beyond me. When we'd met, because I was a product of a divorced home, I knew my family was dysfunctional. I'd subsequently learned through the years that intact, miserable families put the capital D in dysfunction.

I still remember when Patrick borrowed my copy of *Bradshaw on the Family* to "browse through" soon after we married.

As he turned the pages, he seemed to become more entranced by the text. I'd fallen asleep, riding the water bed waves—yes, he actually brought one into our marriage. And yes, I got rid of it as soon as I could, donating it to Goodwill in the same load as the orange velour sectional and the poker-playing dog poster that he still denies he had. He did.

In the morning, he'd said, "You know, babe, I think my family might be dysfunctional." Really? So sweet, so innocent. Since then, we've made loads of progress understanding, or trying to, what makes each of us tick. And we've both agreed that the less his family knows about ours—the four of us—the better.

Back to my future.

So, according to the Association of Staging Professionals, I would need to take a two-day Accredited Staging Professional Classroom course to become certified. Problem is, they won't offer a class in my area until December, and that will still be two hundred miles away. My business could be booming by then. I turned my attention to one of the other 1,580,000 Google results. One of the posts told me I could just watch HGTV's *Designed to Sell* and pick up tips. Another link led me to believe that perhaps my life experiences to date equaled a PhD in the field. I was an expert at home staging already.

On the next site I found a three-day online course for home-based professionals—that was me, a home-based professional—at the end of which I would have a designation I could show my clients . . . all for $1,795. At the next click, a blog told me why I should never pay to get a designation and that training was a waste of money. Argh.

Another site asked me: "Did you know there are one million real estate agents and decorators who consider themselves staging experts?" No, I didn't. I gulped and clicked away from that site pronto. On yet another site I discovered the valuable information I was looking for: The going rate for home staging consulting was between $75 and $150 per hour, depending on the region. I learned I should always take before-and-after photos of each project and build a portfolio online and off. That sounded fun, and I already had a great digital camera I used to capture my boys and their lives.

I was snooping around on my seventh staging site when Melanie came into the kitchen. Her brown hair was up, of course, and she was wearing an oversized tee shirt emblazoned with "Ethanol is Corny" and a stylized ear of corn.

"Can I have some coffee?" she asked. She wasn't smiling, but she wasn't grimacing, so that was a plus.

"Sure, help yourself," I answered, tamping down the urge to correct her and have her say, "May I have some coffee?" See, I was in tune with my inner teen, I thought, and added as I watched her pour the tar, "Beware, it's strong. Patrick made it. Let me make you some eggs or something, okay?" Oreo stirred under my feet. He stretched out, making sure Lucky Carp was positioned between his paws. He looked like he was praying to the fish. That just might help me.

"Probably we should talk about my 'issue,'" she said, making quotation marks in the air.

"Come on over and have a seat," I answered. Remain calm, I reminded myself. Part of the peculiar characteristics of anorexia, I'd learned, is strong denial that there is a problem. I figured since Mel had been in treatment before, she'd at least realized there was an issue. That was good, right?

"I just don't understand why my parents aren't cool, like you and Patrick," she said. "I mean, they'd never let me just hang out with Gavin."

So much for the eating disorder. I guess Gavin was the issue we were going to discuss. "So are you and Gavin serious?" I asked after she'd sat down next to me at our round kitchen table. She held the cobalt blue coffee mug in her hands and smiled at me.

"As serious as a fifteen-year-old can be, Aunt Kelly. He's really nice. And supportive. I don't know what I would've done without him this past year. All in all, it's been hell." She took a drink of her coffee.

"What's hell, honey? School? I know Grandville High School is brutal, clique-filled, and really tough." Earning the "best school district in the state" designation was accompanied by all the pressures of an elite private school.

"No, school's fine. I still have straight A's. It's home; it's my mom and dad. They're the hot mess. And I guess I didn't know it was getting to me until lately. It did, or it has, or it is . . . I don't know. I loved volleyball, and now they won't let me play. Gavin's my best friend, and my folks don't like him."

I sat for a moment, making sure my next words would be supportive. I took a deep breath. "I have a friend who was in almost the same situation as you when she was in high school. Thing is, back then nobody even helped her. Heck, her best friends made fun of her, taunted her, and spread really awful rumors about her just because she was so thin. We didn't know that much about anorexia, other than Karen Carpenter had died of it. Once you get stuff sorted out, Melanie, you'll be back on the team. I've asked my friend Beth—we called her 'Bony Beth,' I'm ashamed to say—to come talk to you. She's doing great now, she even has a newborn. But years ago, she was just like you."

"Nobody is just like me, Aunt Kelly. Did your friend's parents act in front of the world like they were married but then ignore each other at home? Did your friend's parents forget she was even there most of the time as they pursued their all-important careers? Did your friend's parents tell her she couldn't hang out with her best friend, even if he's a guy? I doubt it. Everybody else has normal parents: a normal mom like you who stays at home and takes care of her kids, and a normal dad who comes home after work. My dad is never there, and my mom doesn't even know anything about my life. So there's probably no way you or your friend do, either. But, whatever."

"Mel, just because they're parents doesn't make them perfect. Trust me. You kids don't come with a manual, so all we can do is our best. And being a stay-at-home-mom does not guarantee you're normal, or that you do the right things for your kids all the time. I do know your mom loves you deeply, that she wants you to feel better, and that she has tried her best to help you." My coffee was cold. I got up to fill up my mug with a fresh blast of tar before rejoining the sulking teen at my table. I finally had a game plan, but it all hinged on Mel's willingness to at least talk to Beth.

"Look, Mel. I know you're feeling a bit neglected right now, but I hope you know I'm here for you. And I hope you'll consider talking at least a little bit to Beth. Your mom explained to me that you've been to counselors and therapists, specialists, and the like. I think Beth is different. She's my friend, and well, it couldn't hurt, you know?"

"Whatever," she repeated.

She'd agreed, albeit half-heartedly. I popped up and decided it was time for some comfort food, at least for me; food in general would be good for her. I pulled out my favorite skillet, sprayed on a generous coating of Pam, cracked two eggs into it, and then pushed down two slices of wheat bread in the toaster. As the eggs fried, I poured a large glass of orange juice and smiled over at Melanie, encouraging a response.

"Is that for me?" she asked, motioning with her arm to encompass the eggs, the toast, the glass of orange juice, and probably, me.

"Yep! Best way to start the day is with a home-cooked breakfast, right?" I said, in my best Kelly Johnson/Martha Stewart voice.

"Maybe if you're on the farm and you're going out to plow. I had a health bar in my room and I'm good to go. In fact, I'm going for a jog. I'll be back in awhile."

"Sure," I said, as she scooted past me and out the door. This is going well, I thought sarcastically, as I prepared to eat a home-cooked breakfast. I wasn't going to plow, but I was going to go to work. As I stood eating, looking out the kitchen window, I watched Melanie stretch her lean body. Then I saw a boy appear in the corner of our yard. It wasn't Gavin, and I didn't know him. Melanie's back was to me, but I could see the boy smiling, flirting with her. Ah, to be young, I thought, and then mentally kicked myself. No way I'd go back to high school again. Would anyone, given the choice?

After I cleaned up my farm breakfast, I called Charlotte and told her I'd do it: I'd stage the Thompsons' house. She screeched in delight—nails on chalkboard. She told me the key to the house was in the lockbox, gave me the combination, and told me to let myself in. We didn't have any time to waste.

1 5

NOT BEING ACCUSTOMED TO WALKING INTO OTHER PEOPLE'S empty homes alone, I was both excited and nervous as I crossed the street and walked up to the front door. I'd left a note telling Melanie I'd be back by noon. What I didn't say was that Beth was coming over for lunch. I'd decided to make that a little surprise.

For all the years we'd been neighbors, I'd only been over to Heidi and Bob's once. I guess they would have said the same. So, turning the key in the lock and walking in felt odd. I had two hours to explore the home and sketch the layout in my notebook. I also had my trusty camera for the "before" shots the websites had told me I needed.

The emptiness was what struck me first—the lifelessness.

"Hello," I yelled, just to be sure I was alone. No one answered, but my own voice echoed back to me. The sky was overcast and the air inside the house felt thick and gloomy. And cold, even though it was a warm summer day. To my left, the empty living room—empty except for a huge flat-screen TV. To my right, what was once a formal dining room. The house was colonial revival, if I remembered my home styles, and was symmetrical throughout.

Straight back, past the formal staircase, was the kitchen. I remembered they'd added on, as most people did with these old houses, changing it from a "servant's kitchen" to an open one with a family room combined. It was a dream kitchen with the works: Honed black granite countertops; cherry cabinets; and sleek, built-in, stainless steel appliances. I walked through the kitchen into the family room and was shocked.

On the wall, in four-foot-tall letters, were the words "lying, cheating bastard." Graffiti, in black spray paint, a mural of pain and heartbreak. No wonder Charlotte needed my help. I walked upstairs and found what had been a girl's bedroom painted in a happy purple. Although empty, it still smelled like a teenage girl had lived there, with remaining scents of Herbal Essence shampoo and tropical body lotion. The two boys' bedrooms were something else. One was painted all black: walls, floors, ceilings. Even the pocket bath between the two rooms was black. The other room was covered with graffiti written in every known color of Sharpie pen. Some of the writing was tiny, some large. Poems and angry song lyrics and none of the words hopeful. The heater vent in this room had been filled with cigarette butts and beer bottle caps.

This house was oozing pain.

The walls of the third-floor master bedroom were painted a light blue. It could have been romantic and private. Neutral and happy—once upon a time.

I checked my watch. I had thirty minutes to get home and make lunch before Beth and baby arrived. Even though I was still full from my farm breakfast, I had an old friend to feed. I hoped Melanie would be home from her run in time to join us.

But first, I called Charlotte.

"This is bad," I said. "It's almost painful to walk through."

"I know. It's the worst I've seen in this price point. But look at it this way: Once you get your feet wet with this, you'll be able to handle anything. Listen, I talked to the folks at Global Furnishings and they're going to let us borrow rooms of furniture off the floor."

"Okay, that's a good start, Charlotte, but how do I get everything done—between now and when?"

"Day after tomorrow works. I'll show the buyers the other listings and save the Thompsons' place for last. It'll buy us some more time. Come on, think of this as your own *Extreme Home Makeover* show, the Kelly edition! Thanks so much. I've got to go, but call me if you need anything. Oh, and once you've picked the paint to cover up all that hideous graffiti, let me know. I have the painters ready to start in the morning."

Now in addition to my Things to Change list, I suddenly had a major "To Do" list. At least this big job plus my new houseguest's needs would take care of curtailing *Law & Order* viewing for the foreseeable future. First item on my To Do list: Tell husband I've taken a job. Second, make lunch and open up dialogue between former best friend and current lost teenager. Third, jump into new career field with confidence and speed, due to deadline looming in two days. I trotted back across the street as I called Patrick.

I got his voice mail. Probably better. "Hey, I just wanted to call and see how your day was going and to mention that I took a job, and the next couple of days are going to be crazy, so if you could be around the house that would be good because I'll probably need your help! Thanks, dear! Love ya!" Phew, I thought as I hung up. I've perfected the art of run-on sentences.

Gotta love voice mail. Great for conflict avoidance. I've read there's even a service you can dial first and then make your call, guaranteeing you'll go straight to voice mail. Once my home staging business takes off, I might need it.

Melanie arrived at the back door the same time I did, and we both made gleeful noises back to Oreo, who greeted us at the door. She looked like she'd just run a marathon.

"How far did you run?" I asked her as we headed into the kitchen and she grabbed a bottle of water.

"I don't know, I just went. I'm hitting the shower."

"Okay, um, and that friend of mine—ah, Bony Beth from high school? Well, she's coming over for lunch, with her newborn. I hope you'll spend some time with us?"

"Maybe," Melanie said, and walked out of the room in a blur of thin legs.

I whipped up some tuna fish salad—I thought that was okay for a new mother but couldn't quite remember—sliced some strawberries, and had made a semi-presentable table arrangement just as the doorbell rang.

Beth looked wonderful, fabulous even. I don't know how she had done it, but she looked even better than she had at our ten-year reunion. She glowed. Even if her husband was gay, she was happy. Heck, maybe that was the secret to her happiness. Whatever it was, I was glad for her and thankful she was back in my life.

After a big hug, much cooing by me over baby Sarah and much wowing by her over my house—I thought, again, maybe I am good at this—Beth followed me into the kitchen.

"Thanks so much for coming over and bringing the baby. Melanie's upstairs taking a shower. I think she ran to Pennsylvania this morning; she told me she was just going to go for a jog around the block." I pulled out a chair for Beth so she could sit and hold the baby. I always forget how tiny they are, fresh out of the oven.

I cootchie-cootchie-cooed for an annoyingly long time, after which Beth had a chance to comment. "Overexercising is another sign of the disease, you know? Do you remember how I was always jogging, even when track season was over? Jogging is also an escape. It gets your endorphins flowing and you don't have a care in the world. I could go for miles."

"But she didn't even eat breakfast."

"Not surprising. If she's a true anorexic rather than bulimic/anorexic, she won't eat. If she's bulimic, she'll eat to pacify us and then she'll throw it up."

"So far, I don't think she's had a bite to eat, except for her health bars, since she arrived yesterday," I said.

"Does she know why I'm here? Why I've come over for lunch, aside from showing off Sarah and catching up with you, of course." Beth smiled.

"I've told her a little bit about you, and what you two have in common. Of course, Melanie doesn't think anyone can relate to her."

Melanie walked into the room.

"What were you saying about me, Aunt Kelly?"

"Nothing, Mel. Come join us."

"Your baby is adorable," she said, ignoring me as she pulled up a seat next to Beth. "What's her name? Can I hold her?"

"Sure," Beth said. "This is Sarah. She's such a good baby. I'll put her in the carrier while we eat and after that you can hold her as long as you'd like."

"I like her name, Sarah. That's pretty," Melanie said.

Wow, I thought, two complete sentences not in response to a question. We were making progress.

Beth and I shared what we thought were hilarious high school stories, each of us observing as discreetly as possible Melanie's peculiar eating method. She took tiny bites and then pushed the rest of the food around on her plate. Some of the tuna fish ended up mounded under the strawberry slices, some in a thin spread, and some, from the look on his face, in Oreo's belly.

"So, you're going to be a sophomore at good ole Grandville High?" Beth said. "I remember that being a pretty good year because it was just before my parents broke up and my life went crazy. Actually, their separation came in the middle of sophomore year, come to think of it."

Melanie shot me a look and then said to Beth, "Do you know my mom, too?"

"No, I haven't ever met her but if she's a friend of Kelly's I'm sure I would like her. Why?"

"Just wondering. My mom and Kelly both think I'm crazy." She slipped Oreo another glob of tuna salad.

"No I don't," I said. "Actually, you're very smart. It's not everybody who can text under the table while also eating, feeding Oreo, and talking."

I thought I saw a smile break through, and then it was gone. She was trying hard to only pout around me, but two could play this game. I was going to hear her laugh someday; that was my goal.

"Well, I've gotta go work on my summer reading," Melanie said, standing up. "I'll let Oreo out, Kelly. Nice to meet you Bony Beth—I mean Beth. Your baby is adorable." And she was gone, Oreo trotting out of the room behind her.

"I thought you wanted to hold Sarah?" Beth asked Mel, while shooting me a look that could kill. Melanie had said Bony Beth on purpose. I knew it.

"I'll hold her next time," she yelled from the foyer.

"How in the world did she know that nickname?" Beth asked me.

Jeez. "I was trying to break the ice, to make her understand you could be her friend, you could relate. I'm sorry, Beth. I'm way out of my league here. I'm just trying to help."

"I know you're trying, Kelly, and you're right. This issue is challenging. Do you mind holding Sarah? I'm going to try to talk to Melanie." Her face was determined, while mine probably showed I was giving up.

"Her room is at the top of the stairs. Hanging fish on the door."

Sitting at my kitchen table, holding an infant, I realized I should feel better now that I had reinforcements. Sure, Melanie was a problem, but Beth had agreed to help, and I was the one who had brought them together. I had accomplished more in the last two days than I had in the past six months. I'd embarked on a new career, I cried less frequently, I hadn't compared myself to anyone (#4) in at least a day, and I had reconnected with an old friend—and fed her. I wouldn't have another conversation with the boys for a week, so I'd have to brag to Patrick and Charlotte. And Dr. Weiskopf. That was enough.

I had things to do, and things to change. And as soon as Beth and little Sarah headed home, I needed to head for Home Depot.

1 6

PAINT SWATCHES AND DIGITAL CAMERA IN HAND, I ARRIVED
back at the Thompsons' house just as the first mid-afternoon
thunder rumbled across the sky. Ordinarily, I love summer storms,
but that's when I am safe at home, not in an empty, graffiti-laden
house. I had a job to do, however, and by golly, I was going to do it.

Once I was inside, I realized it would be dark due to the storm.
The kitchen had overhead lighting, and Heidi had left the dining
room chandelier behind, but other than that, there weren't lamps
anywhere. I'd just have to go with the color scheme I'd designed at
Home Depot. Without light there would be no chance to second-
guess my choices.

I had decided to add rich color because the walls in the entry
hall, dining room, and living room were all an uninviting light tan.
Red for the dining room and entry hall and a deep navy for the
living room would do wonders. I needed to liven things up in the
kitchen, so I had picked a sunshine yellow. I finished taping paint
swatches to the appropriate walls downstairs, and I was walking
toward the entry hall when I heard footsteps—upstairs.

I realized I hadn't shouted out my hello as I had reentered the house. "Hello!" I called. Rule number one in home staging: Make sure you announce yourself.

"Who is that?" a gruff voice said from the top of the stairs. "Who let you in?"

Shoot. "Oh, hey, Bob, it's Kelly. Kelly Johnson, from across the street," I chimed sweetly in my best Kelly Johnson/Donna Reed voice, all the while sliding quickly toward the front door. He moved rapidly down the stairs and beat me to the door, blocking my exit. He had a bottle of Jack Daniels in his right hand.

"What are you doing in my house?" Bob asked, the slurring doing little to conceal the anger in his voice.

"Well, hey, good question. Charlotte hired me to stage your home. That's when we get it all fixed up to sell fast," I said. And smiled.

His eyes looked crazed, beady, and not at all happy with me or the situation.

"Should I call her and have her talk to you? Or would it be better if I just left?"

"No, stay. Charlotte must've gotten too busy to tell me she was letting you in. It's cool. Wanna drink?" Bob stuck out his arm and offered me a swig from the bottle.

"Ah, no, thanks. I've got a lot of work to do here." Stupid, stupid! I'd just insulted his home.

I was shaking, but wasn't sure why. Heck, he was my neighbor. But I'd never seen him like this. Sure, he'd been through a lot, but he was also freaking me out, between the booze and his stare.

"Well, I'm going to just finish up and get the place ready for the house painters," I said, backing away from him and the front door. I turned and hurried up the stairs, rapidly taping the paint chips throughout the second and third floors. Now what, I wondered, pausing to catch my breath. There was only one staircase and it would lead me back to Bob. I listened but didn't hear a sound. Maybe he'd passed out somewhere in the kitchen? I took a deep breath and rushed down the stairs to the first floor, and freedom.

Bob was waiting in the shadows of the living room, and he stepped out to block the front door again.

"Yeah, well, the bitch did this to me. Never should've left my first wife. Lust—gets you every time. It's karma, don't you think?" He moved closer to me, his whiskey breath assaulting my nose. I stepped back until I was against the dining room wall. "I've always thought you were more my kinda woman, Kelly, more than Heidi ever was. You know, all perky and perfect. We used to joke about how you all had the perfect little family up there, up above us on the highest hill. Do you wear aprons, little Kelly?"

With that Bob grabbed me with both hands around my waist and pulled me in close.

"I've always wanted to kiss you. Tasty, like a snack cake."

"Bob, really, please," I pleaded pushing him away with all my strength as his face kept getting closer. He'd pressed his lower body into mine and we were touching from thigh to chest. My heart was beating so fast I thought my chest would explode.

"You know, I think your husband was hot for Heidi. I watched them during a couple of block parties. That's why this feels so right with us," he said. Then, as he tried to take another swig out of the bottle, he stumbled backward.

I was free. My legs hadn't run in decades, but suddenly they propelled me through the entryway and out the door, down the driveway, and across the street. Before I knew it, I was standing in my own foyer, soaking wet from the rain, shaking and sobbing.

I climbed the stairs slowly and went straight to my bedroom.

I needed a hot shower. Maybe I can't handle this businesswoman stuff, I thought. Who knows what would've happened if Bob hadn't fallen backward? From my bedroom, I could see over to his house. The front door was now closed. I hoped he had left. I didn't care that he was drunk and possibly driving somewhere. I didn't care about him at all.

1 7

AFTER A LONG, HOT SHOWER, I KNEW THE BEST THERAPY was to get back in action. I couldn't let the unsettling episode with Bob stop me on my first assignment.

Per Helen Reddy's advice, I roared my favorite lines from her hit song as I got dressed. I always feel better when I sing, as long as nobody else is listening—except Oreo. He tipped his head, looking at me while raising one ear, a clear sign to me that he enjoyed the performance.

Everybody has setbacks in business, I told myself. Near misses . . . almost rapes? Well, maybe not that, but close calls. I needed to toughen up, get back in the saddle. The storm had blown through and the late-afternoon air felt refreshing. I had dressed quickly in another new outfit from Clothes the Loop: black True Religion jeans and a black and white summer sweater, accessorized perfectly by the Dogeared Karma necklace I'd chosen. What comes around goes around, I thought, although I wasn't quite sure how Bob fit into that mantra. I decided to focus on the positive.

As Doug and I headed to the Global Furnishings store, I

called Charlotte to yell at her. I got her voice mail. For once I was not satisfied talking to a machine. But I did.

"You didn't tell me Bob lurks around his house drinking Jack Daniels all day," I yelled. "You could've mentioned him to me and vice versa. Jeez." I hung up. I think this was my first business argument in years. It felt good. Cleansing.

Time in the furniture store was my dream come true. I simply walked from showroom to showroom with the owner in tow, telling him what items we'd use at the house. Pretend shopping—creating a new home without spending a dime. I picked contemporary couches and chairs in yellow and off-white for the family room. It was going to be bright. I added a sisal rug and that room was set. Some colorful plates and accessories would help the kitchen countertops spring to life. A formal cherry dining room table with matching chairs, a Venetian-looking smoked-glass-and-gilt mirror for the wall, and the dining room would shimmer. In the living room, I'd selected two soft velvet tan couches, a marble coffee table, and an amazing Oriental rug. Mirrors and uplighting would bring light into the room, while crystal candle holders would adorn a Venetian banquet table. Upstairs, on the second floor, I selected furniture that would make the bedrooms just right for a young family: white wood bunk beds, area rugs in primary colors, and accessories that held the promise of happiness. I would turn the master bedroom into a beach-themed retreat with more sisal, white slipcovers, and dark mahogany furniture. I couldn't wait to see it all come together at the Thompsons'.

As I left the furniture store and started the drive back home, I finally called Patrick. I had pulled over to the side of the road, underneath a weeping willow tree at the entrance to the park by the river. I locked my doors so nothing bad could happen. No more negative events today, I told myself, looking down at my Karma necklace and trying to think positive, peaceful thoughts.

As soon as I heard his voice, I started sobbing. When I didn't stop, couldn't stop, he became frantic on the phone.

"Kelly, please, tell me where you are, babe. I'll come get you. What's wrong?"

"I'm at the park, by Scioto River. In my car. Please come."

And he did.

18

I MADE IT HOME A LITTLE AFTER SIX O'CLOCK IN THE evening of my third day on the job.

Charlotte had made certain Bob had moved out of the house and promised not to be back. Then she personally escorted me the first time I stepped back inside. Patrick took off from work and was my personal assistant the day the painters came. Charlotte also extended the original deadline an extra day. All in all, things were good, and as Patrick and I discussed, they could have been much worse. As it was, I was shaken up, but unharmed.

At least I now knew I could run if I needed to, and pretty fast at that.

As I turned the corner, I found Patrick and Melanie busy in the kitchen.

"Congratulations!" Patrick said, and came over and gave me a squeeze. "You did it! Your first assignment under your belt, and you didn't even tell me you were looking for a job!"

"Congrats, Aunt Kelly," Melanie said, too, and she seemed sincere. "I'm going to go over to Beth's tomorrow, to help with the baby and all. Okay?"

"Sounds great to me!" I said, winking. "I'll be on the job site all day."

As I regaled the two of them with my stories of decorating prowess, I noticed Patrick was distracted.

"What is it?" I asked him after Melanie had left the kitchen.

"I just can't let it go, what he did to you," he said. "I called Bob. He acted like he didn't even remember, denied anything happened. I'm just sorry I wasn't there for you, babe."

"Oh, Patrick, really, I'm okay. He was drunk, probably lonely. His wife left him, his house was covered with graffiti, and it's being sold out from under him. I can see all of that now. It's okay, we're okay. Truly," I said, and gave him a big squeeze. I loved how he loved me.

"You know I'm going to worry about you, now that you're working, going to strangers' houses. Especially with your new hair. You really do look great."

"Wow, thanks," I said. Who knew bangs would make such a difference? Wrinkle coverage, I guess. Watch out, Linda Evans. "Listen, Charlotte and hundreds of other women in real estate go to strangers' homes every day and she's never had a problem. She said they offer some self-defense classes at the Board of Realtors and even at the country club every once in awhile. I've already added that to my Things to Change list. It's #11. Didn't you see it in our bathroom?" I asked.

"Yes, yes, I did," Patrick said, and wrapped me in a big embrace. "And I think that's a great idea. All the women at the firm took a class last month. The YWCA offered it, and their instructor came to the office. I should've thought to have you come."

He hadn't, of course, because that would have meant Patrick pictured me outside the home, which I don't think he had for years. Now he would. I smiled. "That's alright. Charlotte and I will do it together."

"Anyway, good ole Bob is in trouble, Kelly," Patrick said after awhile of silent hugging. "His marriage ending isn't the only thing he's facing. He's got sole custody of those kids, and his business is in trouble."

My jaw dropped. Patrick was the last person to know any gossip, or to care. "How do you know?"

"Stag room. Besides, now he's made it my business to watch his every move. He dropped out of the club, and he used to be a fixture. Guys talk sometimes, just not as much as women do."

"You talk more, it's just not deep," I said. "I'm really over what happened. Reminded me of being trapped alone with a drunk fraternity guy in college. Scary, but manageable." Kathryn had burst into the room where the guy had pinned me to the corner. She'd found me just in time. This time, I reminded myself, I'd gotten away on my own.

"Yeah, well, you can deal with it your way, but if that sonofa . . . if he ever comes near you again, I swear—"

"He's not at the house, hasn't been since. You know that. I'm sure he's embarrassed," I said. "Are you ready to head up? I need to meet the furniture vans over there at seven in the morning tomorrow. And Patrick, thanks for being around so much for the last few days. It means a lot."

"I'll always be here for you," Patrick said. "I'm proud of you for getting back into the work world, if you're sure that's what you want to do."

"Of course, I'm sure. I mean, Bob's not changing my mind. I think I have reached a place and time in my life where I need to focus on a passion of mine, be out in the world as more than just a wife or mom. Home staging seems to be a good fit. I'm taking it one day at a time. In fact, that's a good one for my list. I took a detour over to my Post-It note pad and wrote T2C Number Sixteen: Take it one day at a time.

"You crack me up. Our whole house is going to be covered with Post-it notes soon," Patrick said, laughing, while he turned out the lights in the kitchen.

"Don't worry. I'll put this on Doug's dashboard," I said. "He still has plenty of room."

"Poor Doug," Patrick said as he walked over and gave me a kiss. "Well, let's head upstairs, then, and I'll give you some real congratulations." He had the "let's do it" undertone.

"What about Melanie?" I asked as we climbed the stairs.

"Good night, Mel," Patrick said through the door as we passed by her room. I may have heard a murmured "night" back, but I wasn't sure. She seemed to be in for the night, at least.

I really didn't feel like it. I was too charged up over the last few days. But, well, after we started, I was glad. Besides, I read somewhere that you can burn more than 150 calories this way.

The next morning, Melanie came over to Bob's house with me, since Beth wasn't picking her up until ten. We're making some headway, I thought, noticing that Melanie was walking right next to me. She seemed happier, and she'd certainly connected with Oreo, who had taken to sleeping on the end of her bed at night. He really was a traitor. Maybe a sheepdog puppy or a precious chocolate Lab would be nice, I thought, glaring at him as I let him out each morning, hoping he could read my mind.

Everything I'd read about eating disorders made me believe that Melanie needed to replace volleyball and her long, solitary jogs with an activity that would allow her to connect with her body and get back in balance. I'd been considering starting yoga again. Perhaps we could try that together?

Leaning on the black granite kitchen island in the Thompsons' now-sunny new kitchen, I broached the subject. "So, Mel, have you ever tried yoga?" I asked casually while also glaring at the furniture delivery guys who had just arrived and already were giving Melanie—sporting what had to be the world's shortest cutoffs and an equally skimpy tie-dyed tank top—lecherous looks every time they carted an item past us. I tried to match their leering with an equally direct "I'm-the-adult-in-charge-and-you're-pissing-me-off" look. It didn't seem to work. I think one of them even leered at me.

"You know, we did a little yoga before each volleyball practice and I kinda liked it. I guess I could try it. When did you want to go?" she asked, big beautiful eyes blinking intently.

"Well, soon. I just need to get the schedule from the club, okay?" I realized that now I'd have to do yoga, too. T2C Number 17: Practice yoga, I thought, and looked around the Thompsons' kitchen for something to write it on until I could add it to my Post-its at home.

"Let me know. I'm gonna go wait for Beth outside. See ya!" Mel said, cruising out of the kitchen and down the hall, leaving gawking movers in her wake, all staring at her retreating Daisy Dukes.

I needed to focus on the house.

It was my fourth day on the job and it was all starting to come together. The painters had worked all day and night, as promised, and the walls were gorgeous. Color and life were coming back into the home. Charlotte arrived—causing a renewed level of ogling, of course, since she was in a tight black miniskirt, high heels, and a breezy white blouse—and after clearing the gauntlet of men she ran over and squeezed me.

"This is amazing. Exquisite. I will no doubt have an offer on it today, thanks to you," she said, turning around in the yellow family room, now cleared of hurt. "I have fresh flowers on the way. And, oh, hi, you must be Melanie!" she said, introducing herself to my teen charge who had walked back into the house, presumably finding it too hot outside to wait there. It was a scorcher. "I haven't seen you since you were a baby."

And that was true, I realized. Time flies. After college, before kids, Charlotte, Kathryn, and I had been in a dinner club together with ten other women. It had been a wonderful year of going out to eat every other month to some of the best restaurants in the city while having great girls-night-out talks. We'd tried to turn it into a book club, but everyone got busy and the group broke apart.

Kathryn had been the first of us to start a family, and Melanie, in her infancy, attended one of our last dinners out. I remembered being in awe of such responsibility: a whole person completely dependent upon you. Kathryn, as with everything else, seemed to take on new motherhood with ease.

"Melanie, Charlotte's girls are going to be in third grade and they're adorable. Maybe you could babysit?" I suggested. Neither Melanie nor Charlotte jumped at the suggestion, so we stood there in awkward silence. I guess I needed to give up on that whole Melanie babysitting idea, but I had loved it myself and made some good money. Oh, well.

"I'm going back outside to wait for Beth," Melanie said, and left.

"Nice to see you," Charlotte called after her. "She's awfully skinny, isn't she?" she added, turning toward me.

"Yes, she is. Do you remember my friend Beth from high school?"

"Didn't you guys have a falling out or something? Oh, wait, no. She was the one who turned into a stick person when her parents divorced, right? She was such a mess. No wonder you guys lost contact."

"It wasn't Beth's fault we stopped talking; it was mine. Our whole group ostracized her. We didn't understand what she was going through, and it was easier to talk about her than to help her."

We were interrupted by a mover carrying the front half of the huge mahogany headboard for the master bed frame. He couldn't believe it had to go all the way to the third floor. I smiled and confirmed it did. Served him right, I thought smugly, chief leerer that he was.

"Oh, wow, that's tough," Charlotte said. "Have you talked to her since high school? Where is she?"

"I actually called her and she agreed to talk to Melanie. I couldn't believe it, after all we put Beth through. Her passion is helping troubled teen girls. She's been talking with Mel, taking her to her house. In fact, once this job is wrapped up, I've got to call her and see how things are going. I've pretty much put her in charge of Mel."

"It's kinda amazing how people trust you, Kelly. I mean, Kathryn just left Mel with you, and Beth accepted your apology and is helping. I put you in charge of transforming my biggest listing. You should feel good about that; that's special."

"You're right, Charlotte. Thanks. But enough about me," I said, embarrassed. Inside I felt good for being there for Kathryn and

Melanie, but extending my motherly love to a teen girl wasn't a stretch, especially since I hadn't really dealt with any of Mel's emotional issues. The person who deserved the most credit was Beth. Maybe her stepping up is what allowed me to be here, pursuing home staging. I believe the saying that people come into your life for a reason. And things happen, like cancer scares, to keep us moving forward, trying new things. Beth's acceptance of my apology and her willingness to help were an amazing inspiration to me.

"Okay. What's next? I'm ready for another project," I said, breaking the silence. "This has been a blast! Give me another hard-to-sell property and I'll turn it around!" I was counting the cash in my head, the feeling of success swelling my confidence even though I hadn't made a penny yet. I could be on HGTV. I could be Home Stager to the Stars, Grandville edition.

"Let me talk to you about that in a little bit, okay?" Charlotte said evasively, looking down at a text message.

"Fine. When?"

"How about lunch today? Are you free? We can go celebrate this remarkable job!"

"Sure. Mel has plans, so let's do it."

"Great. I need your advice on something, too," Charlotte said. "Let's meet at Lindey's at one!" And she was gone.

19

"IT'S COMPLICATED," CHARLOTTE BEGAN. "IT WASN'T SUPPOSED to happen this way."

We were sitting outside at Lindey's, one of my favorite cafés. Fortunately, outdoor fans stirred the air around us, the huge Linden tree that was the restaurant's namesake provided a green umbrella above us, and cool air from inside was escaping through a propped-open door, reaching our table in gentle waves. This was my first time to sit and relax since I'd started scurrying around to finish the house. I had to admit, the Thompsons' house did look transformed and exquisite. Maybe that was my word for what I would create for everyone who hired me: an exquisite home.

Charlotte had been talking and I hadn't been listening. "Sorry, can you repeat that? Just what are you talking about?"

"I'm surprised you don't know already," she said, stirring her gazpacho. It was a good thing it was a cold soup; as long as she'd been stirring, it would have been cold anyway.

"Okay, really, just say it. We've been friends forever. You know I will support you no matter what."

"Bruce and I are in love—"

"You're married to Jim and you're in love with someone named Bruce? Oh my gosh—THAT BRUCE?"

"Shhhhh!"

Served her right, I thought. People should stare. They will stare. She had just told me she was in love with the husband of one of my best friends.

"We're going to keep it quiet," she said, "but we plan on getting divorces and moving in together—me and the girls. He sooo understands me," she cooed. "Why aren't you saying anything?"

"What can I say? Kathryn's daughter, Bruce's daughter, is staying at my house right now, you just met her for the first time since she was an infant, and you're having an affair with her dad? Oh, my—"

"It's not an affair. He is my soul mate. Jim and I have been over for awhile; we both could feel it end. We tried marriage counseling, but it just wasn't there anymore. Then, with his work, getting laid off . . . I mean, he needs a change, too. He needs a change in his life. He's just not happy."

"Not happy? Probably because his wife found a different soul mate!" I said, loudly, on purpose.

"Shhhh! You aren't handling this well at all. I need a friend. You told me you were committed to more friend time. Isn't that on one of your Post-it notes? And we have our business to think about," she said, and patted my hand.

I discovered that when you are in shock it is hard to move your hand. I left it there and said, "Kathryn is also a friend. I'm caring for her daughter. What about them?"

"Kathryn knows."

"What? No she doesn't. You were both together at my house . . . Oh my—that's why you left when she arrived."

"Well, she doesn't know it's me, but she knows it's someone, and by the way, she's got someone else, too." I was stunned. First, all of my friends were having passionate, illicit sex, some with each other's spouses. Second, suddenly I was trapped in the middle of a huge drama, and finally, I was disgusted that another friend would find Bruce even remotely acceptable.

But then I realized I didn't know all of the facts and that I would be breaking life lesson number one about saying anything bad about husbands and boyfriends if I slammed Bruce. I clammed up.

But what about Melanie? No wonder she's a mess. And what about Kathryn? Where was she? I'd called her a couple of times to check in and had gotten only voice mail; she hadn't called back. I assumed she had been in touch with Melanie; of course she had been. I wonder if Bruce had? What did Melanie know? My head was spinning.

"Okay, do you know where Kathryn is?" I asked.

"Nope, but I think she's with her mystery man, out of town somewhere. Shouldn't you know? You're in charge of Melanie, right?"

Right. Melanie. Who had a mom MIA and a dad soul-mating with my other best friend.

"Look, Kelly, I know I just dropped a lot on you. But I really couldn't keep it from you anymore. Please. I'm happier than I've been in a long time, maybe ever. Can you at least be happy for me? Jim and I are handling this like adults. It will be fine. Bruce and Kathryn will work things out. Let's talk about our business."

That's what I'd come to lunch for, but then I'd walked into *General Hospital*. I realized I had clenched my jaw, tight. I forced myself to release my jaw by jutting my bottom lip forward. Not attractive, but necessary to minimize dentist visits (T2C #2). Charlotte just stared at me.

"Does Melanie know all of this?" I asked.

"No, she doesn't. Bruce or Kathryn can tell her when the time is right. Can we focus on home staging?"

"Okay, tell me which houses need my staging touch and I'll think about it. This all seems like quite a mess, though."

"You're not really involved. We will all live happily ever after, you'll see." Her hand still covered mine. It was heavy; it felt like she was squeezing my heart.

"If Kathryn hasn't told you anything," she said, "then please, let her come to you about this. She and Bruce are talking soon, sometime in the next couple of days, to figure things out. I know you care about all of us and that you're the common friend here and it's hard. But it will be okay."

"Okay," I repeated after her. I guess my quest for a midlife new start was nothing compared to all of this. Perhaps Charlotte needed to be preaching in Spanish instead of poaching Kathryn's husband? "Do you speak Spanish?"

"No, I wish I did. Why?"

"Just wondered. Listen, Charlotte, I've got to go," I said. I stood abruptly and walked out of the restaurant. I figured she could pick up the tab.

20

AT TIMES LIKE THESE I NEEDED A WISE AND THOUGHTFUL person to talk to. Not having been to church since the boys finished preschool, I didn't have a lot of options. It's not that I didn't believe I could talk to God; I do and did. It's just that I was in the mood for dialogue and instant answers, and my experience in the God area was that revelations came more slowly. My second appointment with Dr. Weiskopf was coming up, but not soon enough.

As I took my place in the driver's seat, closing Doug's door behind me, I found myself punching my mom's number into my cell phone. I'd never asked her for relationship advice. I'd always been sure of what I wanted the moment I met Patrick. It was, to oversimplify, love at first sight with him. I think that was the way it was for my mom with my dad. But now, since their divorce, he was in the land of the unspeakable between my mom and me; too much bitterness erupted if the topic arose. But maybe she'd come through when it wasn't about either of us. Whenever I'd needed her most, she was there.

Maybe I just hadn't asked enough?

As far as I could remember, my mom hadn't offered an opinion about anything since the boys were babies. She had opinions about baby rearing—feeding schedules, baths, and the rest—that were invaluable when David arrived without care and feeding instructions. During those first months with son number one, my mom was amazing, even if I had a nagging fear that she'd abscond with my infant because I was such an unnatural mom in comparison to her. As I'd grown into my role, she'd pulled back. Later on, she'd taught my boys how to plant seeds and grow tomato plants and squash in our backyard. Her love of gardening resulted in my own hydrangea pride. When she moved to Florida to be near my sister, I was crushed.

"Hi. Take me off speaker phone. I can't hear what you're saying, and you'll have a storm there tomorrow," she said as soon as I uttered "hi."

So much for the freedom of Bluetooth and hands-free driving. I didn't like to drive with my ear glued to the phone, so Doug and I pulled over and he became my phone booth. Oh, and now I remembered why I didn't call during the extreme seasons. In the winter, it was a constant update on my wind chill and her balmy beach walk. Summertime: my tornado warnings and her lack of hurricanes. Mom and I talked best in spring and fall, when it was gorgeous in the heartland.

"Hey," I said, picking up my phone. "Better?"

"Much. So what's wrong? What's going on?" Had my mother become psychic? "Something happen at camp?"

"No, no. The boys are having a blast. It's . . . well, me," I said, finally. In my family, I was the funny one and Sally was the sweet one. I got my drive and strength from my dad and I credited my mom for my decorating prowess. She was the creative force in my life. But truly, and usually, she was the one asking me for advice, not the other way around.

I found it interesting, reflecting now, how easy it had been for me to toss in the career I'd worked so hard for to become a stay-at-home mom, just like my mother had been. Had trying to live up to my dad's version of me been an artificial propellant behind me all of my childhood and young adult years? A version that used humor to cover my exhaustive overachieving? I worked three jobs during college and always at least two during the summer. Even as I made my way up the rungs at the top public relations firm in the city, I'd had a writing career on the side. I was like the Energizer Bunny, going and going and going. Did I mask underlying unhappiness with constant motion? Was my teeth grinding replacing the frenetic energy of my earlier years?

Or was that the real me—the me before marriage and family? Or is who I am now, with two kids and an exquisite home, the real Kelly? Could I find a peaceful and fulfilling balance with a great family life and a job? So far in my life, it'd been one or the other. All in or all out—nothing in between.

"What is it?" my mother repeated. "How can I help, Kelly?" She sounded genuinely concerned and, I'm sure, more than a little surprised at my revelation of a weakness.

"Remember when your friends were going through divorces and midlife crises and all of that?" I began, imagining her standing in the kitchen of her perfectly decorated home in Florida, looking out over the lake behind her house: her silver-gray hair short, her body toned and tanned from gardening and long walks on the beach.

"Yes, well, those times in your life are hard to forget. Are you and Patrick okay?"

"Yeah, we're fine. It's just that all around me marriages are breaking up; people who said they would love and honor each other forever aren't. The boys ask me about it all the time, and now a close friend just told me she's discovered she's the soul mate of another close friend's husband and I don't know what to do."

"Well, as you know, I'm no expert in all of this just because I'm divorced. I'm so glad to be through the pain of that time. The only thing I do know is that what I have today, in my friends, is more valuable, perhaps, than any judgment one way or another that I could've made against them when we were in our thirties and forties. I never drew lines in the sand, even with friends who were unfaithful to their spouses. Even with friends who abandoned me when your father and I split up. You just don't know what's really going on in a marriage unless it's yours. And sometimes, even then, you're the last to know. Just look at mine. I read on Yahoo that 45 percent of fifty-year-old men and 46 percent of fifty-year-old women will eventually divorce. Only half of all couples reach their twenty-fifth wedding anniversary. Your father and I made it to eighteen. I'll send you the link."

My mother was a fount of wisdom now that she'd discovered the Internet. It wasn't just weather anymore.

It seemed almost impossible to stay out of the middle of this situation, but Mom was right; I had to try. I had to be Switzerland. One year Patrick's law firm trip was to the Swiss Alps. And one night we had eaten in a cave high up in the mountains. A huge Swiss horn called us into the cave for our meal, and folks in traditional costumes began serving our dinner. Then my claustrophobia hit and I had to run out into the mountain air. I loved the cheese fondue, though, and could move to Lucerne and just sit by the lake all day, drinking wine and eating cheese and rich, Swiss chocolate. I could braid my hair, milk cows . . .

"Kelly, you still there?"

"Yeah, Mom, sorry. I think you're right. I need to just focus on myself, let my friends' lives play out, and be there for them however I can."

"Exactly. So, what about you? The kids are at camp, and you've got your whole summer free. You're a talented gal; you should start a business. I just read that a woman starts a business in the U.S. every sixty seconds. You're so good at design."

"Funny you should say that. I just finished my first home staging job today."

"What is that?" Mom was clearly not hip to the trend.

"Google it. It's where you make a home more appealing to sell. Declutter, depersonalize, de-whatever, or rather, in this case, add furniture and paint to make it presentable."

"Sounds perfect. You need a slogan, or a whatchamacallit. They say right here in the story that you need an elevator pitch. Oh, and a website and business cards. This is so fun, dear. How much money can you make? Maybe I'll be your Jacksonville consultant! There are a surprising number of homes on the market down here. Atlantic Beach and Ponte Vedra Beach. I could declutter them!"

"Maybe so, Mom," I said laughing. "And you're right. I need a business plan. So far, I've just been relying on Charlotte for business, but I could work for any real estate agent who needs my services."

"Oh, you're working with Charlotte. That's great. Kelly Does Home Staging!"

"That makes me sound like I'm a stripper, Mom."

"Okay, well I guess it could just be Kelly Johnson Home Staging. You need an Internet site. Oh, and then I can Google you! You should get going on that right now."

I loved how she still had one of those telephones hung on the wall in her kitchen with a cord that had been stretched to an alarmingly long length due to my sister's kids—and occasionally mine, during our visits south—playing jump rope or tug-of-war with it. She swung it herself when she was excited, and now I thought I heard a "thwump."

It was time to head toward home. I had a mission; I needed to launch my business. Charlotte had her thing, Kathryn had hers. Now, I'd have mine, and where they would all intersect, nobody could predict. But as long as we remained friends, and as long as I remained neutral, it would work out fine.

"Mom, thanks so much. Oh, and please don't mention any of this to Sally. She still talks to a lot of people in Grandville, and well, this was shared in confidence," I said, thinking about my sister and her mouth.

"She'll be so proud of your business, though," Mom protested.

"No, not that, the part about Charlotte and the affair."

Oh no.

"You didn't tell me Charlotte was having an affair! Why, that seems so unlike her," Mom said.

I shoved an imaginary foot—a big hairy one, coated with dirt—into my mouth.

"Well, that just goes to show you, nobody is immune," Mom went on. "Who is it with? Do I know him? Jim's such a nice boy. You and your sister were both in their wedding, right?"

"Look, Mom, this is soooo important. Not a word about this to Sally. Not a peep. Promise?"

"Yes, dear! My lips are sealed, except about your business. I'll do some research online for you, too!" Mom's, phone cord was thwumping her kitchen floor loudly in the background. "Now go get that website built, a business card designed, and send me a copy online. You know how to do that, right?"

21

ASIDE FROM THE CHARLOTTE SLIP, THE CALL WITH MOM
was motivating. And decisive. Once I arrived home, I called Patrick and asked him to file for my LLC license as a sole proprietor.
Then, he let me "borrow" the law firm's IT guy to help me register
the name of my company—KellyJohnsonHomeStaging.com—as
a URL. I then turned my attention to writing the copy points for
the best home-staging website in the business. Credentials: minor
in fine arts; my years with the public relations firm and countless
freelance projects; interior design for private clients (myself, my
mom, and a couple friends, but I would make it sound bigger than
that); and a life-long resident of Grandville. That sounded pretty
impressive. All of that information could go below the fold and
next to my professional headshot.

Right . . . I don't have a professional headshot. Oreo, can you
work a camera? No opposable thumbs, you say? Drats. Well, Patrick would have to take a photo of me when he came home from
work.

The top of the page would be the hydrangea, of course, and the
middle? Well, I suppose the photos of my first job. Before on the

left; after on the right. And the copy: Just imagine what I could do for you. This home sold in under 10 days, and your client's can too. Let—no—allow me the privilege of working with you. Experience exquisite home staging.

I liked it. Simple, but compelling. Heck, I'd have my home staged by me if I were moving.

This was becoming real. I was starting my own home-based business.

I smiled as I looked around my kitchen and took stock of my sunshiny Post-it notes, beaming their life changes at me. I quickly wrote T2C #17: Practice Yoga, and attached it to the kitchen wall in one of the few open spots. I was getting a job (T2C #14) by creating a business. I hadn't had time to miss my Italian getaway, and I was sure I'd be successful enough to plan a vacation for the four of us soon. I'd done a remarkable job on T2C #6; in fact, I hadn't watched an episode of *Law & Order* in a couple of weeks. I'd been fairly good at keeping self-deprecation to a minimum (T2C #10), and although I had stormed out on Charlotte, I had joined her for lunch and listened (T2C #5). Now that I had both rows of teeth protected, I should be well on my way to accomplishing T2C #2, the minimizing of dental visits. I grabbed note #7 and crumpled it up. A better alternative than getting paid to link exchange students with Americans would be—I wrote it down—Take home staging course and earn designation. The new T2C #7.

I felt really good. I was on my way to finding the real me again. Maybe it wasn't one or the other: hard-driving, full-time businesswoman versus fully devoted, stay-at-home mom. Maybe I could combine them—both parts of me.

Patrick was golfing this afternoon and Melanie was still at Beth's. Oreo looked at me like he really needed attention—shiny eyes, fish in mouth—so I headed upstairs to change into tennis shoes. T2C #12—cardio exercise—actually sounded appealing to me. And, as a bonus, I was losing weight. Sure, I'd had an anorexic living with me, but that wasn't it. Well, not all of it. I was learning that losing weight wasn't about a diet for me; it was more about taking responsibility. It's really a whole new feeling when you realize you're in charge of your life, your thoughts, and your actions—or inaction.

I can no longer hold my thyroid responsible. Nope, if I continued to pack on the camp pounds, I'd only have myself to blame. Okay: yes, I had sent away for *The Thyroid Solution*, a book that promised weight loss without cutting calories, stress cured, hair loss reversed, anxiety halted, fatigue conquered, and depression defeated. Unfortunately, after reading the book, I discovered I am not one of the 24 million Americans who actually have the condition. It would have been a great excuse, though.

On my way past Melanie's room, I heard a faint telephone ring. Her cell phone was lighting up on her bed. I'd never seen her without it, omnipresent appendage that it was. When a cell phone rings, one must answer it, I justified.

Just when I reached for it, though, whoever was calling disconnected. I noticed that Melanie had missed a screen full of texts and phone calls. Since I was here and she wasn't, I clicked on the first missed text. I knew a cell phone was a window to the teenage soul.

"LOL lame like ur parents," said somebody named Tom.

Scroll up, I thought.

"Clueless," Melanie had typed.

"no worry about Johnsons?" Tom asked.

"yeah prolly," Melanie answered.

"k. let me know when. 2mrow?" Tom asked

"No Gavin's over later," Melanie keyed.

"Let's just meet 2nite?" Tom had typed.

So, what was that all about? Tom wanted to plan something for tonight, whoever Tom was, but Gavin was coming over. So Melanie had suggested later, maybe tomorrow night. And was I a clueless Johnson?

The previous text series was from Kathryn, checking in on her daughter. They had a great exchange, full of love and support. That made me smile. Before that was a digital dialogue with Bruce, and it was the same kind of thing: love from a dad to a daughter. Well, that was good. I had no idea Melanie was in such constant contact with her folks. It made me glad, and jealous that I wasn't able to be with my boys. This whole unplugged thing at camp was starting to get on my nerves.

Oreo and I heard the front door open at the same time. Rather than bark and charge down the stairs to greet Melanie, however, I quickly tossed the phone back onto her bed and dashed to my bedroom. I quietly closed the door and then took a deep breath. That was a close call.

At least I wasn't quite so clueless anymore.

That evening as Patrick and I sat down for dinner, Melanie breezed through the kitchen and headed outside to the backyard. She semi-smiled on her way by. I'd given up trying to force-feed her or mention the fact we were having dinner; it seemed obvious. I guess my belief that Melanie was just an innocent, lost kid had been altered by the text messages. If she could call people who were hosting her and trying to help her, "clueless," then what else was she saying, texting, and doing behind our backs?

"What is it?" Patrick asked, noticing my grimace.

"Oh, I was just thinking I need to add to my Things to Change list. Number Eighteen: Don't be so gullible," I answered.

"Oh, just ignore her. It's going to be fine. Um, by the way, I noticed the pills in our bathroom cabinet from a doctor I've never heard of," Patrick said, looking at me intently.

Busted.

"Why are you taking an antidepressant, Kelly? I didn't know you were unhappy. Why haven't you told me? I thought we had a great life?"

"It's hard to put into words, Patrick, but it's not about you or us or our home. I love you and the boys, of course. I just feel like something is missing. That I'm not living all the way. I think working could really help, and I know the medicine is already making me less weepy. I was tired of feeling on the verge of crying all the time," I said, not sure I was explaining any of my feelings quite right.

"Dr. Weiskopf is great, incidentally. The breast center staff recommended her to me after the biopsy. I found her card again a couple of weeks ago and just decided to give her a call. Things have been so hectic, I haven't had a quiet moment to tell you."

"Do you want me to come with you, to see her?" Patrick asked, being protective and forceful and there.

"No. Not now. This is my journey, and I need to do it alone. The good news is that I'm feeling better, and I'm excited about the future. I can see it, envision it now."

I spent the next few days learning more about home staging. What I'd discovered was both encouraging and, well, discouraging. A woman blogger wrote that the minimum investment to get started was $20,000. She spent thousands on furniture and accessories, storage, and warehousing for at least three houses' worth of items; she purchased art and had her own moving truck, and that was all before advertising expenses.

I couldn't begin to invest that much in my start-up. Given the economy and Patrick's warning that we needed to take it easy, I couldn't jeopardize our family's finances with that type of cash outlay. Another woman wrote how she'd invested $10,000 her first three months in business, with $2,000 of it wasted on a worthless certification.

Maybe all the naysayers were trying to keep new people out of the business? One home stager complained that home staging was mostly free work and there were too many people trying to do it. She wrote that she spent most of her time educating clients and the real estate community about what the value of home staging was: to sell houses faster, for top dollar. Well, that part I understood. And she ended her little tirade by telling whoever was reading her blog—that would be me at that moment—to pick another field.

I finally decided that no matter how many scary or negative articles and opinions I read, I could do this and that I would give it a try. With that, I closed my laptop and went to get ready for my appointment with Dr. Weiskopf.

"I think my bathtub is nearly filled back up," I said to Dr. Weiskopf as I settled into her comfortable couch. It was true, I felt better. But it was still weird being here, being "shrunk." Before coming in, I'd looked around the parking lot, making sure no one spotted me. I wasn't sure why I felt I needed to hide the fact I was seeing a shrink, but that's how I felt. I could imagine Rachel and the gang having a field day with the information: just something else for her to talk about, to reinforce her feelings of superiority to everyone else, especially me.

When I was sure the coast was clear, I'd rushed into the office. Funny, I hadn't worried about seeing anyone else in the waiting room, but a woman was sitting in the corner, next to the window. Dr. Weiskopf's cute assistant looked up and smiled as I signed in. Soon after, he called me in. The other woman had remained there, staring out the window, and never looked up. Maybe that's how we're supposed to act in the office: pretend we aren't really here? If we didn't acknowledge each other, maybe we didn't really exist in each other's lives. When I had glanced at her, it seemed as if she was trying to melt into the wall. I'm not sure I am ever that still.

"That's great news, Kelly," Dr. Weiskopf said. "I'm glad you're feeling better. How is the rest of your life going?"

"That's a rather open-ended question," I said, and then laughed nervously.

Dr. Weiskopf simply sat and watched me. Finally, she spoke. "Betty Friedan called it 'the problem with no name' in *The Feminine Mystique*. It's that feeling of wanting to do more, to be more than a housewife. It's okay to challenge yourself and to think about your life. I think that's part of what you're wrestling with here, Kelly."

"I just finished my first home staging job and really liked it, aside from the creepy owner of the house who sort of attacked me, but it was nothing I couldn't handle," I blabbed rapidly. "Patrick and I are really connecting, but Melanie thinks we're clueless, and maybe we are, but she is spending time with Beth so that's good. My mom said to be Swiss when it came to my friend Charlotte's affair, so I'm trying to, but I wonder if going into business with her is wise." I stopped to take a breath.

She smiled. Wrote a couple of notes. Looked back at me.

"Kelly, it is important that you don't stretch yourself too thin. I know you're feeling better mentally, but you've suddenly taken on a lot, not the least being a job. Take your time, see how it pans out. You don't need to make business commitments immediately. You've done a remarkable thing uniting Melanie and Beth and allowing them time to work together, with your support. Make sure, in all of this, you are doing things for you. Things to keep you balanced and healthy. It's easy, especially during times of change, to feel anxious. It's important to stay grounded and true to yourself."

"I am. I feel good. Busy, but busy in the ways I want to be. And challenged. Excited. I still miss the boys every minute, but I don't spend every minute dwelling on it. Melanie and I are actually going to take yoga together. All in all, I'm good." And that's how I felt.

Dr. Weiskopf suggested we meet again in a month, which I took as a sign that I was in a "not so crazy" category of patient. Clearly, the good doctor needed to keep her calendar open for people far more miserable than I was, and in fact, I didn't feel miserable at all. My problems weren't uncommon or insurmountable, neither the depression nor the feeling of unrest under the surface. Now I knew Betty Friedan had named it a long time ago. I left, all smiles, waved so long to the hunk behind the desk, sneaked a peek at the corner, noted the woman had vanished, and dashed back to Doug, fairly certain no one had seen me.

22

RESEARCH FINISHED, TODAY HAD BEEN SPENT FOCUSING on the fun part of my new business: the marketing. With my background in public relations and a little bit of design skill honed by helping out at various charity events and school fundraisers along the way, I was ready to design my own business card. The font: Batang. The color: a light blue.

As I sat on my porch in the mid-afternoon sunshine daydreaming, I decided a hand-drawn hydrangea, modeled after the ones in my garden, would be my logo. At the completion of each job, I would leave a bouquet of hydrangeas for good luck. I'd found a website design and hosting firm I'd liked, sent them over the copy I'd written, and they would have a few possible layouts for my homepage within the next day or two. As I ran inside to grab my sketchbook and my watercolors, Melanie walked in the door.

That wasn't surprising, but the smile she wore was. "Hey, Kelly!" she chirped, and she bent down so Oreo could kiss her cheek and drop his Lucky Carp at her feet. "I've had the best day!"

"That's great. So have I! Hey, I signed us up for yoga. It starts today—this evening at 5:30, actually. Twice a week for an hour each session. It's the beginners' class, so they said we'd be fine."

"Okay, I guess. Gavin's coming over tonight, but I'll tell him to come a little later." She sat on the floor with Oreo in her lap. Looking at her, watching her cuddle the dog, I felt that pang again. But if I'd had a daughter, she'd probably think I was clueless, too, I told myself.

"So, um, I guess we'll need to leave here in a couple hours to head over. I'm working on business cards. Want to help?"

"No thanks. I'll be in my room. Let me know when it's time to go," she said, slowly getting up. "Oh, and Kelly . . . Beth is nice."

"Yes, she is," I answered to Melanie's back as she headed up the stairs. That was as close as my beautiful lodger had come to starting a conversation. At least that was something. Maybe I could call Beth and find out what I was so clueless about. I stared at the art supplies I'd collected to use in working on my business cards. But instead of starting there, I knew I would not be able to concentrate on them until I had talked to Beth.

"You just need to keep being patient," Beth explained as I expressed my exasperation with Melanie's lack of real communication. She'd been much more friendly, loved helping out with Oreo, and even spent some time downstairs with Patrick and me in the evenings. But the fact was, most of the time she was either hiding in her room, jogging, or hanging out with her boyfriend—or the young man who lurked in the bushes in the corner of our yard.

"The thing is, I think she knows more about what's going on with her parents than she is letting on," I said. I'd told Beth everything Charlotte had confided in me, knowing it was having or would have an impact on Melanie's life. "And she's in contact with

both of them. Sweet, loving text messages on her cell phone . . ."
Oops.

"Kelly! You really can't spy on her. That would destroy any trust you are trying to build with Melanie."

I felt like a two-year-old being scolded. I needed a peanut butter cup. No, I could handle this. "Here's the thing, though, Beth; she says I'm clueless, but I'm not sure if it's in general or about things she's up to that I should know about."

"Well, time will tell, I guess, but I do have to say she is starting to open up to me. And she's wonderful with Sarah. I wouldn't worry so much. I think the yoga class is a great way for you two to keep building your relationship. I'll encourage it on my end. She's coming over again tomorrow," Beth said.

"And how about you, Beth? What can I do for you? You don't know what a blessing you've been."

"This is what I want to do. You're giving me a chance to work with someone, one-on-one, the way I couldn't at the hospital. Really, thanks to you, Kelly, I'm developing protocols I'll be able to use to help so many more young women, I hope."

"Speaking of yoga, by the way, remember ninth grade girls' dance group? The talent show?"

"How could I forget? You were the only one who did the entire dance having started on the wrong foot. What that did to our chorus line! But with yoga, it's your own pace, so don't worry. Maybe I'll join you two sometime, when Sarah is older."

I was still laughing as we hung up. Laughing felt good, even when I was laughing at myself. Shared memories, even embarrassing ones, are what keeps friendships alive, or in this case, makes sure they're reinvigorated. Hopefully this evening I wouldn't become the yoga class clown.

❋

"Seems to me the only people who enjoy yoga are people who are already flexible," I said to Melanie as we walked out of class. Sure, I'd tried to keep T2C #4 in mind the entire, agonizing sixty minutes, including the warm-up and the cool-down. But with walls of mirrors surrounding us on three sides, not comparing myself to the thin supermodels and perfect A-team tennis moms all around me was impossible. Apparently, all of the over-exercisers from the club considered yoga their relaxation after four hours in the gym or long tennis matches outside. I, on the other hand, thought it would serve as my primary means of exercise. It could; it was tough.

"I thought it was nice," Mel said as we climbed into Doug.

"It was nice spending some time with you, even though you could touch your toes and my forward bend consisted of touching my knees," I said. Yoga seemed to be a natural for Melanie. And she looked amazing in her color-coordinated, light-pink outfit. My Ohio State University sweat pants didn't seem quite right, but I wasn't about to go for skintight workout clothes.

"So, tomorrow night would it be okay if I had a few people over, Aunt Kelly? We'll stay in the basement and keep out of your way."

"Sure. Do you need snacks or anything? Can I help you get ready?"

"Oh no, really, nothing like that. We're just going to chill, kick back," she said.

"In other words, leave you alone?" I asked, smiling. I'd picked up the panic in her voice. "No problem. Maybe Patrick will take me out to dinner. Oh, I've been meaning to ask, Mel. Have you heard from your mom lately?"

"No, not at all. But that's okay."

I wished she'd stop lying to me, but I let it go.

Later that evening, sitting outside on my favorite couch on the porch with Patrick, I brought up Melanie. Her request to have people over to "chill" didn't faze him. He thought it was a great idea. Then I brought up her absentee parents again, and the fact she'd lied about hearing from them.

"If it bothers you, call Kathryn," he said. "Melanie must have a reason. Maybe she thinks that if we think her parents have abandoned her we'll go easy on her, cater to her every whim. Oh, wait, that's what you're doing."

I gave him the look, and he winked. "I know I'm doing the same thing," he quickly added. "She should have some chores or something around here."

I guess I should try harder to connect with Kathryn, but heck, she needed a break. I'd called a couple of times and left messages, rambled on about how great Mel was doing, but now that I knew Bruce was screwing around with Charlotte, it was really awkward. Patrick didn't know that minor tidbit. I just couldn't bring myself to tell him yet.

"Here's the thing. Kathryn said she and Bruce were having troubles, and hopefully they would straighten something out while Mel stayed here with us. But I did think she'd check in once in awhile. I didn't expect Kathryn to up and disappear."

"Well, she'll get in touch when she's ready. Besides, you have a business to worry about," Patrick said as he took my right hand in his. "I'm so proud of you. What's your next step?"

"I need to get the word out to all of the real estate agents in town. I've started to design my business card. And now that I've registered my URL, I've hired a design firm and can't wait to see what they come up with for the site. Actually, it makes sense to work my magic for all of the real estate agents in town, not just Charlotte," I said. There. Take that, Charlotte, you tramp, you.

"I thought you and Charlotte were going into business together?" Patrick asked.

"We were, but I realize I need a broader base. I was thinking about hosting a cocktail party and inviting all of the real estate agents in town. Our house does have a certain snob appeal. When we put it on the holiday tour for the Diabetes Association fundraiser last year, there were long lines waiting to get in, remember? What do you think?" I loved my husband and his opinions, most of the time. Especially if he agreed with me.

"I think it's brilliant, but I also think you and Charlotte make a good team. You definitely need to make sure Charlotte will let you take folks over to the Thompsons' to show off your masterpiece. Speaking of that, can we go over and have a little peek? I haven't seen your final work yet."

The sun was performing its magnificent red, orange, and dark pink setting number. I was proud of my inaugural home staging. Surely taking Patrick over wouldn't be against the rules. And I knew Bob wouldn't be there; he hadn't been spotted anywhere in Grandville since our encounter.

"I'd love for you to see it. Can you look over there and see if anybody's car is in the driveway? I don't think Charlotte has any showings this late, but you never know. I'll go leave a note for Melanie in case she and Gavin wonder where we are." Like Melanie would care, I thought.

"Coast is clear!" Patrick said as I walked back onto the porch. We headed over. The sun had fallen below the horizon, and it was almost dark. I'd set new lamps on timers, and lights glowed in the windows of the front two rooms. I hadn't needed to be told that one of the keys to making a home welcoming was lighting. It was actually the most important component. That, and pleasant fragrances.

I turned the combination on the lockbox and extracted the key. We both looked around a little nervously.

"I feel like a criminal, but I'm certain it's okay to show you, right?" I said, key turning in the lock and door opening.

"Right," Patrick said, stepping past me in the entryway and admiring the transformation. "This is wonderful, Kelly. What is it that Charlotte says? You have exquisite taste. She's right."

I gave my biggest fan a squeeze and then showed him—with great pride and in even greater detail—around the first and second floors. The fresh flowers Charlotte had sent over made every room smell fabulous. I realized we'd been talking in hushed voices, as though we were intruders or something. As we rounded the corner to head up to the third floor, I heard a sound.

"What was that?" I asked.

"Dunno," Patrick said, passing me and heading up the stairs. "Wait here."

Yeah, right.

23

I MADE IT TO THE THIRD FLOOR RIGHT ON HIS HEELS, SO MY body blocked Patrick as he turned for a hasty retreat. The stairs being narrow, I just couldn't react that quickly. We both stood, transfixed, at the top of the stairs. Directly in front of us in the master bedroom were Charlotte and Bruce. In my beach-themed bed. At least they were under the covers.

"My God!" Patrick exclaimed. "Charlotte? Is that Bruce with you? Where is Jim?"

His shock was a bit bigger than mine because I already knew the scoop. But seeing it, them, in person, here?

"Hi Patrick," Charlotte said, pulling the covers up under her chin. "Jim isn't here. We're separated." She said it matter-of-factly, as if we'd just met her in the grocery store, in aisle 4.

I averted my eyes and said, "Sorry for intruding. I just wanted to show Patrick what I'd been working on, and, well, we had no idea you'd be here. Clearly. I'm sorry. I don't know all the rules about home staging yet, I guess. We should be going, Patrick." I tugged on my husband's hand but he wasn't moving.

"Um, say, you two, if you could keep this situation on the down low we both would really appreciate it," Bruce muttered.

"Oh, sure, Bruce," I said, suddenly fiercely, inexplicably furious. I hopped back up the two steps I'd descended and faced him. He pulled the sheet up to his chin in self-defense. "And I'll be sure not to mention the fact that while you're over here your daughter is next door at my house, trying to recover from a serious mental and physical illness that I have had to learn far too much about, yet you seem to be oblivious to; that and what your lack of care and self-centeredness are doing to her and to your wife. But sure, Bruce, I'll keep all of this on the down low. I wouldn't want word to get out that you're a horrible husband and father. No, I'll just let that be blatantly obvious as I try to explain to your anorexic daughter why her father, who happens to be across the street having sex with a woman who isn't his wife, hasn't visited her once since she's been staying with us—"

Patrick started to pull me down the stairs but I was still yelling. "—And Charlotte, I expect to get paid whatever it is you said I'd get paid by helping you turn this bastard of a house around so you could sleep in it with a son of a bitch. And you can just kiss that idea of a business together good-bye!"

We were down the stairs and I was sobbing. I can never yell and get mad without crying. It's such a curse, and it always totally undermines my point. How and when had my mad/sad reflexes gotten tangled? Patrick had his arm around me and was mumbling something in my ear about letting it go and going home when Charlotte, wearing what had to be Bruce's shirt and boxer shorts, grabbed my arm. She must've literally flown down the three flights of stairs behind us.

"Oh Kelly, there's more to the story here, I promise. I love you, and I didn't mean to hurt you. I'm proud that we worked together on your first job, and I can't wait to have a business together. Bruce bought the house. This house. For us and the girls. Isn't it wonderful? We were just celebrating! You helped make this all possible, Kelly."

Patrick stepped between us and said, "Congratulations, Charlotte, but I think right now Kelly and I need to get our bearings in our own home. She'll talk to you later." He grabbed my arm and pulled me toward the front door.

"Bye, neighbors," Charlotte said quietly as we walked out. Patrick slammed the door behind us.

As we made our way down the walk, down the driveway, across the street, and to our home, we were silent. It was a time for reflection or perhaps, as Patrick squeezed my hand tighter, for thankfulness.

When we reached the comfort of the porch, Patrick motioned for me to sit down and he went inside. He called for Oreo, and before I knew it, I had eighteen pounds of unconditional love licking my cheek. He enjoyed the salt of my tears. I just enjoyed the company and love. Patrick was back a few minutes later with two glasses of wine and a lit candle. I'm not sure how he did it, but everything he grabbed was color coordinated: blue stemware and blue candle and even cocktail napkins in blue and white toile. We'd make it past our twenty-fifth anniversary, I was sure of it.

"Well, that was something," Patrick said, sitting down next to me on the couch and receiving his own big lick from Oreo. "I hate that," he added, grinning and wiping his slobber-laden cheek.

"I hate that, too," I echoed, misunderstanding what Patrick had referred to. "I mean, jeez, Charlotte only told me about her and Bruce the other day, and then we had to see it. I think she just wanted a decorator for her love nest. I was royally used." My tears were dried up, and now, since I didn't have to yell anymore, I was mad.

"You knew about Charlotte and Bruce? Why didn't you tell me?" Patrick asked.

Yes, why didn't I? "I promised I wouldn't tell anyone," I said, knowing I'd told my mom and Beth. "Well, actually, I was trying to sort it out. I think telling you would've made it too real."

"It's certainly real now, that's for sure. I just wish I hadn't seen them together in bed." Then he chuckled. "They did seem to be enjoying the romantic atmosphere you created, though."

"Yes, well, that's the thing. I loved the project. I think I'm really good at this home staging thing. But I don't trust Charlotte. I don't think I can work with her. Business, like anything, has to be based on trust, right?"

"Right, but I don't know if this is a sign you can't trust her. I think it may be simply that she's in love. Oh, that reminds me. Hold on, I'll be right back."

As I rubbed Oreo's tummy and admired the candlelight dancing on the ceiling, I thought some more about Charlotte. It wasn't wrong for her to find love; it was the sneaking around behind their spouses. The most troubling part was Kathryn and Melanie. How were they affected; how would they be affected? It's not that I wished Charlotte anything less than happiness; it's just that I didn't want her happiness to cost my other friend hers.

"Okay, close your eyes," Patrick said, rejoining us on the couch. I did as instructed and heard him placing something on the coffee table in front of me. "Open!"

On the table he'd stacked five books, and as I smiled at him, he said: "These should take care of T2C #3: Buy a Suze Orman book. I got you one of hers, as well as these others for women starting their own businesses. I liked this one the best: *Real You Incorporated: 8 Essentials for Women Entrepreneurs.*"

How did I get so lucky, I wondered?

"To your future!" Patrick said, and we clinked our glasses.

24

I'D STAYED UP LATE THE NIGHT BEFORE, SKIMMING THE BOOKS Patrick had bought me. It was a wonderful exercise in self-discovery and inspiration. It turns out a lot of us women are out there looking to put our passions into action. It was good to know I wasn't alone, particularly when I was feeling betrayed by Charlotte. Well, actually, I guessed she felt the same since I'd yelled at her last night and told her we weren't going into business together. We were in a standoff. One thing I had going for me: there were more real estate agents than just Charlotte in Grandville. But I'd also read it was tricky to get a real estate agent to even consider using your services if they'd never heard of staging before. The key would be to reach out to the entire real estate community. Patrick had suggested I enlist Melanie to help and she had actually agreed. She'd called all of the biggest real estate companies in town and asked them if they'd consider encouraging their agents to come to a cocktail party on Summit Road. The incentive was a tour of two of the street's most famous properties, one of which recently sold at asking, for cash. While she was handling the calls for me, I smiled at my business card mockup.

Kelly Johnson Home Staging

Exquisite transformations

I liked my business tagline and the design of my business card, featuring the hand-drawn hydrangea. I decided to start writing a business plan, and whenever I got stymied, I'd reach for one of the books Patrick had given me.

I couldn't believe it when Patrick walked through the door at 6:30 that evening. Time had flown. "Hey how's my favorite home stager doing?" His enthusiasm and support were the best. He'd even written the boys at camp—one-way email—to tell them I had a huge surprise to tell them about so they'd better ask to make a special call home. "They should both be on the telephone, which should be ringing in about ten minutes."

I didn't have the heart to tell him that the boys would think the news was something else they'd been waiting to hear: that we built a pool.

Oh well, at least I'd get to hear their voices, and they'd be happy voices until they heard the real news. And, though they'd be disappointed, they were old enough to fake support. I hoped so, at any rate.

"Hey guys, what's up?" David asked as soon as we answered, both on separate extensions in different rooms of the house. Remarkably, David had not only made a point to be on the phone but also bumped his own little brother and taken the receiver first. At the moment, we were his top priority, way above nature hikes. It wouldn't last.

"Hi Champ! We have some great news!" Patrick said, bursting with enthusiasm.

"I know, I know, that's what you wrote me in the email. And?" David said.

"Yes, about that; you haven't written once," I said.

"Mom, I know, alright? I'll write. What's the news?"

"Your mom is starting her own business!" Patrick said.

"No pool?"

"Nope," I said.

"Bummer. Well, good luck, Mom," David said. "I'll tell Sean what the news is. He'll be kinda bummed, too. We thought it was the pool."

"I know. That's okay," I said. "I love you."

"Son, you should be proud of your mom," Patrick said.

"I am, Dad. I'm proud of both of you. Hey, I'm on the travel-ing basketball team. I think I'll get the award this week at camp-fire! Did I tell you that? I've gotta go. Oh, and Sean is on the team, too, so he'll have to talk to you later. Love you! Bye!"

"Sorry," Patrick said, looking disappointed as he rejoined me in the kitchen. "Kids are selfish sometimes."

"That's their job. Later, when they're grown-ups, they can pre-tend to care about things they don't really care about," I said. "They really want a pool."

"Little shits," he said, laughing. "So, it's date night out tonight, remember?"

"Are you sure it's okay to leave Melanie and let her have peo-ple over?" I asked.

"Sure, we won't be late. Go get ready and I'll take a look at your business plan, if that's okay?"

Melanie hadn't materialized yet, and I assumed she was still at Beth's. As I passed by her room, her open laptop beckoned me with its quiet glow. I noticed a pink Post-it note on the wall next to her bed. It read, "One day at a time." I smiled.

I would respect her privacy for now, but I wasn't going to remain clueless forever. Was I?

Yes. We both were. Mr. and Mrs. Clueless.

We were in Doug, heading home after a wonderful dinner at our favorite romantic restaurant, The Refectory. Housed in an 1890s church, it featured fabulously rich French cuisine and an amazing wine cellar. We were happy, chatting about the new exhibit coming to the Wexner Center the following week as we turned onto Summit, our street. Two blocks from our house we noticed that somebody must be having a party, because cars were parked along both sides of the road for as far as we could see.

And then we both knew, of course, the party was at our house. My enlightenment coincided precisely with the moment I happened to glance at the dashboard and notice T2C #18. Yes, gullible and clueless.

We couldn't pull into the driveway; cars were packed in it. Patrick drove up onto the lawn and jumped out. Framed by our headlights was a teenage boy who looked a lot like one of Bob and Heidi's kids. He held a bottle in one hand in the same sort of pose Bob had been in the night I'd fled from him.

"Ah, hey, Mr. Johnson," the boy muttered.

"Who is that?" Patrick asked.

"Tom Thompson, you know, from across the street. Mrs. Johnson redid my old house. Looks great, Mrs. Johnson," he added, looking at me.

"What's going on here, Tom?" Patrick asked as I followed both of them toward the house.

"Not much, really. Just a few kids kicking back, you know," he said, and then, like magic, he disappeared into the bushes next to our house. He was the boy who'd been talking to Mel when she'd headed out for a jog, I realized. I wondered if he was the one who'd suggested the party in the first place, the one whom she'd been text messaging. I wondered why he was in the neighborhood at all, when he lived at his grandparents' house now.

As we approached our side yard, word had obviously begun to spread that we had returned. Kids were running across our backyard, disappearing into the night. I tripped over a beer can, and then came across an empty fifth of vodka. I just kept following Patrick as teenagers scampered away like mice.

"Where's Melanie?" Patrick demanded, grabbing the next girl who was on her flight to freedom.

"Who's Melanie?" the girl asked, scared and wide-eyed. Patrick dropped her arm and she was gone.

We'd made it to the backyard. The doors to the walkout basement stood wide open. I suddenly wondered where Oreo was in all of this chaos and hoped he hadn't run away.

"Patrick, what about Oreo?" I said, running up next to him.

"He's fine, I'm sure. He's a smart dog. Probably hiding," he said to me, and then yelled, "Melanie!"

We walked into our basement and confronted a pool table covered with empty beer bottles, chip bags, and pizza boxes. The floor was sticky to walk on. We'd created a mini-kitchen in the basement, for parties and entertaining. Patrick kept the fridge stocked for law firm events. The refrigerator door stood open, and the entire beer supply was gone. I hadn't even thought of it until now. All of the cabinets had been ransacked, too. I knew there had been a lot of alcohol stored on the top shelves, but I had no idea how much.

Around the corner was the room where we had a flat screen TV and a huge leather sectional. This was the boys' favorite spot in the whole house. They'd play their various gaming systems on this TV and use the entire space for sleepovers. Right now, it smelled like a fraternity house after a huge keg party. And it looked like it, too.

Only one person remained in the basement, on the couch. It was Melanie. She looked like she'd passed out.

Patrick grabbed her by both shoulders and shook her. "Wake up, Melanie, wake up," he said in a voice that would scare me and the boys but only made Melanie's eyes flutter behind her lashes. I checked her pulse and it was fine. She was breathing.

"Patrick, take it easy," I said, and then rubbed her cheek. "Melanie, it's time to wake up and go upstairs. Come on."

She stirred, and finally opened her eyes. She rolled to one side and then threw up—all over Patrick, the couch, and the floor.

25

I FOUND OREO HIDING UNDER OUR BED. HE CAME OUT to me with his tail between his legs, shaking. Poor guy. He'd been terrified.

I took charge of getting Melanie to take a shower and then got her into bed. It seemed like she'd vomited most of the alcohol she'd consumed, but I had no way of knowing. I'd need to check on her throughout the night. I also didn't know if she'd had anything else. Were kids doing drugs at our house, too? I had no idea. Clueless.

Patrick finally made it upstairs after my second visit to Melanie's room, a little after two in the morning. We were both exhausted, disappointed, and upset. We fell asleep without saying a word.

I woke up late and in a panic at nine in the morning. Patrick had left a note saying he'd gone to the office. I rushed down the hall and found Melanie still asleep. As I had done with my boys when they were babies, and as I had all through the night with her, I checked to make sure she was breathing before I quietly closed the door.

I decided I had to find Kathryn. Not expecting anything but voice mail, I called the same number I had been calling, and this time she answered on the first ring.

"Is something wrong with Mel?" she asked, panicked.

"No, no, she's fine," I fibbed. I would save the party story for later in the call.

"Oh my goodness, Kelly. I'm the most horrible mother in the world. And the most horrible friend. I am so sorry. I dump my morose teen on you, and then I don't even call. I know it's wrong, and I'm so sorry. I just needed a break."

I heard the distinct sound of water in the background.

"Where are you?" I asked.

"Montana. Didn't Melanie tell you? I asked her to be sure to let you know, in case you needed me. I haven't been checking voice mail."

"Montana?" I asked, thinking maybe I'd heard wrong. "Ah, no, Melanie didn't mention it. By the way, what's that sound, Kathryn?"

"I'm sitting next to the most glorious river, looking down through crystal clear, mountain spring water to river rocks with fabulous colors like burned orange, shiny gray, and this really hard-to-describe light blue," she said.

I was, meanwhile, standing in my kitchen looking out over my backyard littered with teenage party debris, and without much effort I could gaze down the basement stairs to a pool table covered with various colors of beer cans and old, greasy pizza boxes. Sometimes, life isn't fair.

"Where in Montana are you?" I asked, trying to keep the conversation flowing and my jealousy under wraps.

"Well, I flew into a place called Kalispell—it's up at the top of the state—and the ranch where I'm staying is next to Glacier National Park. It was thirty degrees last night," she said. "But it's beautiful. I'm surprised my cell phone works so well. We aren't supposed to have them, but I needed to keep in touch with Mel and the office, or well, anyway—"

"Kathryn, are you okay?" She sounded like she was crying.

No answer. How was I supposed to stay mad if she was sad? Argh.

"Melanie is doing fine, Kathryn. She's spending a lot of time with a friend of mine from high school who specializes in counseling girls with eating disorders. Beth's amazing, and I know she's made some progress with Mel already. Oh, and Melanie and I have done yoga together, so there's that. I think we're growing closer." I didn't mention that she'd also found me clueless and my house the perfect place to party unchaperoned. Why hadn't she told me her mom was out west?

Focus, I told myself. Right now you need to cheer Kathryn up, not bring her down more. What's a few white lies among friends? It was times like these, even after all these years, that lighting up a Virginia Slims still sounded good.

"So, how long will you be in Montana? And are you wearing cowboy boots as we speak?" I asked, trying to lighten the mood.

"Well, it's a thirty-day program, but I didn't think I'd even come. My assistant pretty much forced me onto the plane. I'm not really good at this, though. You just don't take a big break in retail, at least not at my company," Kathryn said. "I've never even taken a two-day vacation unless it wrapped around a work trip."

"I'd say it's about time, then, for you to take some time for yourself," I said. "It sounds like you need it, Kathryn. And Melanie is fine."

What I wanted to ask was, "Um, did Bruce plan on spending time with her at all while you're in Montana? When were you going to let me know you would be gone for a month? Do you know Bruce is sleeping with Charlotte and they're moving in across the street, into the home I staged exquisitely? Is there anything else I should know about Melanie, like does she often drink until she passes out? And how do you deal with her boyfriend? Why don't you like him, by the way, and what's her curfew?"

Instead I gave Kathryn my undivided attention. "What's your program like? What do you do all day?"

"It's about getting your life back in balance. They have yoga, horseback riding, and counseling. There is a lot of Native American spiritual healing, too. I feel more at peace than I have probably ever been in my life. I'm going to come home a warrior," she added, laughing.

She was going to need to be.

"Sounds good," I said. "Everybody needs a little warrior in her life!"

"Oh, shoot, they're ringing the bell for breakfast. It's eat now or wait until lunch. The food is all organic, healthy. Frankly, I'm craving French fries, but I'll make it through."

I could picture her then, finally smiling, which came through in her voice. "The blue sky, fresh air, mountains—that all makes up for the lack of fried foods," she said. "There are these amazing delphiniums growing right outside my cabin window; they remind me of your hydrangeas—they're that purple-blue color— and hummingbirds are everywhere."

"Sounds perfect," I said. "Relax. Enjoy yourself. I'll keep Mel as long as you need. And, uh, are there bears in Montana?"

"Yep, we take these sticks and bear spray on our hikes to ward off grizzlies and black bears. Kinda adds an extra level of intensity to this back-to-nature experience. Oops, I think they've spotted me chatting. Gotta go!"

And she went, before I could say good-bye. I decided to try Sean on his cell, just on the off chance he'd not had it confiscated at camp yet. He answered on one ring, too. I was on a roll.

"Hi Mom," he whispered.

"Hi baby! How are you? I can't believe you still have your cell." It was so great to hear his voice.

"I have it on mosquito; grown-ups can't hear it ring. But I can't talk right now; it's camp craft. We're making a huge fire. I love chopping wood," he said.

"I miss you and love you tons."

"Same here, Mom. Gotta go or they'll take away my phone," Sean said, and then hung up. His brother didn't even take his phone to camp. But Sean, a true digital kid, can't totally disconnect from technology, even when it's banned. It made me feel good to know now I could at least sneak him a call or a text message every once in awhile. His to me last year were short: "Need pillow. Luv ya." So far, this summer, he hadn't needed anything, I guess.

So, with my sons still happily tucked away in the mountains of Maine and Kathryn tucked away in the mountains of Montana, it was time to get back to my life. I'd need a little warrior attitude myself once Melanie woke up.

The doorbell rang. Oreo was barking and growling; not a good omen.

I opened the door to find Rachel holding an empty bottle of what appeared to be tequila.

"I think this belongs to you," she said, thrusting it toward me.

"I'm a wine drinker, Rachel," I said in my best warrior tone.

"Are you aware the entire street, for blocks, is littered with filth from the party you hosted last night?" She pointed the tequila bottle at me with one hand; her other hand rested on her hip.

"We'll get it cleaned up. Don't worry. Here, let me take that for you. Have a good day," I said, and slammed the door. That felt good.

When I turned around, Melanie was sitting on the stairs. Oreo sat next to her. Both of them were watching me, waiting for me to do something, say something.

Nope. Not this time.

Finally, after what seemed to be minutes but was probably seconds, Melanie said, "I'm sorry."

I stood still. Quiet.

"I made a mess. I let you down. I'm not sure how it got so out of control?" she said, and then she started crying. Big sobbing sounds were coming from her rail-thin body, and well, I just couldn't be the warrior anymore. I sat down next to her on the stairs and she moved into me. I put an arm around her and she gave me a hug. I gave her time to cry, and when she'd finally begun to calm down, I knew it was time for a real talk.

26

"LISTEN, MEL, I KNOW YOU'RE SORRY FOR THE PARTY AND all, but there's more going on here. I hope the time you're spending with Beth is valuable, and I hope you're telling her the truth. It's really important. It's important for you and me, too."

"I know, it's just that . . ."

"It's just that what?"

"I mess everything up. I'm a mess. Nobody loves me. They—my parents—put me with you like a dog at a kennel. I mean, that's how it feels. I don't even know where they are," she sobbed.

"Yes you do."

She looked over at me, but didn't acknowledge the challenge.

"I just talked to your mom and she's doing great. She said she's talked to you, and that you knew she was in Wyoming, of all places. You know she loves you more than anything. I know you know that," I said, looking intently at Melanie, who simply nod-ded. After a brief pause she said, "Montana."

"What?"

"Mom's in Montana."

"Right. That's me, being clueless again." Melanie showed a

flash of recognition, but she knew better than to say anything more.

We sat in silence for a moment. I'm not good at that, so I jumped back in.

"I told your mom, if it was okay with you, that I'd love to have you stick around until she gets back. That should give us some time to clean—I mean clear things up. Get better at yoga and stuff like that."

"You didn't tell Mom about last night?" she asked quietly.

I shook my head no.

"Did you ever screw up, Aunt Kelly? I mean, you know, get into trouble?" Melanie asked me after we'd sat in silence awhile longer.

"Oh my gosh, of course."

"Really?"

Okay, so I'd read all of the studies that told me parents should lie to their kids about their own underage drinking and the like. It's giving your kids permission to do the same the logic goes. Well, since she wasn't my daughter, I figured I could go ahead and tell her a little bit of truth.

"My first time drinking was a peer pressure situation, like always. I hated the taste of beer, so my friends made me screwdrivers. Actually, Beth and I were the target of the party since neither of us had tried alcohol yet. We both ended up really drunk. I don't remember much else. My boyfriend drove me home and propped me up at my door, rang the doorbell, and drove away before my mom opened the door. My parents were convinced I had done heavy drugs because I kept saying something about a white pill. Actually, I had a headache and wanted aspirin. I felt terrible. Probably about like how you feel right now?"

"I feel awful. It's nice to know you aren't perfect. It's just hard to imagine you or Beth getting drunk together or being out of control. You seem like you have everything together, you know?"

"I'm far from perfect, my dear. The more you get to know me, the more imperfect I'll be. The thing I've learned in life is that you grow more through the bad things that happen to you. You know the old saying: hurdles are for jumping. It's true. Once you get past the mistakes, the bad choices, you can learn a lot from them. I know you're a good girl, Mel. I want to trust you, but in turn, you need to be truthful with me. No more lies, no more hiding. I needed to know where your mom was. You knew where she was and didn't tell me."

Mel looked at me and nodded.

"It's about time we stop walking on eggshells around each other, don't you think?" I said, standing up and pulling her to her feet. "It's going to be okay, it really is. Change comes in small steps. I'm learning that myself. I think, just maybe, we're both at a crossroads and we'll help each other through it. How about we give breakfast a try?"

"That actually sounds really good," Melanie answered.

After our first real meal together, I suggested we call Beth and have her come to my house for a change. Melanie agreed, and headed outside with an extra large trash bag to start collecting party debris in the backyard. I called Beth and filled her in.

"She's a really smart girl," Beth said evenly. "I'm surprised that happened last night. But maybe it'll make her more open to connecting with you. She'll feel guilty instead of entitled for awhile."

"We did have breakfast together for the first time, and she ate some scrambled eggs," I said, proudly, although I knew Oreo ate most of them.

"Good for you," Beth said. "That's a good sign. I've been there; I know."

"Has she opened up to you at all? She must have," I said.

"We're making progress, but I can't talk about confidential discussions. I'll be over in a little bit."

"As I've told Mel, what helped me the most was finding someone to talk to, someone who'd been there, who understood," Beth said calmly. She'd settled onto the couch in my living room, and she was nursing Sarah. For once, Melanie had agreed to allow me to sit in on their talks, so my only job was to keep my mouth shut.

"For me, it was a woman named Amy at a counseling center called The Bridge. I'd stumbled upon it while I drove to my summer job my junior year in high school. She'd had anorexia; she could relate. I went because it had gotten so bad that my boyfriend was threatening not to see me anymore. He couldn't stand watching me starve to death. I went there to get help because of him, but it ended up being for me."

"That's why Gavin came over a few nights ago," Melanie said. "But we had a fight. He said I wasn't trying." Melanie looked down. "I guess that's why I agreed to have the party with Tom. Just to hurt Gavin, show him I didn't need him. But I really do." She had started crying, quietly. Oreo stood up from his spot beneath my feet, ran over, and jumped into her lap. "Gavin said we'd have to break up if I didn't start eating."

And at that, Beth smiled at me. I guessed we'd just made progress.

"I didn't know you had the same thing happen to you," Melanie said to Beth, almost the identical words I'd been thinking. I kicked myself again for not being there for her. "I guess that's why you understand what's going on with me."

"Anorexia sneaks up on you," Beth said. "It's a subconscious decision to exercise control over something—sometimes the only thing—you have total control over: your body. My parents' divorce triggered mine. All of a sudden, everything I'd known fell apart. For you, Mel, the dynamics are sounding much the same."

That was a revelation to me: Anorexia was not a conscious choice. "So you didn't just decide to stop eating?" I asked Beth, but I was also asking Mel, I suppose.

"No. But I remember loving the control over food and over my body. It's all tied to self-image, self-esteem. It was hard for me to talk to anyone, explain what was wrong," Beth added, and Melanie nodded. "No two people with eating disorders are exactly alike. There are many triggers, many causes. It's better to just look ahead, focus on getting better. I did. Mel will."

Yes, she will, I thought. With that, I excused myself because I had to plan the open house that would introduce my new business to Grandville's real estate professionals. Melanie and Beth smiled. I think they realized Kelly Johnson was becoming a force to be reckoned with, business-wise; at least I hoped so.

Patrick blew in from the office in a horrible mood. I'd been working in the kitchen since leaving the counseling session and was shocked to see it was already six o'clock.

"Hi, love, how was your day?" I asked in my best Kelly Johnson/ Laura Petrie wifely voice. If only Patrick could be more like Dick

Van Dyke and see the humor in the situation at hand. But then again, I don't think Rob and Laura Petrie had teenagers around.

"Where is she?" he demanded in a gruff, husband-who'd-spent-the-previous-night-chasing-teens-from-our-house-and-yard voice.

"Who?"

"You know who. Mel." Then he hollered. "Mel!"

It looked like Melanie was feeling the effects of the night before, too, as she walked into the kitchen. Her eyes were blood-shot and her hair, usually swept up, was hanging in strands all around her face. She looked like she'd been napping.

"Hi Uncle Patrick. I'm very sorry about last night," she said. She looked even tinier to me than usual, and I felt the urge to stand up and run to her side. But I was practicing being Swiss. So I remained seated.

"Let's sit down at the table with Kelly and talk about this," Patrick commanded.

He was intruding on my business planning, but my desk was, after all, the kitchen table too. I tried to smile equally, calmly, at both of them.

"That party last night was unacceptable. Do you realize that if any of those friends of yours had gone off and killed themselves or somebody else while driving drunk we would've been responsible? Do you realize how hard I've worked to be respected, trusted as an attorney? I fielded I don't know how many phone calls this morning from members of the country club complaining about the mess strewn all over the course."

"I'm so, so sorry," Mel said, and she started to cry. "I'll clean it up."

"No, you can't. The club had to open today so they cleaned it.

You will be cleaning our yard, though, and the entire neighborhood."

I looked at my husband and felt so sorry I'd added this stress to his summer, to his life. "I'm sorry, too," I said, reaching out to touch his hand. "Mel did get started on cleaning up the yard this morning, Patrick, before she had a long session with Beth."

"Good, that's a start. Look," Patrick continued as he turned and faced Melanie, "you're going to start pulling your weight around here. You'll do chores, help Kelly get ready for this huge party she's planning, and act like you're part of this family. Do you understand?"

"Yes," she muttered.

"Kelly, give Melanie a list of tasks; I saw you have one started in your business plan. Melanie, you can finish cleaning the backyard before it gets dark. And, if any of those so-called friends of yours who attended the party actually are friends, they'll get over here and help you," he added before standing up and walking out of the kitchen.

Mel's head was down on the table.

"I'm sorry," I said to the top of her head. "Patrick doesn't get mad often, but when he does, phew! Stay out of the way."

"He's right. I messed up. I need to finish cleaning the backyard. I'll make this right Aunt Kelly, I will." She stood up, grabbed a big trash bag, and headed out the door.

Watching out the window as Mel carefully maneuvered through my flower beds to pluck out trash and beer cans, I was glad Beth had come over before Patrick had erupted. Melanie had taken responsibility for her actions and she seemed okay with being given things to do around the house and for my party. Was it too much to hope that things would turn out fine?

27

TWO DAYS LATER, I WAS COMPLETING THE FIRST ASSIGNMENT for the home staging designation online course I'd enrolled in when Melanie came into the room wearing a broad smile. I was making progress and so, it seemed, was Mel.

"I'm going to Beth's," she announced. "She's picking me up in a few minutes."

"Okay," I said, trying not to feel hurt. In the past forty-eight hours we'd started to get attached, my troubled teen and I, helped along by doing yoga together after a huge workout picking up all the party rubbish that was strewn throughout the neighborhood. She and Patrick had done a great job of avoiding each other, so far, but she had cleaned up and she was helping with the party. He hadn't seen her in action, but I made a point to tell him about her helpfulness whenever I could, as a good Swiss Miss would.

"Aw, don't look sad, Aunt Kelly. It's just that Beth understands what's going on with me. She's been there, really been there. Thanks again, by the way, for helping me find her, and for helping me clean up the mess," said Melanie, giving me a hug: a bony, gangly, beautiful hug. "Did you know Beth specialized in eating disorder treatment when she got her doctorate?"

"No, I didn't. I'm embarrassed to say I didn't even know she had a doctorate. I'm so glad. I am. You know I'd do anything for you, and now you know Beth would, too. You aren't alone, even though you sometimes feel like it," I said. "Oh, and the Gavin situation?"

"Better, too. He knows I'm talking, getting help," she said. "He's going to stick by me. Just maybe not the way he did before."

"What do you mean?" I asked.

"Well, before, we'd go to lunch at school every day. I'd chew gum and he'd eat. That's just what we did. He said he wouldn't do that again; just sit by and watch me hurt myself."

"You're lucky to have him as a friend who's practicing some tough love, Mel. And that also means there'll be no more backyard rendezvous with Tom Thompson, right?"

"Uh, right. You know, he's the one who said it would be okay to have a few people over. He'd lived in this neighborhood and knew you and Patrick, so I trusted him. And I was so mad at Gavin. It didn't seem like a big deal. But it was. I'm really sorry I let that party happen."

I gave her a bear hug. It felt really nice to be needed, but I knew I could stand alone, too. I wasn't really sure what I was supposed to do next for her, but I was pretty certain Melanie and Beth had this figured out. I was just along for the ride; the chauffeur, so to speak.

"So, tonight for dinner, would it be okay if I sat with you and Patrick? Hopefully Patrick isn't still super-angry with me. And, would you mind if Gavin joined us?" she asked, knowing the answer would be yes.

"My only question is what will you eat?"

"Can we make it simple and easy to digest? That's what Beth recommends. Soup. A casserole. Pretty much baby food. Baby steps; that's what we're working on."

"Your wish is my command," I said. "I know just what to

make. We'll have some tomato basil soup, Caesar salad, and some crunchy French bread. Maybe Patrick will stop by La Chatelaine on the way home. Sound okay?"

"Sounds perfect. Thank you. Just don't be sad if I don't eat a lot. And Aunt Kelly, can you find out before dinner if Patrick's still mad? If so, maybe we should wait for another night."

"Nope, he's fine and tonight's a perfect night. As for the food, I get it. Baby steps."

Dinner began as what can only be described as a perfect meal with two teenagers. We all talked naturally and Melanie ate—not a lot, but a respectable amount. I was really warming up to Gavin, too, and realized that David was just a few years away from having his own girlfriends, and the problems that went with them. This was good practice.

Patrick seemed to have gotten over his anger, but not her betrayal of our trust. He covered it well, but I knew he was wrestling with it. For me, the party fallout had brought us closer, Mel and me. We were talking. Patrick and Mel just needed to get to know each other better, I reasoned.

Next week, Melanie turned fifteen-and-a-half, old enough to get her temporary driver's license. Shocking. I couldn't picture her driving, couldn't imagine that responsibility right now. Gavin, a year older and already driving, would be her teacher. Sometime between the soup and the Caesar salad, I asked if Melanie had heard from her parents—either one.

Gavin shot me a look, and Melanie nodded her head yes. That meant, I supposed, some text messages. At least she'd acknowledged they'd been in touch this time. Okay, time to shift subjects, I thought.

"So hey, Melanie, aside from phone calls, what else would you like to do for the party?" I asked. "I could really use help getting this business off to a good start."

"Kelly, your business is important," Patrick said suddenly.

"Of course it is, honey," I said, smiling at him.

"I could help with food. I'm actually a great cook, Aunt Kelly, believe it or not," she said, and smiled at the irony. "I used to help the nanny get dinner ready. I really like it."

"The problem is, Mel, Kelly would depend on you to do what you said," Patrick said, "to cook or help, whatever, and then, what if you let her down? What if you pulled what you did the night we went out to dinner? Then what would she do? Are you ready to face up to responsibilities?" Patrick threw his napkin into the center of the table.

The other three of us sat frozen in place.

Melanie was the one who spoke first. "Uncle Patrick, I know I let you down. I let all three of you down," she said, looking at Gavin. "It won't happen again. I am getting better. I want to help Aunt Kelly."

"I hope you mean that," Patrick said, and then picked up his plate and walked out of the kitchen.

I believed she did. Since her breakthrough, which of course was attributable to my amazing friend, Dr. Beth, and the fact she'd had the party at our house and now felt guilty, Melanie had been a different kid. She'd put the scale back in my bathroom to torment me (per Beth's instructions). Beth actually told me to pitch the thing in the trash, but I just couldn't break the chains. Beth also told me Mel was recording her successful meals and her setbacks and reviewing them daily with her. And, perhaps most exciting of all, Beth was talking about quitting her job at the hospital and opening her own eating disorder clinic. With this much entrepreneurial spirit around me, I couldn't be wrong in going for it—in a big way.

I didn't want Patrick's explosion to hurt our momentum. So, perhaps doing what I'd just counseled myself against, I made excuses.

"Melanie, Patrick is just stressed over work. Gavin, you and Melanie go ahead and go for a walk and I'll get the dishes."

"You know, he's right," Melanie said quietly.

"I am right," Patrick agreed. He'd walked back into the room and was leaning against the island. "Thank you for your apology. I'm new to this, too."

"Come on, Mel, let's help get the dishes and then we could take a walk. And like we talked about, you're going to need to make amends for the party," Gavin said, looking directly at Melanie. She nodded.

"We'll handle the dishes, kids," Patrick said. "And you don't owe us any money for the party. Nothing was damaged, just some alcohol gone. And we needed to replace all of that anyway. Helping with Kelly's party will be a great way to repay us."

"I'll make it right, and I'm not going to let you down again," Melanie said, standing to help clear.

"I know you will," I said to Mel. I smiled at Patrick. I could tell he wasn't quite convinced.

After we cleaned up the kitchen, Melanie and Gavin went to the porch and—I was sure—from there to the hammock. Nothing better than that, I thought jealously. My choice after letting Oreo out? Go find Patrick and make sure he was calmed down.

As I walked into the bedroom, he was in bed, reading.

"You know, Kelly, we should also invite title insurance contacts of the law firm, mortgage brokers, home appraisers, and home warranty business owners to the party. These are the people who refer a ton of business to the Realtors," Patrick said. He'd been researching my new business almost as much as I had.

Nice try. While it was great to know I had a mini-team behind me—including Oreo, who wagged his tail at me, probably wondering if I'd brought any table scraps upstairs—I was mad at how Patrick had handled his feelings about the party in the middle of the first civil dinner with the four of us.

"I know you're mad," he said, putting down his book and taking off his readers. "The thing is, I can't keep my feelings pushed down like you do. When I feel it, I express it. I'm sorry, but that's the way it is."

That's probably a healthy way to be, I thought, but I was still mad at him for his outburst. And at myself for being gullible. And especially at Melanie for putting us in this position.

"Come over here. It looks like you need a hug," he said, and he was right. I did.

The next morning, after a carefully planned breakfast with Melanie, based on Beth's handwritten notes—one-half cup of yogurt, any flavor; fresh berries; two slices of wheat toast—one of us was full (her), the other was still hungry (me), and both of us were ready to tackle our huge assignment. Mel was excited to be the official calligrapher, and along with Beth, she was going to hand-address all of the invitations for my launch party. I'd picked a shiny silver envelope. Inside was the invitation, printed on thick white card stock with a silver border. The blue hydrangea was growing from the bottom left-hand corner, and the words were printed in silver ink. With just a week to go before the date—next Thursday, 7:30 pm—we had to get all six hundred invitations out today. We'd follow up the formal invitation with an Evite that Melanie had set up online for me. That way the guests who we had email addresses for would hear from me twice.

Beth and Melanie set up at the kitchen table. The baby slept in her carrier on the floor at Beth's feet, Oreo on his mat below Melanie's chair. It was so cute I had to take a photo.

"My business—our business—is official as of today! Smile!" I said and snapped a couple of shots. I gave them both a warm hug before being shooed away. Clearly it was going to be a calligraphy and counseling session, and I needed to scram.

I'd been working on a vision board up in my bedroom, and this was the perfect time to finish it. Oreo heard me leaving the room and followed behind. I guess he knew I was the one who needed him most today.

"CAN I GET YOU GUYS ANYTHING?" I ASKED, WALKING INTO THE
kitchen, hoping I hadn't disturbed them. I saw Melanie reach for a
tissue from a box that had appeared in the middle of their invitations, envelopes, and address list piles. "Oh, I'm sorry. I didn't mean
to interrupt."

"It's okay, Kelly, come on over here," Beth said. "Melanie and I
were just talking about her mom, and how sorry she feels for her.
We're working a lot on Mel not feeling responsible for her parents,
remembering that she's the child here."

"That's absolutely right," I said.

Melanie just nodded and half-smiled my way. She seemed
suddenly intent on addressing the next envelope on her list.

"Melanie, Kelly and I are going to take a walk around the
block, if you don't mind watching Sarah," Beth said. "We won't be
long. I just need a stretch before diving back into the invitations.
When I come back, you should take a break, too, if you want."

"Sure, you guys go ahead. I'll look after the baby," she said.

As we walked down my driveway, I said, "You must really trust Melanie, leaving her alone with Sarah. With all that happened this week at our house, I doubt Patrick would trust her with Oreo. And he wouldn't trust her alone there at all."

"She's trustworthy, Kelly. She just made a poor decision. That Thompson boy, Bob and Heidi's son, was messing with her, acting like he was her friend. He just wanted to get into your house, destroy what he thought was your perfect family," Beth said. "Melanie showed me the text messages to that effect."

"Wow, that's sad," I said. "I need to figure out how to explain this to Patrick."

"No you don't. Melanie is going to do it when the time is right. She needs to be comfortable talking with him, build a relationship with him, as she has with you," Beth said.

I felt like telling her not to hold her breath, but maybe Mel and Patrick would build a relationship someday.

We both saw Charlotte at the same time. We stopped. Beth looked at me; I looked at her. Charlotte, dressed impeccably, was replacing the "Make an offer" rider with an "In contract in less than 10 days!" sign.

What to do?

"Let's head down the other way," Beth said, doing an about-face and heading back to the other side of my circular drive.

That worked for me.

"So, can you tell me anything more about what's going on with her parents?" Beth asked as we reached the first crossroad. "All I know is that it has something to do with your friend with the yard sign over there, and now, her mom is in Montana."

"Right. Well, I've just been figuring all of this out, slowly, myself. It's not like I got any information or instructions from Kathryn when she handed over her child." I was surprised at the anger in my voice. We were walking at a brisk clip and it felt good. I was determined not to have a woman who had just given birth outpace me. I just hoped I didn't start panting and embarrass myself.

"Bruce is self-absorbed and mean. Driven and successful, yes, but mean," I said. "Kathryn is brilliant. Aside from being gorgeous, she's broken through the glass ceiling many times in her career. She's always in motion: on buying trips to Paris, to Asia. I think she's been afraid to slow down. All that said, she's a great mom and a great friend."

"Are they getting a divorce? Because Melanie would be fine with that; it's just the not knowing. No one is talking to the poor girl," Beth said. "She is doing a great job with her issues and her priorities, as you know. She's relaxing, eating finally. But the last step will be some honesty between her and her parents."

"I agree. I just don't have the whole story, though. When I talked to Kathryn she was so fragile, I kept the conversation light. Charlotte, well, she's told me she and Bruce are together, and that they were soul mates. Apparently, they're moving in next door together," I said, realizing I was spilling the beans but knowing it would all be out sooner or later. Probably sooner. Grandville didn't keep secrets, and clearly neither did I.

"Well, isn't that interesting? Does she have no shame? I mean, she's friends with Kathryn, too, isn't she?" Beth asked.

"Yes, but as my mom so wisely told me recently, we don't know the whole story and we need to stop blaming the women all the time," I said. "I am telling you, Bruce is a snake."

"Well, whatever," Beth said, slowing down a bit. I was panting, and I couldn't hide it anymore. Maybe I'd need to add some cardio (#12) to my yoga (#17). "We need to tell Mel about all of this, as honestly as we can," Beth said.

"No. Kathryn needs to get back, and then her parents can tell her. You and I need to keep working on Melanie, getting her better," I said, hoping I was right, believing I shouldn't be the one to share the Charlotte news with Mel. "And speaking of Mel, we should head back." Before I drop over, I didn't add.

"Yes, the truth would be nice, coming from her parents. For once," Beth said, as we rounded a street corner and headed back. "Kids always know more about what is going on than their parents think they know. They're naturally intuitive, because they haven't been told yet not to trust their intuition. So, does Melanie know the whole truth of her dad's infidelity? No. But she senses enough. And she worries a lot about Kathryn, I can tell you that. Kathryn needs to grow up, take responsibility for her life, and start being a parent again. And so does Bruce."

"Agreed. But Kathryn has to take care of herself first, and it seems that is what she's doing. Bruce always has put himself first, so that's no surprise."

And with that, we power-walked back to my side door, and both of us glanced once more at the yard sign proclaiming Charlotte's success.

The rest of the day was consumed by stamping, sealing, and then mailing the six hundred envelopes at the post office. What a fabulous start to my business dreams. I wondered when I'd begin to make money instead of spending it, but I figured it would be soon. Heck, Charlotte owed me big time for decorating what was now her new home.

That night, Gavin was taking Melanie out for a surprise dinner at what had once been her favorite restaurant. He was confident (especially after a little coaching from Beth) he could help Mel figure out a comfortable meal.

When Beth headed home and Melanie headed upstairs to get dressed for her date, I decided Patrick and I deserved a night out on the town. I called him at the office, and he agreed. This time, we knew, we wouldn't come home to a teenage drunk fest.

We were tucked away in a romantic corner of another of my favorite places to dine. Tony's is an amazing Italian restaurant nestled in the oldest part of the city. The building itself was once an old brewery in the German Village section of town. The food is a combination of old-world recipes and modern-day marvels. We'd seen a few acquaintances as we were escorted to our table. When the owner came over to greet us—I vainly suspected it had something to do with my rather fabulous purple dress, which I noticed fit less snuggly than it had before—Patrick pressed me to give Tony one of my new business cards.

Tony congratulated me and in his thick Neapolitan accent said he would be happy to recommend my services to everyone, as I was a woman with exquisite taste. My business sounded so exotic and sophisticated when he said it. Well, actually, everything sounded wonderful when he said it. Maybe he should come to my party and just walk around, enchanting people.

After thanking him and ordering, Patrick said, "Bruce called. He wants the firm to represent him in his divorce. Can you believe he had the balls to phone me? After how I saw him last?"

Yes, I did believe it. "You told him you had a conflict of interest, right?"

"Morally, I am conflicted, but the firm isn't. Kathryn hasn't hired us. Can you call her and find out if she needs representation?

Otherwise, even as a partner, I think I'll be overruled. The chance to work on Bruce's personal affairs may lead to more business with Majors Entertainment. You know how that sounds to some of the other partners."

"Well, I'll call Kathryn then. Right now. It's two hours earlier in Montana. I'll be right back."

Outside in the parking lot, I placed a call to Kathryn. This time she didn't answer, so I left a message. Not having thought through this call until the moment I heard the beep, I stumbled along. "Hi Kathryn, no worries, it's me again. Mel is fine. It's just that Patrick got a call today from Bruce, and, well, he wanted representation and I thought if you did—Patrick, rather, thought he would like the firm to represent you—but if you have another option, that's fine, too. I hope Montana is lovely. Call me as soon as you can," I said and hung up.

If she didn't know she was getting a divorce before, she certainly did now. I felt awful. Panicked, I hurried inside and back to the table. The appetizers were there and Patrick was waiting patiently.

"What did she say?" he asked, digging into his carpaccio.

"I got her voice mail. But the problem with that is I left a message," I said, stirring my minestrone.

"That's what it's for," he said, smiling.

"No, listen, what if she didn't know he was calling attorneys? What if I just ruined her life via voice mail?"

"She's a grown-up woman who dropped her teen daughter off at our house and left town for Montana?"

"Yep, Montana. A program to find balance and things," I said.

"Okay, she's in Montana where she's rediscovering herself. I think she knows something is wrong in her marriage," he said.

"Enough about Mr. and Mrs. Bruce Majors for now; let's enjoy our meal. David called me today."

"He did? I spoke with Sean, briefly, but only because I called him. What did David say?" I asked, feeling jealous.

"That he needed more money in his camp store account." We both laughed.

"Well, at least they need us," I said. "And the way I figure, asking for money is almost like saying 'I love you.' Cheers!"

29

IT HAD TO HAPPEN SOONER OR LATER, I SUPPOSE, BUT I HAD hoped it would be after I had had a chance to talk to Kathryn. Being somewhat dense at times, I hadn't asked for the name of the ranch she was staying at in Montana, in case of an emergency. So, all I had was the message I'd left on her voice mail.

That, and Bruce ringing my doorbell first thing in the morning.

Melanie was still asleep. Patrick was at work, and Oreo was barking furiously. Maybe I'd told him a little too much about good old Bruce, or he sensed it, even through the front door.

I opened the door.

"Hi Kelly. Listen, I know how you feel about me, and I'm sorry about the other night, but I want you to know that I truly appreciate your help with Melanie. And I wondered if I could see her. Oh, and here, these are for you."

He thrust a bouquet of yellow roses at me. The sign of friendship. I hated roses.

"Ah, thanks. Melanie is still asleep, Bruce. Do you want to

come back later? Oreo, stop it!" I was afraid Oreo was going to eat Bruce's leg if he stepped any farther into my house.

"Hi Dad," said Melanie, her sleepy voice coming from above us at the top of the stairway.

"Mel Belle, how are you?" he said, brushing past Oreo and me and turning on the charm, which his daughter, it seemed, was not immune to.

"Hi Daddy," Melanie repeated warmly as she rushed down the stairs and accepted her father's embrace.

"Why don't you two go sit in the living room and I can bring you some coffee?" I suggested, feeling nauseous. I really couldn't stand Bruce Majors. "I'll just go put these in water and be back in a few minutes."

"Thanks, Aunt Kelly," said my teenage borrowed daughter.

Oreo and I fumed all the way down the hall to the kitchen and then I called Beth.

"Help! He's here!" I said as soon as she answered.

"Who is there? Oh, Bruce? The dad?"

"Bingo. What do I do?"

"You hang out there, don't leave them alone for long, and be there for the aftermath when he leaves. Sarah and I can be there in an hour or so. I'm waiting for the dishwasher repair guy. They said I'm the first stop. Just keep things calm, okay? And that goes for you, too."

Pot of coffee brewed, roses placed in vase, I breezed into the living room and right into a private moment. They were sitting facing each other on the same couch. Melanie's back was to me.

"Excuse me, but would either of you like coffee?" I asked.

"No thanks," said Bruce.

"No," said Melanie, without looking at me. I wanted to see her face, but I couldn't.

"Well, if you need anything, I'll be in the kitchen." As I turned to walk out, Oreo trotted over and leaped into Melanie's lap. Sure, she needed him more than I did, but I still called him a turncoat under my breath.

When the telephone in the kitchen rang, I jumped. It was mid-morning, not the customary call time for telemarketers, so I decided not to use my gruff salesperson-stopping voice. I did remain on guard, however. For good reason, it turned out.

"Hi Kelly," Charlotte said. "Is this a good time to talk?"

Argh. Could I hang up on her? No, even if I wanted to be that mean, I wasn't. Besides, I needed my paycheck.

"It's fine, Charlotte. As a matter of fact, I was wondering when you would be paying me for the staging job I did for you."

"Good. Okay. Well, I called your house because I was afraid you wouldn't pick up if you saw it was my cell," she said. "Here's the thing. What a mess. I'm really sorry about you and Patrick finding Bruce and me in bed, but we do love each other and we are getting married. Jim knows. Kathryn knows. Melanie knows, or should by now."

"Yes, I think she's finding out right now, in my living room, but you already knew that, didn't you? This is all so well choreographed, Charlotte," I said, slowly pulling the petals off the yellow roses. I had made quite a little pile so far.

"It might seem contrived to you, but it's heartfelt. It's hard to know how to handle these delicate situations. But love finds a way."

Ick. Be a friend, I told myself, to help Charlotte and to get the scoop to help Melanie.

"Charlotte, where are you right now? Are you at the Thompsons' house calling me?" I asked.

"Yes, but it's my house-to-be," she said, sounding defensive.

"Stay there, I'm coming over," I said and, after telling Melanie I was going to the home makeover house, I headed out the door. Too bad if Bruce knew what I was up to. In fact, I hoped he did.

I had to admit, the house suited them.

At least it appeared to be ideal for Charlotte and the girls. The twins, after giving me gleeful hugs, went back outside to play on the zip line. As I followed Charlotte into the all-too-familiar kitchen and saw the light bouncing off the sunny yellow walls, I gave myself an imaginary pat on the back.

"You really did a beautiful job here," Charlotte said. "That's why Bruce decided to buy it for me. For us."

"So this wasn't a setup from the beginning? I need you to tell the truth here, because either I'm charging you just for staging or for a complete interior design job. Actually, maybe both."

Charlotte shifted a bit in her seat. She was wearing white pants and a white and pink linen blouse. As always, she looked radiant. But as she shifted in her seat and avoided my gaze, I realized that for the first time I could remember, we were uncomfortable with each other.

"I had no idea Bruce would even consider it," she said.

"I've known you for twenty years, Charlotte. You're lying. Knock it off." I started walking around the kitchen, admiring the items—especially the hand-painted Italian plate I'd selected to grace the countertop.

"Okay, sure, I showed it to him, told him all the great things you were doing to bring it back to life. But, just for your information, Bruce was here, with me, long before you were," she said defensively.

"Oh, I'm sure he was."

"Look, Kelly, Here's the check for the home staging. I guesstimated the hours you spent here and paid you at the high end of the scale: $200 an hour. And here's another check, part of my commission, actually, for the interior design help. Global Furnishings will send you another commission check based on the fact we're buying all the furniture you used to stage the house."

I was actually somewhat amazed. "That's really generous of you, Charlotte."

"Seriously, Kelly, I couldn't have shown this house to anyone except Bruce without your help, and your decorating closed the deal. For us. Once I saw it come together, I couldn't let anyone else have it. That is the absolute truth." She handed me the two checks. "Let me know if I didn't calculate the time right."

"Thank you. And thank you for helping me launch my own business. Here's my card," I said. "Say hello to Kelly Johnson Home Staging LLC."

"But, Kelly, I thought you and I were going into business together?"

"Yes, well, and I thought we were the kind of friends who didn't hide secret lives from each other. But I guess we're not." Ooh, that was snarky, I said to myself. "Anyway, I figured I needed to get my feet wet with my own business first, build up a client base and then maybe partner with someone. Everything I've read said I should go into a business as an equal partner. Right now, you have all the clients."

"But this was my idea! You wouldn't even know about home staging if it wasn't for me," she squeaked. We were staring at each other across the island countertop.

"You're right. Thank you for the idea. But I had been looking for my next step, for something to keep me busy as the boys got older. And this plays into all of my passions. So I need it to be mine," I said firmly. "And Charlotte, I'm just not sure—right now at least—I could trust you as a business partner. Melanie is staying at my house, for goodness sake. Her mom is one of my best friends."

"You've got to be kidding me. Do you understand that half of the real estate people in town would never pay you to do a service like this? They don't even get it. Most of them think they have better taste than anyone else. It's just not easy out here. They won't trust you. You need me!"

Just then the twins burst through the back door and asked for more lemonade. Charlotte turned away from me, reached into the refrigerator, and poured two Italian coffee mugs full of lemonade for them.

"Would you like any?" she asked after the girls had chugged theirs and run back outside.

"No thanks. What about the girls, Charlotte? How much do they know? You don't have to answer, of course. You can just tell me to head back home."

"They know Jim and I are getting a divorce. Jim has agreed to give me full custody until he finds a job and gets back on his feet. He's in a really bad place right now," she said, pulling out a bar stool and sitting down next to where I was standing.

We were on the same side of the kitchen island now. And suddenly, I felt a little bit sorry for her. Not a lot—just a little.

"The first thing that happened with Jim was his own business failing two years ago," she said. "He'd acquired another paper distributor in Cleveland, and borrowed a lot of money to do it. That would've been fine if the price of paper and gas hadn't started to skyrocket the moment the deal went through. That's when the drinking started. At first it wasn't so bad. I thought it was a phase.

"You know that we sold the business last year, but like most people, you probably didn't know we had to. We only made enough to cover the business debt and keep the bank from taking our house. That's why I've been in real estate full time. Problem is, real estate is in the dumps, too. And I'm new to the business. It's going to take awhile for me to get to the Jane Smith Team level, you know?"

I nodded, recognizing the name of the multigenerational real estate powerhouse Charlotte was referring to. It was headed by a woman who was maybe five feet in heels, but tough as nails in business. All of her daughters and daughters-in-law worked with her now. They were the queens of Grandville real estate. I hoped they had checked yes on the RSVP invitation to my launch party. I wouldn't let Charlotte's words dissuade me; Jane Smith and company would trust me, I knew they would.

She took a drink of lemonade, and continued. "Jim had to apply for jobs for the first time in his life. That's really hard for a man who'd always owned his own business. It had been in the family for three generations, and he was the one who lost it all. He couldn't even talk to his dad; doubt he has yet. And, he had a wife and two kids to support. He got offered the job as head of sales for Comqual as a favor from his dad's friend who is chairman. But when the layoffs came, he was the last in and the first out.

"To sum it all up, the last two years have been hell, and nobody knows any of this. Jim wouldn't allow me to talk about it. Not to anybody. We tried counseling, but he wouldn't open up there either; thought it was a waste of money."

Charlotte was crying now, and so was I. I hadn't known. How could I? She'd never told me. Here I was, thinking her life was perfect, when actually it had been crumbling around her for years.

"Jim's wishes aside, why didn't you tell me, Charlotte?" I asked, quietly. I'd run and grabbed a roll of toilet paper from the powder room, and we both tore off hunks. As I asked the question, I realized that I hadn't told her about my cancer scare, either. We had both been adrift in our own misery, but we hadn't reached out to each other. Why did we isolate ourselves in times of stress, instead of connecting? Why hadn't Kathryn reached out to us earlier? Probably for the same reason. We all could have helped each other out so much, and we hadn't. It wasn't too late, though, I said to myself.

"Jim told me not to tell anyone," she said. "If people in Grandville had found out, it would've made the value of his business even less. That, plus the fact of having everyone staring at us in pity. Frankly, if they had called the note before we found a buyer, we had talked about just packing up the girls and whatever would fit in our two cars and leaving town in the middle of the night.

"Of course, that was early on, during the threat of bankruptcy. Jim's total deterioration into self-pity and alcohol abuse came after the sale, and more recently, the layoff. I just couldn't take it anymore. For too long I had no one to talk to. I was so lonely. So scared. And then, Bruce and I met. Remember the Michaels' huge Christmas party this year?"

30

"YEP, IT'S STILL THE TALK OF THE TOWN," I SAID, NOTICING HOW at the mention of Bruce, Charlotte's eyes had come back to life. It made me sad that Bruce Majors could find a way to reach out to my friend, but I hadn't even known there was anything wrong.

"Jim was somewhere, totally loaded. I was standing alone in the Michaels' entry hall. I must've been looking at the paintings—they have some fabulous art in that home—and a man's voice says beside me, 'I believe that's an Alice Schille.'

"I turned and saw the most handsome man I'd ever met, enjoying a painting by one of my favorite artists, and my heart went crazy. I know I blushed," Charlotte said, chuckling at the memory. "He went on to tell me how he was a Schille fan, and that he had an original sketch and watercolor by her hanging in his home. We talked and talked, and ended up taking a tour of all of the art in the home. I still hadn't seen Jim, and Bruce said his wife had gone home with a headache."

"Kathryn gets migraines when she's stressed. Happened all the time in college when we were roommates," I said. It was a lame comment, but I thought I should at least put her name out in the room.

"Yeah, I know, Bruce told me. Those are awful," Charlotte said, but her thoughts were back at that Christmas party. "So we ended up for some reason sitting together in the window seat of what had to be a guest suite off the kitchen. It was just Bruce and me. He reached for my hand and when he touched it, a tingling sensation traveled through my entire body. I'd never felt that way before. Ever."

"Uh, I think I should be getting back. I'm so glad you told me a little bit about what was happening and what brought some of this about." I really didn't want any more romantic details.

"But Kelly," Charlotte said, grabbing my hand. "We didn't kiss that night. We stood in that room and slow-danced to the Christmas music being piped through the house. It was the most amazingly sensual experience. But nothing happened. Not really."

"Well, it seems like there was, ah, is, major chemistry between the two of you, and that's great. I just wonder, though, if a man cheats on his first wife, does that mean he's destined to cheat on his second?" I knew it wasn't nice to say it, but it was a valid concern.

"Oh, no, Bruce and I are soul mates. We'll be together forever."

"Well, there you have it," I said, more flippantly than I intended. "I really do have to run, Charlotte. Oh, and before I forget, I'm having an open house, a cocktail party, next Thursday to launch my new business. You'll get an invitation, of course. I'm assuming I can bring people through this house to show off my work? I was thinking I could have small groups leave my house and come over to yours. We can limit it to just the first floor, or if you'd be willing, the whole house would be great."

"What part of your house will you be showing?" Charlotte asked.

"Oh, just the first floor. I mean, it's not really the star of staging."

"I don't know what Bruce will say. I'll have to ask him. I mean, the house is off the market now, and well, I'm not sure I'm comfortable with you launching your business at the expense of mine."

"At the expense of yours? What are you talking about? You asked me to stage this home. I put my life on hold to do it. I discovered a business I had never thought of, which I've thanked you for. I think this is enhancing your business, not detracting from it."

Now I was truly mad. I could feel the tears welling up. Why couldn't I express my anger without getting teary? Thinking that made my eyes well up more. T2C #19: Learn to yell without crying.

"You see it your way, of course. But if you offer your services to all of the real estate agents in Grandville, then you are cutting into my business," she said. "This was my idea, not yours. I really can't believe this!"

"Well, neither can I," I shouted as I walked out the front door and headed back home.

Tears ran down my cheeks as I crossed the street and headed up my driveway. Bruce's car was gone, and that was a good thing, because there's no telling what I might have done to it. I pictured hurling a rock from my garden through the windshield, but I doubt I would've done a thing if it had still been there. I was as effective at revenge as I was at anger without tears.

Oreo greeted me at the door and I called for Mel. No answer.

I searched the kitchen for a note. She would've left a note if she'd gone somewhere with her dad, right? I headed upstairs and found the door to her bedroom closed. The back-up fish hung from the doorknob. I went to my bedroom to put on new makeup, including Orgasm, of course, so I wouldn't look like I'd been crying while commiserating with the woman Melanie would be calling stepmom for the rest of her life. I took a moment to review my vision board, with all of its hope and promise of things I loved and looked forward to doing. And then I took a deep breath and headed back down the hall to her bedroom door.

I knocked.

No answer. Oreo started to whine.

"Mel, it's me," I said as I gently pushed open the door.

At first, what I saw didn't make sense. Melanie wasn't on her computer; it was lying next to her on the bed. She had found an old sleeping bag somewhere and was lying on it, her iPod earphones in her ears. Oreo jumped up on the bed and licked her face, but she didn't move.

That's when I saw the bright red blood that oozed from her wrists and pooled in the creases of the navy sleeping bag. Oreo whimpered and stood on top of Mel's still skeletal body, licking her face.

I screamed and ran to the telephone in my room. I dialed 911 and spoke to the dispatcher, who told me to get towels and try to make tourniquets around Mel's wrists. Everything started moving as if in slow motion. I'd felt for a pulse, willed one to be there, and then the sirens were in my driveway and the paramedics were hovered over her. They put Mel on a stretcher and carried her away to the ambulance, and I followed. Everything seemed to be a blur. At the last minute, I closed the door so Oreo would stay.

Because I wasn't family and couldn't ride with Mel in the ambulance, I started to walk toward my car, my hands shaking so badly I couldn't operate Doug's door handle.

I called Patrick. He told me to wait there and he'd pick me up. So I did, all the while looking at my hands and my shorts and my shirt, all covered with my borrowed daughter's blood.

Beth and Sarah joined Patrick and me in the awful waiting room a little before Bruce and Charlotte arrived. The ER doctors had insisted a parent be called, and since they told me Melanie was stable, I decided not to call Kathryn right away. She still hadn't returned my call from the other night, and perhaps we could handle this situation better without her. The insurance was under Bruce's name and company, anyway, so he was the natural choice. The psych ward doctor and the ER doc made it very clear that Bruce would not be allowed to see Melanie until after Beth and I had a chance to talk to her.

I had stretched the truth just a bit to position Beth as Mel's doctor, the one in charge of her care for anorexia, and played up Bruce's philandering as the reason why his daughter tried to kill herself. It worked.

"Dr. Beth Merwin," said the ER doctor, whose coat said he was Dr. Marsh, and we all looked up. "Dr. Merwin, if you could come with me, please, Melanie is asking to see you."

"Of course," Beth said, handing me her sleeping baby and giving me a look that asked, "Can I pull off pretending to be this type of doctor?" I just smiled back.

"What about me?" Bruce said, standing up and charging toward the door.

"Your daughter does not want to see you right now, sir, and as her doctor, I will be abiding by her wishes," Dr. Marsh said calmly. Clearly, he'd been through this before. "As I told you, she is stable and I will keep you updated on any issues. We will be recommending to Dr. Merwin that Melanie be placed on the psych ward for evaluation and monitoring. Suicide rates for anorexic women are more than double the rate for the general public. There's a strong link between the two."

He turned and escorted Beth through the magical doors of access at the end of the hall, and Charlotte, Patrick, the sleeping Sarah, and I sat in silence as Bruce paced back and forth in front of us.

"This is bullshit. I don't know what you've been telling her, Kelly, but I love my daughter more than anything. You've turned her against me, and I don't know why."

"Bruce, that's not fair," Charlotte said. "Kathryn asked Kelly to take Melanie in. This isn't her fault at all. In fact, until today, Melanie was doing great."

"Oh great, Charlotte, so you're taking their side, too?" Bruce said, shaking his head and looking disgusted.

"Calm down, Bruce," Patrick said, standing. "Your dramatics are adding more stress to an already tense situation. Don't blame people who love you, who have gone out of their way to help your family. My wife has been taking care of your daughter while you've been fucking around, and whatever else. Just calm down and sit down."

Bruce shot Patrick his angry look, which made me nervous.

Charlotte either didn't notice or was used to it. Patrick just gave it back to him.

"I'm going to take the baby for a walk," I said, leaving the two men in a staredown and cooing to little Sarah as we started down the hallway. This couldn't be a healthy place for a six-week old, with all the illness and sadness and death.

Dr. Marsh appeared at my side. I guess it was the rubber-soled shoes, but I hadn't heard him at all. "Dr. Merwin would like you to join her in the patient's room, and she said to bring the baby; it's feeding time. Let's go through these doors so we don't stir up the father, shall we?"

31

"HI AUNT KELLY," MELANIE SAID WHEN I WALKED IN THE room. She was lying in the second bed of a double room, the first bed being occupied by a large man with an equally large family. I pushed my way through his crowd to get to her bedside.

"Hey Mel," I said, stroking her head. She was so white and frail. Her left arm was hooked up to an IV, and both wrists were wrapped with heavy white bandages. She looked terrible. "You scared me so much. I'm so glad you're okay, honey."

"I'll be right back, Melanie. Now that Kelly's here, I'm going to go feed the baby," Beth said, leaving us alone, except for the large group just on the other side of the curtain. They were all surprisingly quiet, so I decided I had better be, too.

I pulled up a folding chair and sat so I was right next to Mel's face. "Do you want to talk about anything?" I asked. Beth hadn't given me instructions when she left, so I was winging it.

"Well, just that I feel stupid. Could we not tell Gavin about this? I know he'd give up on me entirely if he knew," she said.

"I think if anyone tells him, it should be you. What about your mom? Should we call her?" I didn't know what to do.

"No. She needs her time in Montana. I'll be fine. I don't know what I was thinking. I just . . . I just feel so hurt, so confused. I had been feeling better about myself, through Beth and all. And then Dad starts telling me how he's found his soul mate, and I don't want to hear about that. What about me for a change? What about what I need?" she said, softly.

"I know. We adults can be really selfish and messed up and needy. We're supposed to be caring for you, but sometimes we only care about ourselves. Some of us just never learned to give love, just take," I said. "I guess your dad was anxious to share his happiness, but he picked a bad time, and a terrible way to do it. I know he's sorry now. I know that, even though I'm not a big fan of your dad. He means well, and he loves you. You're his only child. It's the same for your mom. They just get it all wrong sometimes. Heck, so do I; just ask my kids. But you know I am here for you, whatever you need, and we'll get through this together. Okay?"

"Okay, and I'm sorry," she whispered and gave me a smile. Then she fell asleep.

Beth joined me a little while later at Melanie's bedside.

"I'm not a medical doctor, Kelly," she said, a little too loudly, I thought.

"I know," I whispered, "but you have a lot more clout as a doctor at a hospital than as my formerly anorexic best friend who I abandoned when she needed me most and who is now the parent of an adorable newborn and who is considering starting a counseling center for troubled teens with eating disorders because that's what she studied and got her doctorate in. So I sort of stretched the truth when I explained your credentials. But it worked. We're here."

"I know. It was a good call; I just felt a little self-conscious. I would've been a great doctor," she whispered back while burping Sarah over her shoulder.

"Yes, you would've been."

We sat in silence for a few minutes, watching Melanie sleep. "Did you ever try to commit suicide?" I asked, an odd thing to ask a woman cradling her infant daughter.

"I thought about it, a lot. The closest I got to creating this much drama was hitting myself with a hammer, trying to create really big bruises on my arms and hands and legs so my parents would notice."

"Oh my God, Beth!"

"They didn't notice," she said, and smiled down at Sarah, asleep in her lap. "What Mel did today was very dramatic. It was in response to a deep ache inside that she just couldn't handle. I think it was more of a cry for help than a true suicide attempt. Think about it: she found the old sleeping bag to lie down on; she was being really careful not to mess up her room—your property. She wasn't checking out for good. She was angry and hurt and she didn't know what to do," Beth said. "I thought she was ready to hear the truth from him, but I guess not. This will be a turning point in her treatment, though. In my case, I had underlying depression. Fortunately, I've been on meds since graduating from college. I'm going to talk to Dr. Marsh about evaluating Melanie for depression. I had suspected she might be suffering from it, but she had been making such good progress until now."

"I'm suffering from depression," I said. There, it was out.

"What?"

"This isn't about me, but I thought I should tell you, since you've shared so much about yourself and it might help Mel. I'm seeing a psychiatrist, and she has diagnosed me with depression," I said.

"Kelly, I just now realized that I never ask you about you. I assume that everything is going along perfectly for you. Perfect home, perfect husband and kids. You know: lovely flowers, the adorable dog, plenty of friends, new business. I'm so sorry that I've never stopped to find out about you."

I squeezed her hand and smiled. "Thank you. I'm doing really well. I am. And you?"

"Good. Better than ever in my life," she answered, smiling at me and then looking down at Sarah. "Really good."

We sat there, quietly, watching Melanie sleep. After awhile, I said, "It's hard to accept that she did this on purpose, that she planned it out with the sleeping bag and everything." I realized I'd talked too loudly. Mel stirred in her bed, but her eyes didn't open.

"No, she didn't plan it out, Kelly; she was just careful to not make a mess. I would never blame Melanie for any of this. It's just that she got so upset today and didn't know how to deal with it. She couldn't starve herself anymore and feel the hunger; that didn't hurt enough. So she went a little deeper, cutting and trying to feel more pain. She doesn't realize this fully yet, though it is what we've been working on, journaling about. It takes years to recover from an eating disorder this severe. But we are making progress. She's eating, and until now, we were moving forward."

"I know. I wanted to explain to you what happened this morning after I called you about Bruce's appearance on my doorstep. Charlotte telephoned and I went over to confront her. I didn't realize I was gone that long, but when I got back, Bruce was gone and I found Melanie upstairs." Suddenly it hit me, and I blurted out: "The scene I walked into was all my fault, Beth. If I had stayed there and watched over Mel, kept things calm as you had advised me to do, instead of fighting with Charlotte, Melanie would be okay right now."

"No, stop. This isn't your fault, Kelly. Even if you hadn't gone over to see Charlotte, she could have done it when you were saying good-bye to Bruce, or cleaning the kitchen, or even taking Oreo for a walk. Neither of us can watch Melanie 24/7. She loves you and loves living with you. None of this is your fault."

Beth smiled sweetly and handed me the baby. "And now," she said, "wish me luck. I'm going to have the talk."

"What talk?" I asked.

"The talk with Mr. Majors about the fact we're committing his daughter to the psych ward for observation, probably for up to a week. Dr. Marsh asked me to come along because he thinks the dad is—what was his word? Ah, yes: volatile."

"That Dr. Marsh is a sharp cookie. I'll stay here by Mel, if that's okay. Could Patrick come here to Mel's room? I know he's worried to death."

"I'll try to sneak him in for you."

"Thanks, doctor." I looked down into Sarah's tiny, innocent face, snuggled in her blanket, pressed up against the dried blood smeared across my white tee shirt. Be happy, baby, I thought. Be happy.

I awoke to Patrick hugging me around the shoulders. Somehow I'd fallen asleep while cradling Sarah on my lap and resting my head next to Melanie's. I don't know how long I had napped in that position, but I'd had time to drool and get a major crick in my neck.

"Sweetheart, she's going to be okay," Patrick said. "The doctor said Melanie will pull through just fine and will have a couple of faint scars to remember all of this by. Now, how about you? Are you going to be okay?"

"I will be, once we get Mel back home, she gets better, and I punch Bruce Majors," I whispered. As I sat up I noticed the curtain was open and the large man's bed was empty, his family dispersed. "Where'd he go?"

"Who?" Patrick asked.

Jeez, I hope he didn't die while I was sleeping right next to him, I thought. The idea gave me the creeps.

Melanie stirred and her eyes blinked open. She smiled shyly at Patrick.

"Hi Mel, so glad you're doing alright," he said, smiling at her. "You sure did give us a big scare. You rest and heal, and we'll be back tomorrow. I need to get Kelly home." He gave Melanie a tender kiss on her forehead. He was the best guy ever.

"Bye, baby Sarah," Mel whispered, as I carried the baby from the room. "Remember, Aunt Kelly. Please don't tell Gavin."

32

I'D COME HOME FROM THE HOSPITAL AND TAKEN A LONG, HOT shower. Patrick had decided to handle cleaning up Mel's room; he had it back to normal by the time I finished my shower. Except Melanie wasn't in it. I doubted it would ever feel the same. I untied the backup carp from the doorknob; I didn't want it associated with the room, either.

The next task was to talk to Kathryn. Maybe I'd just drive to Montana, I thought, until I checked the distance: two thousand miles, or about thirty hours. I'd keep calling. I had called her direct dial number at the retail giant's corporate office but her voice mail was a strange, non-personalized computer voice that simply said, "Leave a message for the person you are calling, thank you." I tried the number three times and got the same robotic snub each time.

I called Kathryn's cell phone again and left a friendlier, though more urgent, message. "Hi Kathryn. It's me, Kelly. So, hey, I need you to call me immediately. There's been an accident. Mel is okay now, but I need to fill you in. Call me ASAP."

Then I called the main number and asked for Kathryn Majors' assistant. There was what can only be described as a pregnant pause, and then the receptionist put me on hold. A few seconds later, I heard a slight click, then:

"This is Susan Standon, Human Resources Director. I am unable to come to the phone right now, but please leave a message and I'll return your call promptly."

I left her a message, too, saying I was trying to connect with Kathryn Majors' office. Fortunately, this time I remembered to leave my phone number.

Then I called the main number again.

"Look, I called a couple of minutes ago and asked for Kathryn Majors's office, but you put me through to the HR director. Please connect me to Ms. Majors's assistant."

Susan Standon's voice assaulted my ears.

"ARGH!" I yelled at the top of my lungs, causing Patrick to yell back from the laundry room.

"Are you okay?"

"NO! I am incapable of getting in touch with Kathryn, her assistant, or even a live human being at the corporate office. Every time I call, they put me into the HR director's voice mail."

Patrick came into our bedroom and wrapped his arms around me. "Hey, calm down, Kelly. You've left messages all over the place. Kathryn will be in touch. Mel's fine. Everything's going to be fine."

"You're right, Patrick, but I can't shake the need to connect with Kathryn. She's in the dark about so many things. Come on Oreo," I said, "let's go do a Google search of guest ranches in Montana. I'm sure we could call a few and ask for her."

"Great idea," Patrick agreed as he followed my loyal companion and me downstairs.

For a state with a population under a million, there sure were a wagonload of guest ranches. About 178,000 Google search results to be exact, leaving me with a big list and no clue how to narrow it down. Oreo looked uncomfortable on the hard floor so I brought over a cushion from the couch for him to lie down on. This could take awhile.

According to the Montana Dude Ranchers' Association, "Once you cross the bridge to a Montana guest ranch, the rest of the world disappears. Reconnect with nature, the cowboy culture, and each other. Warm hellos . . . tearful good-byes." That certainly seemed to be the case for Kathryn. In fact, I wondered if she would cross the bridge back to her real life?

I read on. "The scenery is spectacular in Montana, the kind that restores the soul. Create precious moments of discovery and learning that will always be with you, whether from the back of a horse, hiking on a mountain trail, or with the fish rising to your fly in a rushing stream." Well, good, she was restoring, learning, and discovering too.

There are three types of these guest ranches: working dude ranches, where visitors actually work with cattle and sheep along with real-live cowboys; dude ranches, where folks do a lot of Western style horseback riding and outdoor activities, even square dancing; and resort dude ranches, which are larger ranches with lots of on-site facilities. I was guessing Kathryn would be at a resort ranch where guests could horseback ride a little and relax a lot. Problem was, which one? There was no way to tell.

All I could do at this point was wait. Maybe Melanie would remember the name of the city her mom flew into or the name of the ranch itself. But that discussion would have to wait until tomorrow, too.

It was 8:00 pm and I still hadn't heard from Kathryn. Melanie's bedroom was back to normal, but I still got the chills when I walked past the doorway. Bruce, Charlotte, Beth, Beth's husband, Ryan—who seemed nice, dressed metrosexually, and was not necessarily gay, I decided—Patrick, and I sat in the living room of my house, a room we had rarely used until this week, it seemed. Of course, baby Sarah and Oreo were included, but they weren't adding much to the conversation. Beth was attempting to explain why the father of the patient was not being allowed to see the patient; legally, we actually couldn't keep him away, but we were trying to, for Melanie's mental health.

"I know Bruce appreciates everything all of you have done," Charlotte was saying. Why she didn't keep her mouth shut was beyond me. "But you have to understand how much he loves his daughter, and he feels so responsible for what happened today."

Bruce shot her that Bruce evil eye, and she stopped talking or even looking at us.

"I understand what you are saying, Beth," Bruce began. "I fucked up. It won't happen again. I'll be there tomorrow and I will see Melanie. And I will be there for her when she comes home. You're right. Her mother and I have been selfish, and in our efforts to avoid each other, we've avoided our daughter."

"You might have avoided her, Bruce, but Kathryn's been a great single parent while you've been doing, well, whatever it is you've been doing," I said. Kathryn wasn't here to defend herself, so I would.

"I've been building an international company, that's what I've been doing," he said, glaring at me.

"Let's stick to Melanie and her needs," Beth interjected. "If you insist on visiting Melanie tomorrow, I insist on going with you. She trusts me. She needs me."

"You realize, Bruce, that Beth has been volunteering her time, every day, to care for your daughter?" I asked.

"No, I didn't know that. I will pay you for your time and your help with Mel. But I don't need an escort," Bruce said, and with that he stood up. "Charlotte, let's go."

"I'll be there, waiting for you tomorrow morning when you arrive, Mr. Majors. Mel's situation is too fragile just now to leave you two alone. I insist on being there to supervise your visit," Beth said. She was standing, facing Bruce with as much resolve on her face as he had on his.

Bruce stared at her for a few seconds and then broke eye contact, heading for the door with Charlotte following like his puppy dog. The sight made me sick.

"That went well," Patrick said.

"He knows where we stand, and that we'll all be watching," Beth said. "In that sense, it was a successful evening." She sat back down with a sigh. "You really should try to get in touch with Kathryn, Kelly."

"I'll call again, first thing in the morning. I'll call her assistant, too, and get the name of the ranch. I'll track her down."

The doorbell rang. We all looked at each other.

Patrick went to the door. It was Gavin.

"Come on in, son," Patrick said and led him into the room where we were all still sitting.

"Is something wrong? It's Mel isn't it?" he said. "She hasn't called me, not all day. She's not online. I was so worried I decided to come by. What is it?"

"Have a seat," said Beth, patting the couch next to her.

I wasn't saying a thing. I promised Mel I wouldn't tell, and I wouldn't. Beth had heard Mel's request as well, but as the professional, she was deciding to spill the beans. She told him the whole story, and as she did, he dropped his head in his hands and began to sob.

Patrick and I excused ourselves and went to the kitchen. Ryan followed us with the baby.

"I don't know how Beth does it," Ryan said. Both Patrick and Ryan were looking at the pile of yellow rose petals and the half-plucked bouquet. "She is so amazing with teens."

"She's amazing with people in general. Did you hear her stand up to Bruce?" I said.

"I'd like to punch Bruce in the face," Patrick said. He was pouring himself a big scotch on the rocks. "Can I get you anything, Ryan?"

"No thanks, I'm fine. I need to get Beth and the baby home. I'm glad Beth has found her passion, but I just wish it wasn't coinciding with Sarah's arrival."

"Sometimes you find out what you really want to do next when you have some time to think," I said. "Being able to take maternity leave is probably the first time in her life that Beth hasn't been working and in her same routine. Not that babies don't take up your time, but you know what I mean."

"Oh, I agree. Beth's already started talking about office space. Anyway, it sounds like she's going to be spending a lot of time at the hospital tomorrow, so she's got to get some rest. At least it's Saturday, and I can be home with Sarah."

"Yep, you're right. I'll go get Beth. Come on, Patrick, we have a teenage boy to talk to, and that's your territory," I said, grabbing my husband's hand and leading him back into the living room. "It's man talk time," I said, winking at him.

"Beth, you need to go home and get some rest," I said in my

best Kelly Johnson/Julie Andrews *Sound of Music* voice as I walked into the living room. "Melanie will need you to stand by her as she faces her father tomorrow. Ryan has taken Sarah out to the car. And Gavin, how about a Coke and a turkey sandwich? Stay where you are and I'll be right back with a tray."

I left Patrick with Gavin and trotted off toward the kitchen behind Beth. I was quite the social butterfly tonight, I thought. Moving people through the house, calming raw nerves, extracting myself when tears began to fall. Was I leaving too much for Beth to handle? I wondered.

"Hey, how are you?" I asked her, once we were in the kitchen.

"Good, thanks; nothing that some sleep can't fix. Gavin's going to stick by Melanie; he loves her, I'll say that much for the young man. She's lucky to have him in her life. All the rest of her friends have dropped by the wayside," Beth said. "I might need your help tomorrow, depending on how things unfold. Don't minimize your role here, Kelly. You are the glue tying us all together. It's because of you we've all been able to rally around Mel. Remember that."

I gave her a hug. "You know how to reach me for anything you need." We walked outside where Ryan was waiting. "I love you, Beth."

"Right back at you, Kelly," she said.

As I watched them drive away, I thought about how lucky we'd been today, how fortunate it was I'd found Melanie in time.

I wondered what tomorrow would bring.

33

AFTER A FITFUL NIGHT'S SLEEP, I WOKE UP TO HALF OF AN empty bed. Patrick had left a note in the bathroom, letting me know he'd headed to the office for an important meeting, even though it was Saturday, and to call him if I needed anything. What I needed was for Kathryn to be in touch, I thought, getting into the shower after making sure my cell phone ringer was up as loud as it would go.

Showered, dressed, coffee made, and still no call from Kathryn, I reached the nurse on Melanie's floor at the hospital and learned Melanie was sleeping and in stable condition. Visiting hours were from three to five this afternoon, she informed me firmly. Well, fine, I was busy. I had a business to launch in five days. On Friday we received twenty-five yeses, and the invitations had been mailed just the day before. That's some impressive postal work and some party-loving Realtors. I liked that in a group. In my experience hosting parties for the law firm, for every affirmative RSVP there were double the number who didn't bother to reply and simply showed up. On that basis, I was already up to a guesstimated seventy-five attendees. Factoring in summer vacations and the like, my goal was to reach two hundred out of the six hundred invited. And that was before counting "and guest."

Now, how would I convince the real estate agents at the party that their business would boom with me in it? I needed to show them proof in the form of before-and-after photos of the Thompsons' project, mounted for display just in case Charlotte and Bruce wouldn't let me use their house-to-be to showcase my work. I couldn't imagine Charlotte wouldn't allow it; I couldn't imagine that Bruce would. Number Twenty on the Things to Change list: Tell Patrick I love him every day, especially because of the little things. And I counted my blessings again (T2C #8).

I walked around the first floor of our house looking for spots to place my new business cards for easy pickup. I'd have the computers—mine, Patrick's, and Melanie's—open to my website and encourage guests to register for preferred status, tonight only, and receive 15 percent off on each of their next five home staging jobs. That was a deal. But what was I giving away? I didn't even know how much to charge. Charlotte had suggested a flat fee, but had paid me for our first job by calculating hours. Turning to the fount of all wisdom, I went online.

"What is the average fee for home staging in the Midwest?" I typed. I was happy to learn I was ahead of the curve in the heartland, because while home staging—or neutralizing—a home has been around for thirty years, that was only in major cities like Seattle, San Francisco, and the other fly-to cities. Grandville being a fly-over place, they hadn't dropped leaflets, so we didn't know. I looked at six sites and discovered home staging pros charged about $100 per hour in the Midwest and spent, on average, fifteen to twenty hours of time working on each home. Fees were higher for a whole-home makeover, where furniture was brought in. I guess that's what I'd done at the Thompsons' house—called, I had learned, "vacant staging"—although I would call it disturbed staging myself.

So, I would charge $100 an hour. That seemed fair to me. I hoped the real estate community agreed. I realized I'd need to become good at estimating the hours required per project. I knew I worked fast, so I needed to be careful not to minimize my price. With my hourly rate established, the next step would be setting up a business process for potential clients. That would require a spreadsheet; I hated spreadsheets. The creative side of my brain rebelled at the notion of all those linear little boxes.

To procrastinate and avoid spreadsheet process-making, I decided to open the check from Charlotte. I hadn't told Patrick about it; I hadn't even taken it out of my jeans pocket. I didn't look at the amount when Charlotte handed it to me. I walked upstairs, sped past Mel's room, getting the accompanying chill, and found my jeans in the dirty clothes hamper. I rummaged around in the front pocket and pulled out the check.

Pay to the order of Kelly Johnson Home Staging. Amount: $15,000.

I blinked, a lot. At first I thought it was $1,500 and I started to fume. After my Internet searches, I knew I was worth more than that. Then I realized what I held in my hand.

I have to admit the dance I danced in my bedroom by myself over the first check for my own business was the best dance in my life. I'm not taking anything from Patrick, but boy, it felt good to feel good about myself. I'd done it! And, there was still a check coming from Global Furnishings.

My first job was at the top of the pay scale. I realized I had nowhere to go but down, theoretically, but still, it was time to celebrate. Based on what I just decided to charge—$100 per hour—she'd given me 150 hours worth of payment, but I'd pulled off the transformation of the Thompsons's house in just five days. Amazing.

I heard my cell phone ringing. I'd left it downstairs. Shoot. I dropped the paycheck, ran down the hall, bounded down the stairs, and raced into the kitchen just in time for whoever it was to go to voice mail. I checked the call log, thinking, Kathryn finally calls and I don't answer. It was David.

"Are you okay?" I asked, calling him back immediately on the camp's main phone number. I was still out of breath from my jog through the house.

"Yep. I'm just calling to see if you could send me a couple more books," he said. "I finished the stupid book on my school summer reading list, and I'm ready for some good stuff."

Be still, my heart. "Are you trying to make my day?" I love it when my kids read. I love picking out new books with them, sharing the classics.

"Mom, listen, I'm not supposed to be calling now, it's rest time, so be serious," David said in his boy-man voice.

"Got it. I'm on it. Expect a book care package within the next two days. No, make that three, since tomorrow is Sunday," I said.

"Thanks mom! And feel free to throw in some candy and root beer. You know that gets me a lot of trading weight around here," he said.

"You got it, super star! I love you," I said. And I miss you so much I want to fly up to Maine right this minute and take you home with me, I didn't say.

"I love you too, Mom. Gotta go. I'm swimming head of the lake today!"

And then he was gone again.

I was okay. I had my business. And the boys would be back in a few weeks. They'd be so proud, and this year I could tell them tons of stories about my summer.

But what if they didn't like having a working mom? What if I couldn't be both successfully? What if my boys turn out like Melanie, feeling ignored for the sake of their mother's big career? Maybe I was starting all of this business stuff too soon? Maybe I should wait until they were in college and didn't need me anymore. Sean would be off to college in just seven more years.

Seven years?

I couldn't wait seven more years, I thought. I loved the project next door, loved changing the Thompsons's ugly house into a fresh, new home. I knew I was good at home staging, and I'd been having so much fun helping to create my marketing materials, overseeing my website design and development, and talking with others about my business. Millions of other women did it. Heck, Beth was doing it right now, with an infant, and she seemed to have no guilt. But maybe she was just too tired to have guilt yet. No, I could do this. I needed to do this—for me. I remembered the fat check upstairs and smiled.

In one of the books Patrick had given me I'd read that balance is internal; that there really wasn't one set formula for how to live your life nor how to handle the wife-mother-businesswoman juggling act. Maybe it was just being tuned in to every role and knowing when one or the other needed to be the focus. My mom hadn't said anything negative about my new career; in fact, she'd encouraged it. I hadn't even realized that until now. She had given my future a blessing and hadn't said anything to make me feel guilty about the boys.

"Hi Mom," I said when she answered. "Thank you."

"For what, honey?" she asked.

"For encouraging me to start my own business. My website is almost ready to go, and I'll send you a link in my next email. I want your opinion about how the site looks and feels. But what really means a lot is that you didn't say anything about my working making me a bad mom."

"Of course not, dear. Having a job doesn't make you a bad mom. It makes you a smart woman, as long as you're doing what you want to do. You're so lucky, Kelly, to have a choice. Most women don't. To not value that choice, to not make the most of it, well, that would be the real shame, dear." I heard the telephone cord thwumping. She'd been thinking about this.

"You and Sally both married great men. But you just never know what the future holds," she added. "I've been trying to get your sister to understand that, too."

"She has to realize it for herself, Mom. Maybe she'll have a wake-up call like I did."

And then I told my mom about the double biopsy just before Christmas, about the job across the street, and about what had happened the night before, with Melanie. I shared everything, and I didn't pretend I could handle it. And finally, I told her about Dr. Weiskopf, and the prescription I was taking.

"I'm so proud of you," my mom said. "It took me until I was sixty-five to really take charge of my life. You know, I'd like to come up for your launch party. Would that be okay?"

"I would love that," I said.

It was surprising, actually, how good sharing my true feelings felt. I was downright giddy. After I'd hung up from talking to mom, I called Patrick. I needed to tell him about the check. And about our child prodigy's reading acumen. I called his private line, and ever-efficient and helpful—but not attractive and definitely married—assistant Jeanne answered. Drats. She said he was in a meeting and would call back ASAP. I could call his cell and he would answer, but it wasn't an emergency. We'd had enough of those.

My cell phone was ringing again. Where had I put it this time? I followed my ring to the laundry room, where I'd left the darn thing after putting in a load. I answered before my voice mail did. Small victories.

"What's up" Patrick asked.

"Oh, it's you. I mean, hi! I was just hoping it was Kathryn."

"Yes, well, she hasn't called, then?"

"No, but I got my first paycheck, Patrick! And guess how much I made?"

"I've got to get back into this meeting; we're getting ready to pitch a new client on Monday, but, um, okay. $5,000?"

"Triple that!"

"Wow, that's awesome. Just one job like that a month and you'd really be in business."

"I really am in business."

"Right you are. I've got to go, but let's celebrate tonight, okay?"

"Yeah, yeah whatever," I said, echoing Sean's favorite saying whenever we told him something he didn't want to hear. I hope Patrick got the gist.

Back to work, I told myself, realizing my solo celebration of my first paycheck could last only so long. I looked back down at my list of business items to tackle and realized I was still facing the need for a process. Surely there was something more fun to tackle.

Publicity. That was what I needed next, and that had been my specialty back in the day. I was planning on taking photos at the party and sending them to the local newspapers. I knew they'd cover a new business opening, especially if I had shots of local dignitaries and luminaries. But what about before the event? Did I still know anybody in the media? During my days at the PR firm, it was my job to connect with key reporters at all the local radio and TV stations, and client-specific reporters at the newspapers. These days, most of the traditional media folks my age who I'd worked with had been replaced by youngsters. Especially at *The Dispatch* and the major broadcast television affiliates. Except, I just remembered, Sherry White. We had worked together quite a bit when I had pitched countless stories to her, and I still had her email address. Sherry was a respected news anchor for the local NBC affiliate, and I knew she'd love home staging. Why not give her a call, I thought? So I did.

"Kelly, that sounds like a fabulous segment for us," Sherry said after we'd spent a few minutes catching up on each other's lives. "Do you want to come in this afternoon? The five o'clock show could use some beefing up, and everybody is so concerned about whether they can even sell their homes if they tried right now."

"I thought you'd like it, Sherry, but should we wait and do the story on a weekday? Don't you have more viewers then? And come to think of it, why are you answering your phone on a Saturday anyway?" I asked, suddenly realizing what day it was.

"Oh, I thought you knew," Sherry said. "They bumped me for a twenty-five-year old. She has the weekday evening anchor job on the six and eleven o'clock shows. A twenty-eight-year old has the 5:30 slot. I've got the weekends, now. That's show business."

"That's stupid. You're one of the most respected names on the air, the most well-known anchor in town," I said, stunned.

"Yes, but that doesn't matter much once the big 5-0 comes around," she said. "I'll understand if you want to pitch it to those new gals for one of their shows. Be my guest. Doubt they've lived in a home except their parents', but they might understand the concept," she said, chuckling.

"Nope, if you'll have me, I'd be honored to be on your show."

"Good. My demographics are better. Older folks, you know, with time on their hands and money to spend."

34

SHERRY GAVE ME THE DETAILS: COME TO THE BACK DOOR, RING the buzzer, the producer will let you in, get there early so we can mic you up, and wear extra makeup. Then she'd hung up. Suddenly I realized I'd just committed to being on television tonight.

Jeez.

To make matters worse, the person I'd usually call for fashion advice was Charlotte, and she was on my do-not-call list. Or was she? My mom's words were ringing in my ears. Stay neutral. Charlotte had just given me a check for $15,000 after all.

I was a nervous wreck. I needed a Reese's big time. I rummaged in my secret drawer in the kitchen and found my tiny packet of solace. I popped first one then the other treat in my mouth and savored the feeling.

The house phone rang. I glanced at the clock; could be a salesperson. I turned on my gruff voice.

"What's wrong with your voice, Aunt Kelly?" Melanie asked.

"Hi sweetie! Nothing, just a frog in my throat. How are you?"

"I'm doing better, and I want to apologize for scaring you. I'm sorry. I just wanted you to know that. And, uh, I like doing yoga with you. I like being with you."

"Mel, you made my day. I'm so glad you're feeling better. You did scare me, but everything is all fixed up and waiting for you to come back. I'll be by during visiting hours to see you, so just keep feeling better."

"I will. Oh, Beth wants to talk to you."

"Hey miracle worker, how are you holding up?" I asked Beth.

"I'm walking out of the room, hold on . . . Okay, well, it went better than expected, actually. Bruce came and he was calm and he listened. We did a couple of hours of counseling, so he could better understand why Mel is taking out all of her emotional pain on her body. He wants to try bringing her home with him," Beth said.

"Absolutely not! Kathryn is the primary caretaker."

"But Kelly, she hasn't even showed up yet. And, really, if she's working on herself and her personal issues, she's not the best choice. Mel needs a stable parent focused on her right now," Beth said.

"Bruce travels 24/7. He isn't stable. He's leaving his wife for his mistress, for heaven's sake!"

"He is listed as the emergency contact on her insurance card and the coverage is through him. He is her father, and he wants to take her home. There is no one who can stop that, including me," Beth said. "Especially since Mel wants to go home with him."

"What?"

"That's what she thinks right now."

"I'm coming over there. It's almost three. You'll let me see her, right?"

"Of course."

❊

I called Charlotte on the way over to the hospital. I had to multi-task; I was up against the clock. Besides, if Melanie was deciding to live with Bruce, she'd be living with Charlotte, too.

"Hi Kelly. I wasn't sure we were talking," Charlotte said, cautiously.

"Well, we are, sort of. Look, I'm driving over to the hospital to see Melanie, and since it seems you're about to be her stepmother, I figure you are up to speed on everything. You are, right?"

"I haven't heard from Bruce all day." The sadness in her voice filled the phone.

"Here's the scoop. She's doing great and they made up, Bruce and Mel. Seems she may even be considering living with him—I mean, you guys. So, that's good."

"Living with us? I'm not sure she'd be a good influence on the girls, the way she is right now," Charlotte said. "I mean, I don't want to sound callous, but I'm just not sure I can handle that. And what about her mom?"

Yeah, well, you should've thought about that before you became soul mates, I was about to say, but caught myself. "Well, now you know all I know, so at least you won't be caught offguard. Take it easy on this one. Bruce feels responsible for the suicide attempt, and he's going to do everything he can to make it up to Mel; at least that's what Beth says."

"Can't you call Kathryn? Get her back here?" She sounded desperate, as if she'd just now realized she'd be inheriting a troubled teen as well as a soul mate.

"Great idea, Kathryn to the rescue," I answered, wondering

if she could hear the sarcasm in my voice. "I've called her numerous times. I'm sure she'll be back as soon as she can. But you can't really expect Kathryn or me to help you and Bruce out, can you? What's that saying, you make your bed, you have to lie in it, or something?"

"Nice. Sorry to cut this short, Kelly, but I have a listing appointment, so I've gotta go."

"Wait. One more thing. I'm going on television tonight. What do I wear?"

"Why?"

"For my new business," I said, gloating. "Sherry White is having me on as a guest at 5:30. So please, any help?"

"Wear the light blue silk top that makes your eyes pop. Simple jewelry. Flatten your hair and use hairspray. The studio lights highlight fly aways. HD makes overdone, caked-on makeup look even faker, so use your mineral makeup. Powder your eyelids so they don't shine, and wear neutral lip gloss. You want your eyes to take center stage," she said in a rush. "I really have to go. Bye."

I'd gotten the television tips I needed and had tipped off Charlotte to boot. Maybe she'd intervene in time for me to get Mel back to my house. It certainly sounded as if she didn't want Mel in her new love nest. As I disconnected the phone, Doug and I turned into the hospital.

Gavin sat on one side of her bed, and Bruce was on the other. Melanie was smiling.

"Hi Aunt Kelly!" she said as both guys looked at me. "Those daisies are wonderful. From your garden, right?"

"Hi sweetie! Yep, I picked them just for you. It looks like you're in good hands here," I said, placing the flowers on the windowsill and kissing her forehead. "Bruce, could I talk to you for just a couple minutes?"

He smiled at Melanie and then followed me out into the hall.

"Have you talked to Kathryn about any of this?" I asked.

"Some of it. We agreed that I would move out of the house when Mel came to live with you. We just hadn't told Mel yet. Kathryn told her I was on a business trip. And then, the next thing I know, she heads to Montana," he said. "I didn't want to go against Kathryn's wishes. She wanted us to tell our daughter together, but since she's gone and Charlotte is your friend and our new house is across the street, it seemed like I needed to fill Mel in.

"I know I didn't handle it well, bursting into your home and telling my emotionally fragile daughter that I was in love with someone other than her mom, and that I was moving in with her and her twin daughters," he added, shaking his head.

"Yeah, that was a little harsh," I agreed. Selfish shithead. "I don't think it is right for you to take Mel to your love nest before Kathryn returns. I think Mel should stay on neutral ground, with Patrick and me, until all three of you sit down together and work this out."

"I appreciate your thoughts, Kelly, but Mel's my daughter, and I've got it under control," he said. "I need to get back in there. Gotta watch those lovebirds."

"Gavin is a great boy. He was there when you weren't, Bruce. I hope you know that," I said. But I was talking to his back because he was already heading into Mel's room.

I followed him in.

While Bruce was getting an update from the cute doctor who'd walked in the door, I whispered to Mel: "Say, do you have your mom's assistant's cell number? I just wanted to give her a quick call."

"It's programmed in my cell. That's still in my room at your house. Her name is Donna, and she's the only Donna in there. Is my mom okay?"

"I'm sure she is, but I need to reach her. I can't remember the name of the ranch where she's staying, do you?"

"I know it's near Kalispell and Glacier," Melanie answered.

"Well, we'll track her down. I know she'll be here as soon as she hears what happened."

"No, please, Aunt Kelly! Mom deserves a break. She's had to put up with me and him—especially him," she said, looking at her dad, and squeezed my hand. "Just let her have peace. I'll be okay at his house. And Beth and I are going to spend a lot of time working to get me healthy. And you're right up the street. And Gavin is here, too." They beamed at each other.

"Yes he is, and so are Patrick and I if you need anything," I said, and gave her a kiss on the cheek. I walked past Bruce and the doctor without saying another word.

As I strolled down the white hallway of the hospital, it struck me again: I'm going on television tonight.

35

CHARLOTTE WAS SO RIGHT. THE BLUE BLOUSE WORKED! I
decided to wear my Dogeared Karma necklace. I hoped it would
help me feel positive and peaceful. I tried on my largest pair of
black dress pants, and they were too big. I moved down to the
next section of the closet and danced a little jig as the smaller
pair slid on and buttoned easily. Wow. As I flat-ironed my hair,
I accidentally touched the top of my right ear. Burn pain on the
tippy top of your ear is uniquely indescribable, especially when
self-imposed. I was completely out of my element when it came
to the high-maintenance, every-hair-in-place, getting ready mode.
I'd been out of practice for fifteen years. In fact, I'm not sure I ever
had it down.

An hour of primping later, I headed for the door. Oreo gave
me the look, but I shook my head and reached for a treat, promising to take him on a drive on Sunday. After all, that's what Sundays
are for, I told him. I wrote a note to Patrick, who had informed me
that after finishing their new business pitch the guys had decided
to play a round of golf. It was okay, because if I'd told him I was
going to be on TV, he would've watched and then I would've been
even more nervous than I already was.

I followed all the back door and buzzer directions and found myself microphoned and alone in the "green room," which was actually a conference room with a TV, so I could see what Sherry was reporting on for the news of the day.

A burst water main at the airport was the lead story. It wasn't really at the airport, however; it was near the rental cars, although the reporter on the scene's urgency made it sound as if a flood would be coming our way soon. Next up, layoffs at the mayor's office. Then, Sherry told us, "Stay tuned. There's been a tragedy in the suburb of Grandville. We'll be back with details after this break."

I hoped she wasn't talking about me.

"Hi Kelly! Great to see you!" Sherry said, breezing into the green room and giving me a hug. "You look great. Nervous?"

"Extremely," I admitted.

"I could tell. You aren't breathing. Breathe. You'll do fine. I'll see you in just a few minutes; I've gotta go. Breathe," she said again, and dashed for the door.

"Hey, wait, am I the tragedy in the suburbs?" I asked.

"Ha, ha, ha, you are so funny!" she laughed.

That wasn't really an answer.

"Welcome back. Tragic news from Grandville today as police were called to the scene of a motorcycle accident. Apparently, the crash happened last night but the accident scene wasn't discovered until this afternoon, when a jogger happened to notice the wreckage at the bottom of a shallow ditch. The name of the male victim who was pronounced dead at the scene has not been released, pending notification of the family. We'll bring you more as information becomes available."

What? I wondered, as the producer tapped me on the shoulder and said I was on. "After that story?" I asked.

"No, after the break," she said. "Follow me, but don't say a word. We're going into the studio and we're live."

My heart was beating so hard in my chest that it was hard to breathe. Sherry's advice just wasn't cutting it. I needed water. And a towel. I was perspiring so much I was sure I would soak my blue shirt. I felt like I was drowning. I'd read that water is a thousand times heavier than air. Was it possible to drown in your own sweat? I'd worked so hard to look good, and now I was blowing—actually drenching—it.

Get hold of yourself I told myself, and smacked the top of each thigh. That was grounding, feeling the jiggle. I touched my necklace, reminding myself to keep positive. We entered the studio from the side. Sherry was behind the news desk, speaking into the huge camera lens as if she were speaking to a person. Amazing.

"And we're out," said the producer next to me, as she pushed me forward and onto the set. We were moving over to the couch, where I would be seated next to Sherry. That would be fine, except for the cameras. Someone came from somewhere and powdered Sherry's face, and then, seeing me, did mine too.

Sherry patted me on the hand, told me to look at her and not the camera, and then we were on.

I don't remember a thing we talked about. I remember talking, and smiling, and swallowing a few times, and nodding, fascinated, and then looking concerned when she read off the dismal housing market stats. And suddenly, we were finished.

"Great job, Kelly!" she said. "Let's do lunch sometime, Okay? Let me know of any other ladies our age starting new businesses. That's where I want to put my emphasis: helping other women over forty. We need it."

"I do know of one. My friend Beth is starting her own

treatment center for anorexic teen girls. She's fabulous and has already made a huge difference in the life of a teen I know," I said, politely ignoring her over-forty comment since I was only thirty-nine.

"Great! Have her call me," Sherry said, walking back toward the set. The producer ushered me out as Sherry retook her position behind the anchor desk.

My phone was ringing as I headed through the door out into the warm summer air. I was high with accomplishment, invigorated by my marketing savvy, amazed that I had pulled it all off today.

"Hello," I said.

"And you didn't think it would be important to tell me you'd be on television today?" Patrick said.

"Well, it just sort of came together and you were golfing and, well, if I told you, you would've watched and that would've made me nervous. Wait. How did you know?"

"You looked beautiful. You talked fast, but you only want to work with fast-talking, intelligent folks, right? That was really gutsy, especially since you just opened for business, um, two days ago."

"Three. And no time like the present. Where are you?"

"I'm at home, fielding phone calls from all of your friends and some from home sellers who want their homes staged. You're going to be busy, Kelly."

"I hope so! Sherry said they'd link our story about home staging to my website where I have that contact form, and that could lead to a lot of business too. They have a lot of traffic. I'm just leaving the studio, so I'll see you in a little while."

Doug and I pulled out of the parking lot and began the trek home. I was so excited I decided to sneak a call in to Sean on the way home.

"Hi Mom!" he said. "I'm over picking blueberries so they can't see me talking!"

"That's great. Hey, guess what? I was just on TV."

"Really? Cool. Are you going to be famous?"

"I hope so. I started my own business. It's for people moving and selling their houses. I'm really excited. So how are the berries?"

"Really good and sweet. I could just sit here and eat them all day."

"Is everything okay?" I asked.

"Yeah. Just a little homesick, I guess," he said. "But it'll be better tonight. It's movie night."

I knew the rules. Don't feed the homesickness by saying come on home. "I miss you so much, too. But we'll be there to get you soon. And then, as usual, you'll be sad to leave."

"You're right, Mom. Hey, good job on the TV show. I learned how to do a loon call, wanna hear?

"Sure." I laughed as the sound of a loon filled my car.

"I've gotta go," he said.

"Great loon! Love you."

"You too."

36

PATRICK HAD A BOTTLE OF SPARKLING WINE IN AN ICE BUCKET on the countertop, and he popped the cork as I walked into the kitchen. "To my wife, the staging star of Grandville," he said, and then poured us each a glass. "Cheers!"

I love sparkling wine: the way it's saved for special occasions; the way the bubbles feel as you drink it and how they look in the glass. I especially love to call it Champagne even if it is domestic, just to honk off the French in my own little way. Sure, they have culture and wine and cheese and Paris. But here in the USA we deserve to call our sparkling wine something more than sparkling wine, I thought. So I did.

"You're so wonderful, Patrick. Thank you," I said as we clinked glasses. I smiled over at T2C #20. And then, of course, the telephone rang.

"This is how it's been ever since the segment aired," Patrick said. "We're going to need to set up a business line for you here at the house. You don't want it all mixed together—and I know I don't. We can let voice mail pick this one up."

"How many calls have been from potential clients?"

"Three, at least," Patrick said. "I wrote them all down for you and told them you'd call tomorrow. I'm assuming, like real estate agents, home stagers don't take the weekend off?"

"Yeah, bummer about that, I know," I said, smiling. "But it will all be worth it when I make enough for that beach house."

"Yes, I could retire, become your assistant, or better yet, just play golf."

"Oh no you won't. Cheers!" I planted a big kiss on his cheek and he gave me the look. It did seem as if our house would be teenager-free and that there wouldn't be any big meetings in my living room tonight. Maybe a little romance was the perfect way to end a business-launch day.

I pulled Patrick by the hand and we made our way slowly up the stairs and then into our room. The sun was still up, but the red glow of sunset was just beginning. We made love slowly, but still enough to qualify as a workout in anybody's book. I even took the top for a change, a position I'd been too self-conscious to take in years. I was turning into a cougar, or was it a tiger? Anyway, it was great.

Afterward, as we cuddled, Patrick complimented me on losing weight. I told him that having an anorexic around had prompted me to think about eating healthier through watching portion sizes and writing things down. I had started doing it with Mel, and I had made a commitment to myself to keep it up. Beth said she'd help me by just giving me copies of the weekly meals she and a nutritionist had planned for Mel. I was exercising, too: walking at least thirty minutes a day, and I had been a regular at yoga with Melanie.

"Maybe if we did this more often I could really get in shape fast," I said.

"Fine with me," Patrick said. "I'm just so glad you're happier. It's great to see your spunk back."

"What? I have always been spunky. What are you talking about?" I was quickly losing the afterglow.

"You've been sort of . . . what the boys call a 'Debbie Downer,' actually, but it's okay. You just needed to figure out what would make you feel more fulfilled, more joyful. And you've found it! You're back in touch with friends, you've started a business, you're getting in shape. All of this provides me with guilt-free golf, by the way."

He gave me the smile that said he was trying to extract his foot from his mouth: the one that said I love you and even though this came out in a bad way, I support you 100 percent.

I couldn't be mad. His hair was messed up—I loved that—and we'd just had great sex.

"You're right. I guess I had to hit my own midlife-crisis bottom. Maybe crying at the dentist's office was the last straw."

"There are worse midlife crisis scenarios."

"Yes, well, what is yours going to be?" I asked, realizing I hadn't thought about that. What if he had an affair, bought a motorcycle, or . . .

The doorbell rang.

"I thought the Johnson Home Counseling Center was closed for the night," Patrick said as I jumped out of bed and raced to the closet for jeans and a tee shirt. I most certainly wasn't getting back into my sweaty TV appearance clothes.

"I thought so, too. Get dressed, please; I'm not going down alone!" I said, and he hopped to it. Good man.

37

OREO WASN'T GROWLING, JUST BARKING, SO HE KNEW whoever it was at the door. He was right. It was Charlotte.

I couldn't tell if she was mad or sad. She looked like she was in shock because her mouth was doing strange things: trying to form words, but none were coming out. I looked behind her and saw that she had left the twins in the car. Jeez.

"Charlotte, come on in. Patrick, take Charlotte to the living room while I go get the girls out of the car," I said, and patted Charlotte on the shoulder as she stood, not saying anything. Just moving those lips.

It was dark outside, but the light of the car popped on when I opened the back door on the passenger side. "Girls! Come on in! You know where the toys are upstairs, and Oreo will be so glad to see you." They both popped off their seat belts and bolted out the door I held open, wrapped their little arms around me, and held tight. They were crying.

"There, there," I said. What in the world was wrong?

And then, I knew. Before Alexandra said it, or maybe at the same time.

"My daddy got dead on his motorcycle," she said, and then sobbed.

"Mommy and Daddy didn't live together anymore, but Mommy still loved Daddy," Abigail said.

"Oh, yes, I know they did. And your daddy loved you too. Here's what we're going to do. We're going to go inside and all sit down together in my house, okay? Oreo wants to hug you both. Come on," I said, walking them up the walkway and into the house.

They ran to their mom, who was sitting on the couch in the living room. I went to find Patrick. He was in the kitchen, pouring two glasses of scotch on the rocks.

"What are you doing?" I asked.

"I see it all the time in the movies," he said. "I think the taste snaps 'em out of it. Charlotte's in shock, Kelly. Don't know how she drove over here. She just mumbled that Jim's parents called to tell her he was dead. Died on the damn motorcycle and that they would handle arrangements. They were so crass as to say they hoped she was happy now."

"Nice. Blame her for this. This is so horrible. Aside from a stiff drink, any other ideas? And what do I do with the girls?"

"Rent them a happy-ending movie on TV; we have that pay-per-view thing. That could help. Put them in Sean's room, with the twin beds. Maybe they'll fall asleep. It's after eleven already."

"You're a regular Dr. Oz tonight. First diagnosing me, now curing shock. I'm impressed," I said, as we walked into the living room and looked at Charlotte and her daughters, who all seemed incredibly small and impossibly lost.

"Alex and Abby, let's see if we can find a movie for you to watch. Does that sound good? How about some hot chocolate?" Coercing children was one of my specialties.

"With marshmallows?" Alex asked.

"Of course. Extra."

"What about Mommy?" Abigail asked.

We all watched as Charlotte took a big gulp of Johnny Walker Red and coughed, but kept it down.

"It's okay, girls, go on up. I need some grown-up talk right now," Charlotte said. Patrick was right, that scotch shot did the trick.

"Uncle Patrick will take you up, and he's an expert popcorn and hot chocolate maker," I said.

"Indeed," Patrick said. They went upstairs.

"Charlotte, I'm so sorry," I said, wrapping my arm around her thin shoulder. I think she'd shrunk in the last couple of weeks. Stress does that to her, and of course, she'd been having some new-relationship, soul-mate sex too.

I wondered what would happen now? She'd need to be cared for, watched, like Melanie. Bruce will have two on his hands, I thought.

"Where is Bruce?" I asked, perhaps a bit loudly, because she jumped.

"He's, he's at a concert they're producing in New York. He's taking the first flight home in the morning. He'll be here tomorrow morning."

"That's good." So much for Mr. Majors not traveling, staying home to take care of Mel. "What can I do for you? And the girls?"

"Can we stay here? I can't . . . I can't go home," she said, and started to cry. At least she sounded like she was crying, but no tears were falling. Maybe she'd used them all up and they hadn't replenished? Does that happen? I'd need to Google that.

"Of course, as long as you need to," I said, thinking she could have Mel's room. After all, they were about to be family.

"I can't go home, it has too many Jim memories. Even though

he moved out, it's still ours. It's us, when we were happier," she said.

I wrapped a blanket around her shoulders, went and got us each a bottle of water, refilled her scotch glass, grabbed a tissue box, and let her talk until 2:00 am. She fell asleep on the couch, and I headed upstairs, my heart heavy with the sadness of a life lost, girls without a dad, the twists of fate, and how, really, you can't take anything for granted.

I jolted awake at ten, totally disoriented and reliving the remnants of a bad dream. I had been shot in a corridor of a hospital, trying to stop someone from entering someone's room. My right shoulder actually ached, as if I really had been shot. How was that possible?

I grabbed my robe and headed to Sean's room. No girls. Panicked, I rushed downstairs to find Patrick, a twin under each arm and Oreo on his lap, watching *The Incredibles*. He really was wonderful. I was able to make it to the coffee pot and out the door toward the living room without any of them hearing me, including my dog.

Charlotte was still asleep on the couch. I quietly gathered up the empty scotch tumbler and water bottles. I covered her up a little better, and pulled the living room drapes closed. Maybe she'd sleep awhile longer. Dreaming had to be better than being awake right now.

With everything under control—as much as it could be—I decided it was time to call Donna, Kathryn's assistant, on Melanie's cell phone. Using Mel's made it more likely she'd pick up. I just had to get up the nerve to go back into Mel's room, a place I hadn't been since the suicide attempt.

So I took a shower to give me time to build up courage. It helped the courage a little and my gunshot shoulder a lot. I needed to hurry, though, as *The Incredibles* couldn't keep the twins occupied forever.

My heart thumping, I walked into our guest room. Amazing how quickly a life can be lost, I thought. What if I hadn't come home in time? I wondered if Jim would still be alive if anyone had been looking after him, noticing he wasn't home.

Happy thoughts, happy thoughts, I repeated to myself as I grabbed the cell phone and hurried out of the room. Luckily, Mel had left it charged. She had twenty-two missed messages. I wondered how many were from Gavin. Great kid. I didn't know if my sons would be able to show that level of love, patience, and commitment at that age. I wasn't sure, but I didn't think I wanted them to need to be that responsible that young.

Donna Without-a-Last-Name was in the contacts as promised, so I pushed send. Sure enough, Donna answered.

"Mel? How are you?" she said. Her voice was warm and friendly.

"Hi Donna, this is a friend of Kathryn's and Melanie's, and I'm calling because I need to get in touch with Kathryn. I thought you might have the name of the ranch where she is staying in Montana." I blurted it out in one long rush of words.

"Is Melanie alright? Why are you using her cell?" Smart cookie.

"She is. Her mom dropped her off to stay with me when she went to Montana."

"Oh, you're her nutty friend Kelly," Donna said. "I mean, she thinks you're great, tells me how funny you are."

Ha, ha. "Do you know the name of the ranch? I've tried her cell, her work number. Hey, that reminds me, I asked for you but got HR," I said.

"Oh, you don't know?"

"What?"

"Kathryn and I were both downsized. It was incredible. She'd spent her life at that company, made them half their money, if you ask me," Donna said. "And not so much as a thank you. Just a big meeting where they pulled us all into a room together and told us. Kathryn was the only senior executive, and they treated her the same as the stupid new assistant. It was awful. That's why I forced her to go to Montana. I mean, what else did she have to do? They only gave us an hour to clean out her office that day. She didn't tell you?"

"No, not a word. She did say she was going to Montana to get healthy, figure some things out."

"Hopefully, she is. I feel so bad for her. She's gotta dump that husband of hers, get her daughter eating, and start a great new business. I told her I'd work for her. She's amazing. Oh, the ranch is called Sunset Wolf Ranch, near a town called Kalispell. I know they do have a phone. Hold on and I'll go get the number."

I'd just hung up with Donna, after promising I would have Kathryn call when she started her new business, when Patrick called for me. The movie was over, Charlotte was up, and it was time for me to help.

"Coming," I yelled, grabbing the ranch phone number and shoving it into my pocket. I tossed Mel's cell onto the bed in her room and headed downstairs.

Charlotte was sitting at the kitchen table. Patrick and the twins were making pancakes—all over the kitchen. It would have been really cute if the situation hadn't been so sad.

"Need some coffee?" I asked Charlotte. "I'm pouring a cup of Patrick's tar for myself."

"Very funny," Patrick said.

"No thanks," Charlotte said.

This was going to be a long morning. I wondered when Bruce landed. I wondered what he would do? Could they close on Bob's house earlier and move right in? That's what I would do, I guess. But you just never know what you would do until you're in someone else's shoes. That must be something my mom said, too. Go, Mom.

I sat down at the table next to Charlotte and suddenly had the urge to start finalizing my website. Stop it, I told myself. My business was not important compared to Charlotte's tragedy. I guess since Charlotte was sitting in what had become the desk chair of my office she was triggering my working girl itch. No.

"The pancakes smell great, you guys," I said, focusing my mind on food.

"Mommy, Mickey Mouse or a flower?" asked Alex.

"Neither. I'm not hungry right now," Charlotte said.

"You aren't ever hungry, Mommy," Abigail said. "Aunt Kelly?"

"Mickey for me; he's my favorite shaped pancake," I answered smiling at the girls, "You should bring your mom a flower. She needs it."

"Okay. Hey, Aunt Kelly, we figured out what to sing for Daddy at his funeral," Alex said, which brought tears to my eyes. "We are going to sing 'Happiness Runs.' Do you know it? Daddy loved it."

Then they sang in unison: "Happiness runs in a circular motion / Love is like a little fish upon the sea / Everybody is a part of everything anyway / You can be happy if you let yourself be!"

The three adults clapped, and Charlotte and I wiped our eyes. Her tears must have reconstituted.

"Go ahead and do whatever you need to do," Charlotte said, looking at me and my laptop on the table in front of her. "Bruce will be here any minute and we'll be out of your way."

"Charlotte, you are not in my way. I love you. And I need to keep reminding you that Jim's accident was just that, an accident, and not your fault. You believe that, right?" I said quietly, holding her hand.

"I think I do."

"Breakfast is served!" said Patrick as he brought our plates to us, and the girls pulled up chairs on either side of their mom.

Bruce showed up an hour later and thanked me for "again taking care of his family." He assured me he'd arrange his work schedule so he'd be here from now on, that "it wouldn't happen again." And then he whisked them away. Bruce explained that he had expedited the closing with Bob, due to the circumstances, and that Charlotte and the twins would move in today. Melanie would be released tomorrow and join them.

I could, of course, imagine each of the girls' rooms. I designed the house perfectly, not knowing how all of this would come to pass. Mel would have the romantic purple room, with its own bath, and the twins would each take one of the former boy residents' rooms and share the pocket bath. Ironically, it was the perfect setup for the newly created family. I just hoped Bruce could live up to his responsibilities. He knew Patrick and I were watching now, so that was something. We were now, after all, the crisis center across the street.

Once they were all out the door, I dialed the Sunset Wolf Ranch. And someone actually answered. A person.

I explained the reason for my call, and I was put on hold.

For fifteen minutes.

I wasn't hanging up if they weren't hanging up.

"Hello?" Kathryn said.

"Oh my gosh, it's so good to hear your voice," I said.

"Kelly, why are you calling? I thought you told me to unplug my phone for a couple of weeks. Is something wrong?" she asked. She sounded stoned or peaceful; whatever it was, she was the opposite of me.

I took a deep breath. "Yes, Kathryn, something is wrong. But it's better now. Mel is in the hospital, but she's okay. She gets out tomorrow, actually. Since Bruce and Charlotte are moving in early, I'll be able to keep an eye on her, even if it is from a vantage point across the street. And, really, you should've told me about losing your job. I would've helped you rant and rave about it, cry about it, something."

Silence.

"Hello?" Maybe I'd said too much.

"Bruce and Charlotte? What are you talking about?" Kathryn said.

I felt, right then, that perhaps I had not heard correctly. "Melanie is fine. The wounds were just superficial. It was all related to the fact that Bruce told her he was moving in with Charlotte."

"I know about Melanie. I got your message and called Bruce. He filled me in. He left out the part about Charlotte," she said evenly.

Really? Really! Why didn't these people keep me in the loop? How am I supposed to know who knows what?

"Kathryn, I'm sorry, I thought you knew. But look, it doesn't matter anymore. Just keep getting yourself where you need to be. All of this will be here when you get back."

"Nothing will be there when I get back. My child, my home,

my job, my husband . . . all gone. It's like starting all over. That's what I've been trying to come to terms with."

"Not exactly. Melanie isn't going anywhere and neither am I. And one of the top things on my list—well, #5 actually—is not to forget the care and feeding of friends. And #15, especially old friends. Friends are friends forever, remember?" I said, quoting a shared favorite song. "And a friend will not say never 'cause the welcome never ends, or something like that."

"Though it's hard to let you go / in the Father's hands I know / a lifetime's not too long to live as friends," Kathryn said, finishing the verse from the Michael W. Smith song. "You know, it's funny, but you were right about Bruce all along. He was so self-centered, focused only on himself and his needs. I guess that made me self-centered in my own way. I needed to show him that I could rock the business world, too. And that's what we talked about, all the time. His production company, my climb up the retail business ladder . . .

"So where did that leave Melanie?" she added rhetorically. "Without either parent fully there for her. Sure, we'd take her on business trips; she'd make a great photo op for his company Christmas cards."

"Oh, Kathryn, you and Mel have much more than that," I said.

"Well, not enough. I left too much up to the nanny, too much time zeroed in on the office. But now that's going to change. I know I can be there, be present for her. I'm getting myself in order, back together. I just hope there's enough time left," she said, and sighed.

"There is plenty of time. Mel's never needed you more."

"And I'm going to be there for her. I can't miss the few remaining counseling sessions I have coming up, for obvious reasons, but

I'll be back soon. They've been great here and I can't tell you how much I appreciate you in my life—holding my life together there. Here in the mountains, I've been learning to live in the present. I haven't been doing that at all in my life. I've been too busy running to the next activity: the next business meeting, the next buying trip, the next school event, whatever. I have to remember, it is all going to work out, I'm just not sure how."

"I agree. And Kathryn?"

"Yes?"

"I love you."

"Bye, love you, too."

PART 3: HOPE

38

MONDAY MORNING: NO HOUSE GUESTS, NO COUCH CON-
sultations. Just me, my laptop, and my to-do list for Thursday's
party. I'd completed section two of my online staging designation
class (new T2C #7), and I'd learned some valuable things about
record keeping and how to explain my business. I also was advised
to consider adding Feng Shui into my practice. I guess I'd consider
it, when appropriate. Feng Shui, essentially, believed in clearing
clutter to create harmonious energy throughout your home. Chi—
positive energy—also flowed through homes with good light and
clean, quality air. I realized I needed to add more houseplants, specifically some palms, rubber plants, and a Boston fern. I'd open all
my windows more often, including before the party.

When it came to the Feng Shui Bagua of homes—defining
which areas are connected to specific areas of people's lives—I'd
learned that if I wanted to bring more money energy into our
home, I'd need to add wood and water to my master bathroom.
Okay, I could do that. I decided I'd add green to the east area of
our house; it was good for balancing family life and improving
health. I should do that over at Charlotte's new house, too. I'd

learned that David was a wood element and he was born in the year of the dog; Sean was fire and he was born in the year of the rat. Patrick was a metal/ox and I was a water/hare. Not sure what all of that meant, but I'd get back to this. I was having so much fun learning about this ancient practice.

I paused the module. I needed to focus on the basics. I had just realized I was expecting, at latest count, more than two hundred invitees plus their guests, which added up to four hundred people, and I hadn't hired a caterer yet. So soon after Jim's death, I wouldn't think of imposing on Charlotte, so I wouldn't be able to show off my only job. I needed a plan B.

The doorbell rang.

Oreo wasn't barking at all, so at least I liked whoever was on the other side. Sure enough, it was Beth and Melanie.

Melanie still had the white bandages on her wrists, but otherwise, her coloring had returned and she seemed, well, back to her normal, if skinny, self.

I gave her a big hug as they came in the door.

"Aunt Kelly, Beth and I have been talking on the way over," Melanie said. "I have messed things up around here and you have a big party on Thursday. I want to help. Put me to work. It's the least I can do. And the added benefit? I get to stay out of the way of the drama across the way. Deal?"

Why not? "Deal," I said.

"Cool. I'll just be in my room. Let me know when you need me!" she said, and bolted up the stairs, with Oreo tagging behind her.

"Traitor," I said under my breath to my formerly trusty steed. Maybe with all my newfound success, I'd get a pony. That would show him.

The phone had been ringing off the hook, and I had let it go to voice mail. I mean, really, who calls on Sundays? People desperate to sell their homes, that's who. But I had a party to plan. They were jumping the gun, or perhaps I had, with my TV appearance.

"Mel seems stable," Beth began as we headed toward the kitchen, "but with Jim's death, it's probably best to allow Charlotte and the girls to get settled in over there, without the pressure to acclimate Mel to a whole new family dynamic."

I poured us both a cup of tar and we sat down at my desk/ kitchen table.

Beth glanced around at all the Post-it notes on the wall, but didn't mention them.

"If you could keep Melanie busy over here for the rest of the week, through the funeral, that would be the best for her and for Charlotte. I've explained this to Mel and to Bruce. He finally listened to me," she said, smiling and taking a sip of coffee.

"Of course I'll keep her. I love her, and I need the help!" I also thought it would give Kathryn time to come home and maybe keep her daughter with her.

"Yes, I'm buying her mom some time, too," Beth said, reading my mind.

"She should be home in a couple of days, so that's great! Oh, and I've got a surprise for you. I told my friend Sherry, the TV anchor who interviewed me about my business, about you, and she'd love to do a story about you and the practice you want to start up. You have to do it. Rent office space. Take the leap. You are just wasting your talent working at that job at the hospital, not specializing. You have a gift, Beth. You need to share it. You can save people, for heaven's sake. All I do is decorate and declutter."

Oops. Broke life-change rule about not being self-deprecating (T2C #10), but I needed to make my point.

"Truth is, these past few weeks haven't felt like work. I know I can help other girls like Mel. I'm confident now," she said.

"You know, I hope it makes up a little bit for my not being there when you needed me in high school."

"Please, let it go. We were kids. I would've abandoned myself. In fact, I did," she said, smiling at me and then looking at the time on her cell. "I've gotta go. Ryan's been with Sarah all weekend, and I miss her something fierce. Call me if you need me, and good luck with all of this."

Yes, that's what I'd need. Good luck and an even better caterer.

I spent two hours ignoring phone calls and researching caterers. I made my list but couldn't call any of them until Monday. Two of them were attached to restaurants, which were open, but the catering manager wasn't in.

During a break in my research I looked out the kitchen window just as a moving van pulled down the street and into the driveway of Charlotte's new house. At least she'd have her things around her, but wasn't that the point of staying out of the house she had shared with Jim? Or maybe the van held Bruce's stuff from Kathryn and Melanie's house?

I decided to stop watching and start doing. I should make a casserole, or something. Maybe I'd call my mom and ask her what to bring to a widow and her two children, even though she was happily with her soul mate and moving into a million-dollar home with all new, perfectly staged furnishings and a few trinkets from her old life.

"Well, I'm just not sure," Mom said.

"Well, Charlotte—"

"Charlotte! Oh my goodness, not that sweet Jim? He was a darling man. He died?"

"Yes, Mom. I told you Charlotte is moving in with my friend Kathryn's husband, Bruce, remember?"

"Yes, I remember that, and you don't have to be so testy."

"Okay, sorry. But the question is what to take over to her, to be a good friend, because you told me on our last call that no matter what, I should side with my friend, even if she stabbed my other friend in the heart and lied to me."

Silence.

"Well, I'm just not sure she deserves anything."

"Oh great, now you're backpedaling on the advice you gave me earlier."

"I am trying my best to have a conversation with you and you are hostile. Maybe you should just go make your own decisions and call me when you can speak civilly."

"Sorry, Mom. Happy Sunday. Tell Sally and the kids hi. And I love you. When are you coming up? I really could use some help."

"I'd like that, if you're sure. They have those nonstop flights now pretty cheap. How about if I come Wednesday? Would that help? The party is Thursday, right?"

"That would be great," I said putting a smile into my voice.

After we hung up, I decided I would take Charlotte flowers. Even I couldn't stand the idea of a casserole in the summer, and I liked to eat. After calling up to Mel and Oreo and telling them I was heading out, Doug and I took the easy way out—or call it thoughtful—and headed to my favorite flower wholesaler. Once there I created an amazing bouquet of vibrant wildflowers in yellow and purple, hydrangeas (naturally), and a few greens. I had brought along a crystal vase and I worked at the cutting table to assemble my selection. I wrapped it with a purple silk ribbon and bought a sympathy card. Inside I wrote: Charlotte, Alexandra, and Abigail: You are in our thoughts and prayers. Kelly, Patrick, David, and Sean. I could've written our Feng Shui animals, Hare, Ox, Dog, and Rat, I thought randomly. I had just finished the card and was stuffing it into the envelope when I felt a tap on my back. I turned around to face Rachel White. Argh. Maybe she was stalking me?

"Oh say, Kelly, saw you on TV. You're big time. No wonder you couldn't be bothered by a little ole baby shower or controlling a teen party," she said, smiling sweetly.

"Yes, well, thanks, gotta go," I said, wrangling the arrangement into my arms and heading to the counter to pay. I watched as Rachel grabbed a potted plant and followed me to the checkout line.

"I'm just distraught over Charlotte's husband. So sad. She leaves him, and he is so upset, he starts drinking. That motorcycle accident. It's almost like suicide. Not wearing a helmet and all. And with those two little daughters," she said, her prying eyes squinting behind her glasses. "Have you talked with them? You're new neighbors, right? So sad for Kathryn, really, her husband shacking up so quickly. And what about poor Melanie? Good thing she survived her suicide attempt."

I imagined pouring my entire fabulous flower arrangement over her head, crystal vase and all. It would feel so good.

"Look, Rachel, it's all very sad, yes, and I don't even know how you found out about it all. But instead of talking about them to me, why don't you do something productive with your—uh—grief. Plant a tree. Pray. Just don't meddle and gossip," I said. I was mad, but I wasn't crying (Wow! #19). "Really, you need a life. Your own."

And then, perfectly exquisite flower arrangement in hand, I grabbed my receipt from the cashier and walked out the door.

I debated about whether or not to ring the doorbell and ended up pushing the button. Bruce came to the door. I handed him the bouquet and told him to call me, for anything. He actually gave me a big hug and said thanks.

I still didn't trust him, but I was warming up.

Back at home, I called Mel from the bottom of the stairs and—miracle—she came bounding down, eager to help. Patrick, back from golfing, stood ready to assist too. It was business time. I assigned Mel to the voice mail retrieval and assigned Patrick to the walk-through. He was a master at party flow; he would know where to place the bars, the food, which door we should leave open, which closed. I also assigned him the task of figuring out our fallback since we couldn't use Charlotte and Bruce's house. I focused on finalizing the website, emailing my last changes to the web design firm, and reviewing the event To Do list. Ever since my PR firm days, I'd created event lists and timelines to carry off the perfect party, whether for twenty-five or twenty-five hundred. I had forty-one items on this list. That was a problem, since the party was in four days.

Melanie joined me at the kitchen table.

"Aunt Kelly, twenty-three people left messages saying they want to hire you to stage their homes," she said, and gave me the knuckle-bump.

"Oh my gosh!" I was amazed.

"You're in business, Aunt Kelly. Big time! Can I work for you?"

"Of course, you already are."

"Where do we start?"

"Scheduling appointments with each of them. But first, we have to tell them our fees up front and make sure they are willing to pay. My rate is $100 per hour. An average job, for an average size home in Grandville, would probably require five to eight hours of consulting. Vacant homes—like what I did down the street—are a different matter, and I'll have to negotiate a project fee. Got it?"

"I'm going to be good at getting people to understand your value," Mel said. "I'm really used to conning money out of my parents. I'm a teenager."

"Funny." She was adorable. "Can you try to schedule the appointments for the homes closest to here first? I want to work mostly in this part of town."

"Of course, Aunt Kelly," she said, and as I watched, she started Google mapping all of the houses. "I'm going to research your callers on some real estate sites and find out if they are already listed for sale, how many square feet their home is, all that kind of stuff. Then I'll be able to picture it before I call."

"Brilliant," I said, and turned my attention back to Thursday night's event. Patrick was busy chopping herbs for his signature chili, which would be our dinner. He'd started it before he left for golf, since he liked his chili to simmer for a long eighteen holes. I'd already called Beth and she said that chili was a perfect meal for Mel. We were all working on our own projects, peacefully busy, when the doorbell rang.

Now what? I thought as Patrick offered to get the door. Oreo wasn't barking—always a good sign.

39

IT WAS KATHRYN, HOME EARLY.

And, I had to admit, the fact of her return made me jealous. I'd really grown used to the idea of a daughter, especially now that Melanie was talking to me. I pushed that aside and rushed to the door right behind Mel to welcome my friend home.

"Welcome home, Kathryn," I said, giving her a big hug.

"I can never thank you enough, for all you've done," she said, keeping her arm around her daughter's waist. Mel had tears in her eyes and she was wearing a smile I'd never seen, one that was glowing from inside.

"Mom, I missed you so much," she said, hugging Kathryn back.

I was clearly the third wheel here. "Okay you two, why don't you head to the living room and get caught up?" I suggested as cheerfully as I could while acknowledging silently that my temporary role as a mom of a teenage girl had ended. I started to well up.

Patrick wrapped his arm around me and walked me into the kitchen.

"You knew Kathryn would be back someday soon, right?" he said gently, knowing I was on the verge of a full-out bawl.

I nodded.

"Not only have you done a great job as a friend, but you and Beth have made a real difference in Mel's life, forever," he said, pulling me to him in a full bear hug.

"You're right, it's just that I'm going to miss her," I managed to sputter.

"She'll be living across the street half the time, remember? And she seems to love helping you with your new business. Why don't you make it official? She could be your first employee," Patrick suggested.

"Great idea," I said and felt a little bit better about losing my teen. "Okay, back to work," I added, pointing him toward his chili pot while I tackled the stack of phone numbers and names that Mel had been working through to set up appointments. I guess I should have looked at them sooner, but I'd been busy handling the party planning. Some of the twenty-three names on the list were folks considered the "who's who" of Grandville. I recognized at least five of the names. Melanie had made notes next to all of the callers, based on the voice mail messages and her online research. Some of the people who had called for home staging services weren't actually moving. That's because in my TV interview I had mentioned that part of my services included rearranging furniture for people looking to change their homes, freshen them up a bit.

I called into the voice mail and started listening to the messages myself. Three of them were creeps who had seen me on TV and wanted me to come over. Mel didn't tell me about those. I hadn't thought about that possibility at all, not since the scary encounter with Bob. The fact was, I'd be going into strangers' homes. I needed to make sure Charlotte and I signed up for that self-defense class soon (T2C #11). I needed to know how real estate agents protect themselves.

Somewhere along the line, Patrick kissed me on the cheek

and said it was time to eat. The smell of chili had permeated the air, and my stomach growled. "Why don't you take a break, start all of this again in the morning? Kathryn's home, you've had a full day already," he said, rubbing my neck. I melted and acquiesced.

"Can you go find Kathryn and Mel, please?" Patrick asked. The chili did smell delicious. "I'll set the table for four if you'll go grab the ladies."

As I walked into the living room, I noticed Kathryn was sunburned and glowing; she looked so much better than when I had last seen her, crying her eyes out in her car in my driveway. She and Mel sat so close together on the couch that they could've been the same person. They were holding hands.

"Sorry to bother you two, but dinner is ready and Patrick is quite excited to share his chili prowess with both of you."

"Oh, we don't need you to feed us, Kelly. I was just telling Melanie we should get her packed up and head home."

"You are staying for dinner. Period."

"By the way, Aunt Kelly, do you need me to get back to work?" Mel asked.

"Work?" Kathryn asked.

"Mel's helping me start my new business," I told Kathryn. "And you know I want to pay you to help me, Mel. Starting tomorrow, until school starts. As long as it's okay with your mom."

"Mom? Aunt Kelly was on TV, and she's officially launching her home staging business this Thursday with a big party at the house. It's really cool and I'm having fun helping."

"Wow, Kelly, I had no idea. Here I've just been talking about myself, not even asking what you've been up to," Kathryn said. "This is fantastic! Maybe I could help, too?"

"I'd love it," I said as we walked to the kitchen. "But I can only afford to pay one Majors right now."

"Once you explain exactly what it is you're up to, I can help with a business plan. I have severance for a year, thankfully, so I don't need the money. I just need something to get involved in. I didn't know how to tell you, either of you, but I was laid off in the last round of cuts," Kathryn said. "The counselors at the ranch helped me work through it, and I know it's for the best. It's just that work had been so much of my identity all those years. I felt lost."

"Mom, we know. It's okay," Melanie said, giving Kathryn's hand a squeeze as we sat down at the table. Her big white bandages had been replaced by Band-Aids, which discretely covered the wound on the inside of each of her wrists.

"Make way for cornbread and the best chili in Grandville," Patrick proclaimed.

"It's so great to be home," Kathryn said. "I actually feel happy for the first time in so long. And Mel knows this, but I just felt like I had to keep going, to prove myself or something. But really, down deep, I was afraid: afraid to do anything different; afraid to get off the treadmill. You know, until I was let go, I didn't know how good change could feel. I just worried about the risks, not the rewards."

"Mom, what are you talking about?" Mel asked, looking at her.

"The point is, you've got to take risks to change," Kathryn said. "And I'm ready to go. I was stuck for too long, in my marriage, in my job. I was on a treadmill, really. Great chili, by the way, Patrick."

After Melanie and Kathryn helped clean up dinner, they packed up Melanie's things and headed back to the home they'd both shared with Bruce, the one they'd be leaving soon as they started over. Kathryn told us at dinner she was thinking maybe a condominium would be fun for the two of them, and Mel agreed, as long as it had a swimming pool. All in all, they both seemed happy, peaceful, and recovering. As long as Beth worked with both of them and Bruce remained cooperative, Mel was going to be fine.

I'd keep an eye on Kathryn. And, quite honestly, I would love her help with my new, suddenly busy business. She'd offered a proposition at dinner—probably promoted by Mel—that if I'd stage her home to sell, she'd help get the business systems rolling and off the ground for the next couple of months. Sounded like a great idea to me, and it would give us a chance to test the waters of working together. I'd heard Kathryn was tough in business, and I didn't want to be overshadowed while pursuing my newfound purpose.

As I headed upstairs to get ready for bed, Oreo climbing the stairs behind me, I wondered if Charlotte was the listing agent for Bruce and Kathryn's house. I guess that would keep it all in the family, but if I were Kathryn, I wasn't sure I'd be comfortable with it. I guess that's life during divorce; things get messy. Or perhaps the mess that was already there came to the surface.

I joined Patrick, my ox, in our room. He, being a low-maintenance man, was already in bed reading. His grooming ritual consisted of brushing his teeth. Mine, on the other hand, would take me twenty minutes on a good night.

I wondered how many hours I'd wasted, washing my face and applying lotion only to wash my face the next morning and apply more lotion? Now, though, with my new sonic cleanser, I was cleaning even deeper each time. Scrubbing off those pesky lines. And with my bangs, I could pass for a youngish middling home stager. That was something, I supposed, but nothing to put on my business card. Thankfully, unlike a lot of real estate agents I knew, I didn't put my photo on my cards.

Just a happy hydrangea for me, thank you.

40

ALONE AT MY KITCHEN TABLE DESK THE NEXT MORNING, I tackled the remaining voice mail. After deleting the overtly disturbing ones, I was left with twenty messages that seemed to fall into three categories. The first and largest category was messages from desperate sellers whose homes had been on the market for months. Most of these callers lived in lovely neighborhoods, and I knew I could help. The second category was from people considering putting their homes on the market and wanting my advice to make their homes ready for sale. I could do that. Surprisingly, the third category of messages covered people who wanted me to stage their homes for events. One had a daughter's wedding at the end of the summer, another was hosting a company party, and a third was planning a charity fundraiser at her home.

Did I do event home staging? Was there such a thing? I guess my background in event planning would make this a natural extension. But I'd have to be perfectly clear that I was not an event planner; that was an entirely different business. I'd call these three women back, explain my fees, and go from there. If they balked at the cost, I'd focus on my core business. If not, I'd add event home staging to my business cards and website.

I decided to call the doyen of society about the fall charity event staging and see what she had in mind. I had to admit, I was intrigued. Mrs. Clark had explained in a very matter-of-fact way that she had enjoyed watching me on the television program and thought I could bring a heightened sophistication to her upcoming party. She'd never had her home staged before an event, just decorated by the caterers and the party planners. She wondered how much I'd charge. So did I.

"Hello, Mrs. Clark?" I asked.

"No, this is her house manager. May I help you?"

"I'm returning Mrs. Clark's call inquiring about home staging services," I said in my most professional yet warm voice, I hoped.

"Ah, yes. She wanted me to inquire about the charges for your services. Do you work for an hourly rate or a flat fee, and what should we allocate in the event budget? The party is on September 22."

Unfortunately, I hadn't gotten to the part in the course where it told me how to price an event at a mansion—and it was an imposing mansion in every sense of the word—so I was sort of stumped. But I knew what I could do. "My hourly fee is $100, and I'd estimate six to ten hours, depending on the requirements of the job. Does that fit into your budget?" I smiled at the conclusion of my first business pitch.

"Please just forward your contract, with your fees spelled out. We'll be in touch." The house manager hung up.

Jeez. She didn't say yes, but she didn't say no. I made a note to get my contract together; I'd seen some samples online that I had forwarded to our attorney. I needed to find out if he'd had any changes. I added that to my business To Do list.

I returned the call about the other two party staging jobs and told them I charged $100 an hour. They both said they would give me a call back after considering their budgets. I put each of them down as a "no" on the spreadsheet.

Next I started in with the desperate home sellers. Marjorie Davis, who lived two blocks over, begged me to come over right away. We made an appointment for 3:00 pm, giving me time to finish making all of the desperate seller calls. My next five calls went to voice mail, where I left an official-sounding message and invited them to visit my website, email me, or call me back. Of the other four sellers I reached, all of them wanted appointments today. I made one other appointment for 4:00 pm, and booked the other three for Tuesday morning.

The "I'm thinking about putting my house on the market" calls were the most interesting. Four of the potential sellers hadn't hired a real estate agent yet. They were calling me first, for my opinion. That meant I had the power to refer these folks to a real estate agent of my choosing. This was a great way to start building my credibility with top listing agents, my upcoming party aside. I'd need to include Charlotte, but I couldn't recommend her exclusively. Not now.

It was just after lunch, and Mel and Kathryn arrived as I hung up from my last call. I smiled, knowing I had a team. My plan was to put Mel in charge of returning other telephone calls and setting up more appointments. Kathryn, if she was willing to do so, would be in charge of the party, based on Patrick's ideas of foot traffic flow. She could handle calling and selecting as well as meeting the caterer.

"Kelly, could I take a look at your spreadsheet, too?" Kathryn asked, settling in at the command center/desk/kitchen table. "I read your business plan, and I have some ideas I'd like to implement. I'm an expert at the business process."

"Ah, yes, have at it, please," I said, blushing a bit as I handed her my hand-drawn checklist.

"You go get ready for your meetings, and Mel and I will handle this," Kathryn said. "Go get 'em!"

Marjorie Davis's home was cluttered with all of the equipment necessary for a family with very young children, starting outside with the Little Tykes toys littering the driveway and the plastic swimming pool on the front lawn—filled, but not in use. Marjorie had asked me not to ring the doorbell in case her children were napping. That had been my other clue. I'm quick, after all. The For Sale sign in the yard was from a do-it-yourself Internet company.

As I walked through the toy maze and up to the front door, I took out my notepad and started jotting down details. I figured, if nothing else, taking notes would help calm me down during my first official home staging appointment. The door swung open and a rather frantic looking brunette ushered me in with a whispered, "They're still asleep."

I nodded and followed her down the hallway to a dark-paneled, dark brown Formica counter–topped kitchen. Hmm. This was an easy fix, I thought. Marjorie seemed diminished in the darkness of her kitchen, swallowed up in brown. We sat at a dark oak table. It was sticky on top from kid crud. Two rolling high chairs were pushed into the corners of the crowded room.

"My husband will be here in a minute," she said in a hushed tone. "We've been at this for six months. Everything we have is in this house, and we just can't sell for less than what we're asking; we can't. Can you help us?"

"I can, but I need to know what you're willing to invest to get the price you deserve," I said. "From what I can tell already, we need to clean up the front, get all the play toys into the back, plant more flowers in your beds, and get that grass watered. You never get a second chance to make a good first impression. If I was a buyer and drove by right now, I'd be turned off. Especially if I didn't have young children."

Marjorie nodded. She seemed open to my opinions, even if they were negative. She looked like she needed help, and I wanted to help her.

"This kitchen needs paint. It's too dark. This is the heart of your home. And all of the photos of your kids, which are lining the hallway on the way back here, need to be taken down right away," I explained. "It's about depersonalization. You need to allow prospective buyers to picture themselves here. They don't want to picture you and your family living here."

Just then Sam walked in and introduced himself. He immediately asked about my fee. I told him I estimated four hours at $100, not including what they'd pay painters or anyone else for tasks I suggested. He said they'd do everything themselves and that was fine with me. I did a walk through of the house, quietly, and sketched a floor plan. I saw every room except the kids' bedrooms. I told both Marjorie and Sam I'd have a plan ready by Wednesday. I knew that was a fast turnaround, but I was excited and ideas were bursting from my pen to the notepad. I knew I could help. As I was leaving, I made one more suggestion.

"Think about hiring a real estate agent to help," I said. "Agents don't like to show 'for sale by owner' properties because even if your sign says you'll pay a commission, they aren't sure. And they end up doing all the work for both sides of the deal because they know you aren't familiar with the process, the legalities, all the contracts, and the like. It is worth the fee, I'll guarantee it. We could list the house with someone next week if you two can devote the rest of this week to the improvements I'll specify. Think about it."

After we all signed the contract (hot off my printer), I left with $250—I required half the estimated fee upfront—and a huge smile on my face. I knew I could help the Davis family.

The second appointment, at a house double the size of Marjorie and Sam's, went just as smoothly. The home was listed with Grandville Realty, a local boutique shop, but the listing was expiring Sunday, and Mr. and Mrs. Wurst—they didn't tell me their first names, and I didn't mind—were going to make a change. As we walked through their elegant home, they asked me for a referral to a real estate agent. I told them that as I drew up their home staging plan I would also spend time thinking about who would be the perfect agent for them. I promised that their plan would be ready at the end of the week. I left without knowing their first names, but with a check and contract in hand.

I drove home, parked Doug, and burst through the door between the garage and the mudroom and started yelling.

"What? Are you okay?" Patrick yelled back.

"Aunt Kelly?" Mel called.

"I'm fine everybody, just excited!" I yelled back as I met Patrick, Mel, Kathryn, and Oreo in the hallway. "I got two jobs today! Two out of two. Look!" I held up the checks and the contracts, like a fifth grader showing off a great report card.

"Congratulations, superstar!" Patrick said, wrapping me in a hug.

"That's a great close rate," Kathryn said, and seemed genuinely impressed.

"I've scheduled four new appointments for you, but they're next week. Mom thinks you should take it easy this week with the party and all," Mel said.

We were having our first staff meeting.

"Caterer is booked. Flowers ordered. Rental table and chairs ordered," Kathryn reported. "Oh, and you have an actual spreadsheet. Can't wait to show you! This is fun."

"Kelly, just let me know when I can retire. It sounds like it'll happen soon," Patrick said, smiling as we all made our way over to the kitchen table command center.

That night, in bed, all I could think about were my two new jobs. Marjorie and Sam's drawing, along with a detailed plan and color chart, was almost complete in my mind. I just had to finish it on my laptop. I propped up pillows and made a desk. Patrick smiled over at me, and then went back to reading.

"How late do you plan to be working in bed?" he asked a few minutes later.

"Until I get this finished," I answered. "Hope I'm not disturbing you, but I am on deadline."

"You're fine, tonight. I hope this doesn't become a regular thing, though. You know I'm a light sleeper. But I do love looking over and seeing you smiling while you work on your computer."

I realized I had been smiling. This was much more fun to think about, I decided, than how much to scrub my wrinkles. Tomorrow, I'd start the Wursts' plan in between appointments. Maybe I should offer Charlotte Marjorie and Sam's listing as a good faith gesture? Perhaps the Wurst's, too.

I was full of faith, I thought, and most of the time, it's good.

SOMEONE HAD DECIDED IT WAS ACCEPTABLE TO CALL OUR house at 7:30 am.

This, to me—a non-morning person who had stayed up late the night before writing the final home-staging plan for Marjorie and Sam—was a completely unacceptable hour to talk to anyone except Oreo. Patrick was long gone to the office. I picked up the phone and used my most grumpy voice, hoping to scare whoever was on the other end into hanging up immediately. It didn't work.

"Hi Kelly, it's Carol from Dr. Bane's office to let you know your bottom guard is in," said the perky, singsongy voice. It wasn't her fault that I got the heebie-jeebies when that office called. "We have time today at three o'clock or four o'clock. Which would you like?"

"Actually, I'm busy all this week, Carol. I started a home staging business and I'm booked, all day, all week long. Let me call you back next week, when I can squeeze in some time."

That felt good. And actually, even though I hadn't been paying attention to it, so did my jaw. My mouth wasn't achy. Maybe I'd stopped grinding my teeth? Maybe I was cured, at least of this particular affliction.

Invigorated by my incredibly full schedule and my relaxed jaw, I jumped into the shower. My first appointment was at 10:00 am, and I had to organize my team before then. Beth was coming over to meet with Mel at nine, as usual. We'd all agreed to keep her schedule intact and in neutral territory, at my house. Kathryn was bringing Mel over; I hoped Kathryn would stay and work. It was beginning to dawn on me that I really needed help.

After getting ready, I decided to call Charlotte.

We exchanged pleasantries, and she shared that the funeral would be in the evening, with a small number of people, and all of the details were being handled by Jim's family. She didn't sound like the Charlotte I knew, but I chalked that up to her state of grief.

"Do you want me there?" I asked, somewhat shocked at how fast it had been planned and how calm she seemed.

"No, I'm fine. Bruce is coming, and the girls will sing, and it will be fine. Thanks, though, Kelly."

She didn't sound fine; maybe she was on some drugs? Bruce had mentioned trying to get her something to control the crying.

"If you're sure, Charlotte—by the way, I had my first meeting about home staging and my clients are a for-sale-by-owner," I said, thinking that would stir up her competitive juices. Or any juices.

"A lot of people try that, even here," she said listlessly.

"Yes, well, they're tired of trying that and want to work with a real estate agent. Are you interested? They are a lovely young couple, with kids a bit younger than your girls."

"Sure, Kelly. How about if I call them later, maybe tomorrow? Would that be alright?"

She sounded like she was sleep talking.

"I'll give them your name when I drop off their plan later today. I'll explain you're busy until later in the week."

I was excited I'd put the plan together a day early. I would put Charlotte's name and contact information at the end of my home staging plan for Marjorie and Sam, along with a note that I would need at least another hour for the final walk through and staging after they'd executed the improvements I'd outlined. I was proud of the presentation and of the ideas. I'd even provided them with paint swatch colors and paint names, and I'd gone onto Target.com and done screen grabs of inexpensive accessory pieces I wanted them to purchase, and where they should place them.

I asked them to paint the kitchen table and chairs white, to cover the table with a plastic tablecloth for everyday kid use, and then to set the table as if for a dinner party when the house was shown. I'd picked out four place settings, place mats, stemware, napkin rings, and even the silverware I wanted them to use. I also insisted on fresh flowers in a vase on the table. The kitchen counters were to be replaced with white Formica and the kitchen cabinets painted white. I'd selected hardware they could order online from Restoration Hardware, or they could head to the store. I had made this type of a plan for each room of the home. Now, it would be up to them to execute.

I was excited to deliver it, so Oreo and I hopped into Doug and drove over. I was pleased to see that all of the plastic toys and even the swimming pool had disappeared. A sprinkler was working in the front yard, and either Marjorie or Sam had been to the nursery. Flats of pink impatiens waited to be planted in the beds leading up to the front door. I suggested adding a hanging plant in the plan I'd drawn up, and I was sure they'd follow it to the letter after seeing how much progress they'd made already.

Marjorie answered the door, a toddler on her hip, and gave me a big hug. She told me they'd make me proud. I waved off her offer to come in, pointing at Oreo doing his frantic panting number in the window of the car. Every time I left him in there he thought I'd forget him. I had, but only once, and it was in our garage. I'd rescued him after two minutes. He was such a drama king.

Back at home, Doug, Oreo, and I arrived the same time as Beth and Sarah did. Kathryn and Melanie pulled in just behind Beth. The gang was all here. Woman (and baby) power working together. I loved that.

Beth and Mel had settled in the living room while Kathryn and I pulled up chairs at my kitchen table command post. She was wearing a light green sweat suit with a peace sign embroidered on one sleeve. "A party for six hundred doesn't happen every day. What a great business launch. Can I see the To Do list? Sounds like we need to check off a few more items. Oh, and I like all of your Post-it notes. They didn't tell me about T2C lists in Montana."

I wondered what they'd taught her at the ranch in Montana. Kathryn was acting far too calm, far too happy and normal. What had happened to the uptight, driven, working woman who was the "Majors" force in the retail world? What happened to the scorned woman who was left by her husband for a tart—well, not a tart—a friend's friend? What happened to the tears over the anorexic teenager? Was Kathryn taking the same tranquilizer that Charlotte was?

"Well, T2Cs are my special creation, but they have really helped me stick to my goals and accomplish some changes in my life. Somehow, though, I'm still not as calm as your ranch visit seems to have made you," I said. "I'm hoping that will rub off on me. And are you sure you have time to help me today? I mean, you've been out of town and all, and with Bruce and the divorce? Not to bring up a sore subject, but I just don't want to impose."

"Impose? Really? You're the one who has been imposed on! I'm doing great and having a blast. Bruce and I are meeting with our attorneys sometime in the next few days. We've let this drag on for years, but it's time to move on. We're hoping to bring about an amicable settlement. Melanie has been through enough pain because of us. We need to have a united front, for her. You know, life's just too short to go through it being miserable. Mind you, I'm not going to get screwed, but if he plays fair with Mel and with our assets, I will too."

I handed over the party checklist with a smile, seeing she'd already crossed off at least half of the items, and Kathryn got busy making phone calls. I'd forgotten how many contacts she had, and I loved watching how quickly a woman who was accustomed to running a multimillion-dollar company could get things done. The best part was hearing her say she was calling on behalf of Kelly Johnson Home Staging.

Today was the last official camp call before we went to Maine this weekend to pick up the boys. I had put Post-it notes—purple ones—on my kitchen door, the back door, and my purse reminding me of the times: 2:10 and 2:20. Patrick's assistant would conference-call us in. I couldn't believe I would be able to squeeze my own little guys in person in a few days. And I couldn't believe they'd be hugging their mompreneur back.

I took the next half an hour to make return calls and booked one more appointment for later in the day. And then, after changing into what could only be called a fashionable white pants suit, because it was, I dashed out the door to meet Ginger Smith of Wellesley Drive. I pulled up to a wonderful Tudor, with a For Sale sign from Real Living in the front yard. I didn't recognize the name of the sales agent on the sign rider.

Ginger Smith was a beautiful woman—about my age—whose home had been on the market, she said, "forever," which translated in actuality to six months, according to Melanie's meticulous pre-meeting notes. But that could seem like forever, I agreed. We talked, and I sat down and walked her through my process and the fees. Her family was moving into their new home a block away in two weeks, and she was frantic. I understood that not many people could afford two homes, I told her.

After we'd walked through her entire home and I'd given her a lot of free tips—use brighter light bulbs, add some plants, hide the photos of the family, and neutralize the smells (cats)—we had arrived back at her front foyer. I presented her with my proposal, an estimate of twenty hours of work, and asked when the listing expired.

"I don't mean to offend you, Kelly, but do you have any credentials? I mean, how do I know that hiring you will make any difference at all? My real estate agent said she's never heard of you or home staging," Ginger said with a sweet smile on her face. "And my neighbor didn't speak too highly of your abilities."

Okay, stay calm and collected, I said to myself. This is just your first business challenge. You know what you're doing. You're halfway through your online certification program, remember.

"Who is your neighbor, and why would she have any idea about my abilities?" I asked, miffed but not crying.

"Rachel White? I know you two know each other. She says she's worked with you on events for years and you didn't seem—well, I think she said she was shocked you'd opened a business."

The high road beckoned, but so did the low road. My yoga practice kicked in and I took a cleansing breath.

"Ginger, I hope you'll consider my proposal, and I would be

happy to refer you to a real estate agent perfect for you and your property," I said calmly. "I require half up front. So, if and when you decide to work with me, sign the contract and mail or drop off a check. Thank you for your time."

High road taken, I smiled and showed myself out the door. I would deal with Rachel soon, but not now. First I had another appointment.

The next appointment was worse. Not only did I not get the job, I think I had been invited there only to hear them complain. Mr. and Mrs. Raunce sat down across from me and told me how much they didn't like real estate agents or anyone else in the real estate business; how their home was a treasure and how it was supposed to be their retirement nest egg. They didn't understand why their agent even deserved a commission after doing nothing.

I didn't understand why they'd called, and said so.

"We just wanted to satisfy ourselves that you're like the rest of them, all full of promises," Mr. Raunce said accusingly from across the early 1970s brass and glass coffee table. I wasn't going to point out for them, at that moment, that the photos crowding the fireplace mantel and the light blue wall-to-wall carpet could be hindering the sales process.

"You're right, I am," I said, and walked myself out the door. I should've yelled, or at least been indignant, but I wasn't that strong yet. I was impressed that I'd handled my first face-to-face outright rejection by making it all the way back to Doug before the tears welled up.

"Oh Kelly, honestly," I said, shaking my head and checking my makeup in my rearview mirror. No streaks in the Orgasm. "You didn't want to work with those grumps." Still, I called Kathryn for moral support.

"I couldn't even believe you hadn't had a 'no' yet. This is good! Congratulations! Rejection is part of sales, and you need to toughen up," she said. "You didn't cry, did you?"

"No. Well, at least not in front of them. I gotta go. I'm still two, one, and one."

"Go get 'em tiger," she said, laughing.

The next two appointments went great: no more friends of Rachel White and no more wrathful Raunce-like folks blaming the housing crisis on me. I didn't know if I'd get either job; neither had signed a contract, but both were respectful meetings.

As Doug and I turned up the street, I saw Bob Thompson walking up the sidewalk. I hadn't seen him since the night I'd let myself into his home and he'd accosted me. He looked thin, but he gave me a big wave as I pulled into my driveway. It was a bright, sky-blue day, and perfect for a walk. But it was also the middle of the day and most men, at least around these parts, were at work. He seemed to be stalking his former life. And, really, I couldn't believe he waved at me.

Too quickly, he was next to my car. I stayed inside Doug, but put the window down a little.

"Hi former neighbor," Bob said, through the crack. "I was just taking a walk down memory lane. Nothing like having your marriage blow up for all the world to see."

"Yeah, it must've been really tough. Must be tough. Heck, marriage is tough. So sorry for your troubles, Bob." But I wasn't. I was being insincere. The jerk had lunged at me, and now I had way too much to do. I made a note for my life-change list. Number Twenty-one: Avoid insincerity—especially when busy.

"Thanks," he said. "Well, I'm sorry if I upset you before. I wasn't myself."

Drats. Apologies melted me. I rolled down my window all the way and asked Bob if he'd like to come in and have a cup of coffee. Of course Bob agreed and followed Doug and me as we pulled into the garage. As we walked in through the back door, Oreo was immediately suspicious and growling. "It's okay, buddy, it's our neighbor," I said to Oreo, searching frantically for his Lucky Carp to throw him off. "Come on in, Bob. Have you met Kathryn Majors before?" I asked as we rounded the corner into the kitchen.

"No. Hello Kathryn. I'm Bob, a former neighbor of Kelly's. Used to live down the street on the opposite side of the road."

"Oh, yours is the home that my soon-to-be ex-husband is sharing with your sales agent and his soul mate," Kathryn said, shaking his hand.

"Jeez, I'm sorry," Bob said, looking as if he'd jump out a window if there was one available.

"Not your fault, and actually, it's working out for the best. Our marriage was over a long time ago, we were stuck, and now he's made the move," Kathryn said.

I thought that was an interesting way to put it, and that yes, it is easy to get stuck in a long-term relationship, whether you stay in it or decide to leave it.

"Why did you sell?" Kathryn asked.

"My wife moved out one day, took all the furniture, and left me with the kids. Said she'd had it with me. She was right. I worked too much, and I missed the kids' growing up years. But it's too late. She's finished," he said. "I couldn't live there, not without her."

I handed him a cup of coffee, and he took a seat next to Kathryn at the kitchen table. Clearly, not a lot of work would be getting done with the two of them reminiscing about their failed relationships. I wondered if now would be a good time to bring up the bad influence that Bob's son Tom had on Melanie. Probably not.

I headed upstairs to change out of my fabulous white linen and into something more home-office looking—AKA, jeans and a comfy tee shirt. Oreo trotted behind me until he spotted Melanie in the living room and abruptly bolted in her direction, tail wagging. Maybe a small Paris Hilton-type purse pooch would be good as his replacement, I thought, giving him the stink eye.

Wearing new jeans—after all, I had company, I rationalized, and I was starting a company—and an oldish tee shirt, I barged back into the kitchen and seemed to have surprised Bob and Kathryn, who were deep in discussion. They both looked at me as if I was in their kitchen. "Hey, hate to interrupt you guys," I said jumping in, taking charge, "but Kathryn, could you update me on where we are for Thursday night?"

"Oh, I should get out of your hair," Bob said, starting to stand up.

"No, it's fine, Bob. Everything that can be handled before the event is taken care of," she said matter-of-factly. "The remaining items are things we have to do or pick up the afternoon of the event. I was just working on your Quick Books for the home staging business."

What? I thought. She's amazing. And she obviously figured out that I'd been avoiding the world of spreadsheets and accounting.

"You need to get your books in order. I installed Quicken.

That way, when you come back with another signed contract, you can enter it into the system immediately, track payments, track expenses. You're launching a big business here, Kelly, if you keep landing three to four jobs a day," Kathryn said. She gave Bob a smile, as if to say, silly creative girl.

"Okay, I know I'm the creative person, and I know I need this, but how am I going to keep this going? I mean, how am I going to do it without you?" I asked.

"I think you're going to need me, and I would love to help. Just give me the rest of the day to get you organized and then we'll go over everything. You handle the sales and create the plans for the clients. Deal?" she asked.

"Deal I guess—okay." I felt like I was adding a business partner before I'd even thought about it. But I did need the help. And neither Mel nor I could do what Kathryn could in business.

"So, Kathryn, tell me more about . . . " I heard Bob say as I walked out of the room. That's great: two damaged folks looking for rebound love in my kitchen/office. That's all I needed. I high-tailed it for the porch and took a minute to breathe. I looked at the beautiful blue hydrangeas. I checked my hummingbird feeders; water was full and clear. I just loved those little birds. I was taking a moment: relaxing, getting in touch with nature. If Kathryn and Bob found each other, so be it. If Kathryn added value to my business, that would be great. I hated working alone anyway. Just breathe, I told myself.

As I took another deep breath, my cell phone rang. It was Patrick's assistant. "I'll put you into the conference call now," she said, and suddenly, I heard Sean's little voice. "Mom?"

"Hi, baby," I said. "I can't wait to see you!"

"Do you think, um . . . I asked Dad and he said it was okay

with him if it was with you. Do you think I could stay just one more week? Please?"

"Listen champ, I didn't agree. I said your mother and I need to talk about it," Patrick interjected.

Of course he had already told Sean it was okay with him, the traitor. Maybe I'd get a sheep dog puppy and a new husband. Everybody else was doing it.

"Please, Mom, everybody's staying and I'm having a blast and if I come home I'll just want to play computer games in my room and this way I'm out in nature and stuff," Sean said.

I had to hand it to the kid; he could spout out a line of reasoning almost as well as I could. Learned from the best, I guess. I missed him so much it hurt, but I knew he was telling the truth. "Hey baby, if it's that important to you, we can push it back another week. I just miss you so much," I said.

"I miss you too, Mom! You're the best! Thank you so much! Thank you, thank you! Oh, and David says thank you, too! He's standing right here, but he wanted me to ask for both of us, and he says he has to go now, so he can't do his call, but he'll talk to you soon! Love you," Sean said, and then he was gone.

"You okay, honey?" Patrick said. Suddenly he and I were the only ones left on the conference line. "You didn't have to agree to it. We can call them back if you've changed your mind."

"No, it's okay. I know they love it. I just miss them so much." At least my mom was visiting. That would help; she's another distraction.

"You have a lot going on Kelly. Think of it this way," Patrick began, trying to cheer me up. "Now you have more time to focus on your business, and you can have fun at the party and really take the time to work all of those contacts you're going to make, since we don't have to get ready to leave for Maine right away."

"Yeah, I guess so," I said, trying not to pout. I'd focus on my business. My kids were happy. I loved what I was doing. It would give me time to finish my online classes (T2C #7) and to take that self-defense class (T2C #11).

When I went back inside from the porch, Mel had finished her session with Beth and was working the phones. She'd begun writing the messages into the three categories I'd suggested, using the new professional spreadsheet Kathryn had created, and she'd flagged hot calls or high potential calls with pink highlighter. A great system, I thought. Kathryn didn't. She wanted to computerize the highlighting too, but Mel and I won.

"This all needs to be entered into an Excel spreadsheet, Mel," Kathryn reiterated. "Let me show you how to do it. It will make things a lot easier."

"Oh, Mom, really."

Now I was certain Kathryn was showing off for Bob. She leaned over Mel and her computer and began typing standing up. Kathryn's green sweatshirt top was fitted, I noticed now, and actually showed off her figure. How was that possible?

Mother and daughter were both beautiful, and Bob was noticing.

"Mel, for now, just give me the hot names to call. We don't want to miss our chance. I don't have anything booked for tomorrow or Thursday," I said.

"We aren't booking anything more for this week, but we can make the calls and set the appointments for next week. For Thursday's big party, I need you fresh and rested and rejection free," Kathryn said.

"Yes, ma'am," I said, and sort of huffed out of the room. I'd make my calls from my peaceful porch, away from spreadsheets and the sexual energy flowing between Kathryn and Bob.

I was one call down—a very good lead; a man, for once, who I was meeting in the morning at his home around the corner, ignoring Kathryn's command—and had one call to go when Charlotte appeared in my backyard.

4 2

I COULDN'T GET A MOMENT OF PEACE AT MY OWN HOUSE.
Oh, well.

"Kelly, is that you?" she asked. Her cheerleader's energy wasn't
back, but she seemed much better than she was last night. "I don't
have my distance glasses on."

"Hey, it's me, come on over," I said, waving her up to the porch.

"I was just checking to make sure you didn't give me all your
hydrangeas," she said, drifting my way in a gauzy white dress. She
looked like a dream feels when you first wake up: cloudy but real.

I met her halfway, on the lawn, and while I was certain Kathryn could see us if she looked out the kitchen window, I hoped
Bob was keeping her distracted. "No worries. I got the flowers at
the florist store, to remind you that I'm right here," I said. "Are you
doing okay?"

"They made me take something yesterday, a white pill, that
sort of makes you feel ethereal. That's the right word, isn't it? I
hated it."

"I'd say it's the perfect word. Stop taking them. And who is
they?"

"Bruce, and I guess Beth agrees. They wanted to keep me calm, to get through the funeral service because Jim's family is being so mean."

"Well, I trust Beth, and I guess you were rather inconsolable yesterday. Come sit down on the porch. I'll get you some water."

"Problem is, I think it's better to just feel the pain. So I didn't take the pills they gave me today. I flushed them. I kept wondering, where does the pain go if you don't feel it? Does it slip away or hang around you, waiting for an opening? Without those pills, I could feel it, remember Jim and the good times we had together. And remember his funeral. So I'm just acting calm to throw them off.

"Guess what I found out?" Charlotte continued. "Jim had just left his girlfriend's house when he crashed his motorcycle, and he wasn't wearing a helmet. She'd just broken up with him, and she said he was going to kill himself on that thing. He proved her right."

"Oh, Charlotte! How do you know all of this?"

"She called me. The woman. She believes it's her fault that Jim died. And here I was, thinking it was all my fault. Maybe it was all his fault, you know? Or maybe, subconsciously, Jim just wanted to die. After she and I talked, I felt so much better. I think it helped her, too. She's coming to the funeral, and Jim's parents don't even know about her. It's better that way, I guess. They can go on blaming me, but I'll know the truth."

"Wow, Charlotte. I guess it is better for you to have heard the rest of the story. I know it makes you feel better, to have connected with her. In a weird way, I hope you and Kathryn can come together somehow."

"If she thinks I am the reason their marriage broke up, I can understand her not wanting to be friends, ever," Charlotte said in her dreamy, ethereal voice. "If she realizes their relationship was gone long ago, like with Jim and me, though, then maybe Kathryn and I have a chance."

She was right. "Let me go grab some water. I'll be right back!" I said perkily and headed inside. I grabbed two bottles out of the fridge and was headed back out to the porch when Kathryn stopped me.

"Why is she here?" she asked.

"Who? Well, I . . . Charlotte is just visiting. I'll take her home soon. They're burying her husband tonight," I stuttered, suddenly feeling guilty.

"I know. It's just that I saw her, outside the window, and I got so jealous and hurt," Kathryn said, tears welling up in her eyes. "I'm trying to let it go. I know it's not her fault our marriage broke apart. But I just wished she had, they had, the decency to wait until we were divorced before moving in together. But at the ranch, they taught me I have to let it go. If I don't, the pain and hurt consumes me. And it will. I can feel that negativity when it starts to come out."

"You're human, Kathryn. What you're feeling is natural. But you're light years ahead of most people because of Montana," I said. "You seem so confident and calm. I'm sort of stuck in the middle here. I just was taking her some water."

"I know. And I'm trying to be calm. I just got thrown off. Seeing Charlotte walking across the grass—that jettisoned me into the past. I've really been working on this, Kelly, before and during my stay at the ranch: staying in the present, focusing on the future."

"That seems so brave," I said. We'd ended up in the living room. I was going to have to redo the whole space soon if people kept using it as a confessional. Perhaps a pew instead of a couch? I wondered what my online Feng Shui tutorial would say about it.

"Well, here's the thing: Holding onto the past only hurts you. I mean, Bruce has moved on, and I need to. I need to realize that this is my life now. I can't change the past, but I can change the moment now. And the future for Mel and me," Kathryn said. "I'm ready."

"Ready for what?" She sounded like she had just come to a decision.

"To talk with Charlotte. To forgive her. To move on."

"Ah, I'm not sure this is a good time for that, Kathryn. I mean, her former husband just died . . ." and then I realized I'd left Charlotte out on the porch for quite awhile. "Oh what the heck, come on out."

Charlotte was curled up on the couch. She looked so small. The sun shimmered through the leaves of the trees as it made its way to night.

"She seems peaceful," Kathryn said. "It would be hard to stay mad at that."

"Yes, it would," I agreed, and then Kathryn and I hugged as she sobbed in my arms.

"It really will be okay, right?" she asked.

"Absolutely. It's always the worst right before it gets to be the best," I said. "I really believe that."

"Me too," Charlotte said. She was still curled up on the couch, eyes closed. "I'm sorry for hurting you, Kathryn. I was selfish and needy. I hope, sometime, we can be friends again."

"Thank you. Someday we'll talk, I'm sure," Kathryn said, and then she turned and walked back inside.

Charlotte and I sat in silence for a few minutes, but then I reminded her she had to go home.

"Thank you for a moment of peace," Charlotte said. "I love this porch. It's like an oasis in the midst of suburbia. I hope to create spaces like this in our new home."

"You will," I said, standing. I'd decided to walk her back. "You know, there's a perfect spot, just off the dining room, where you could add French doors and a little garden." I'd been imagining it during the home staging. It would be, well, exquisite.

"So, tonight at the funeral, you are going to stay strong, right?" I said.

"Right."

"You are going to hold your head high, right?"

"Right. Even though Jim's folks think I'm a slut!"

"You're not, though, Charlotte."

"Are you sure? I slept with Kathryn's husband, I broke Jim's heart." She stopped and looked at me.

"You were looking out for yourself and your girls. Your heart was in the right place, and so yes, I'm sure, I'm sure," I said as we crossed the street and walked up to her house. I didn't leave until I had handed Charlotte over to Bruce, who greeted us at the front door. I was glad he'd noticed she was missing. Probably the twins were looking for her, I thought.

"I'll take care of her," he said. "I promise you."

"You said that before, with Melanie, and then you went out of town," I said, unable to hide my disappointment.

"I know, I know, Kelly. I don't know how to convince you of this, but everything has changed for me. My priorities are with Charlotte and Mel and Charlotte's girls. I'm going to do this right this time. I just named my right-hand man president of the company. He's taking over day-to-day responsibilities. It took all of this to make me see that I was a selfish bastard," he shook his head, looking at me intently while still holding Charlotte in his arms. She looked up at him adoringly.

Meanwhile, I was looking at him suspiciously.

"You have been right about me," he said. "About not trusting me. But from now on, I'm going to prove you wrong. I am."

"I hope so," I said, and waving my arm in the general direction of my house added, "There's a lot of healing that needs to take place around here."

"I know. And I can do my part. Beth and I will have some sessions, and she's going to help Mel and me. All I can do is be here for Charlotte. And I will be." And with that, the new Bruce Majors nodded his head at me, and he and Charlotte walked back into their new house.

"You'd better," I said to myself as I walked slowly back home. Remembering T2C #18—don't be gullible—and immediately adding T2C #22—trust your instincts—I thought, for once, I believed in him.

43

GAVIN PULLED INTO THE DRIVEWAY AS I WAS WALKING AROUND the house to go in the back door.

"Hey Kelly," he said, and we gave each other a hug. I couldn't wait for the boys to meet him.

"I'm glad you're here," he said, looking down at his tennis shoes.

"What's up? Are you proposing marriage?"

"No," he said, turning bright red before he realized I was kidding. "It's just that Mel's mom doesn't like me very much. I mean, before she went away and stuff, she would yell at Mel for staying on the phone with me, and she wouldn't let us go out or hang out together. I think she blamed me for Mel not eating, and you know, I was the one trying to help her. I mean, it's true, I would let her chew gum and watch me eat lunch, but I didn't know what to do. Now I do."

"Beth and I have both talked to Kathryn about you, and she is in a better place now, too," I said. "Come on in, Gavin. It's going to be fine."

We walked in the door with my arm looped in his. He was

blushing, I thought, but I was enjoying a borrowed boy since mine had abandoned me for another week in the woods.

"Gavin," Melanie shouted as she jumped up from the bar stool and gave him a hug. I thought at that moment about the purity of their love, that first-love devotion and passion.

"Hey buddy," Patrick said, clearly bonded with the teen. It seems he'd been awaiting another male's arrival to venture into the kitchen/office. He'd been hiding upstairs since he'd arrived home from work.

"Gavin," Kathryn said. "It's wonderful to see you." When she reached him, she, too, gave Gavin a hug.

He grinned at me over her head. "Hi Mrs. Majors. Wow, you're tan."

"I've been spending a lot of time outside, in Montana. And one of the things I learned there was to admit when I'm wrong. I'm sorry to have mistrusted you," Kathryn said. "I was worried about my daughter, and I didn't know if you could handle everything she was going through. I should've given you more credit, young man. Thank you for all that you've done for Melanie."

"That's okay, Mrs. Majors." Gavin was now blushing even more deeply.

"Um, hate to break up this love fest—it's a great scene for a Lifetime movie—but I have a huge party to host tomorrow evening, a business to start, and, well, all of you are a part of it. So let's focus on me, okay?" They all laughed.

After everybody gave their updates—everyone being Mel and Kathryn—Gavin and Mel took off for dinner and the movies. After they'd left, I suggested to Kathryn that she and I sit on the porch and talk about going into business together.

"Patrick, you can be the attorney who puts our deal together, okay?" I said. "Let's get outside. It's perfect porch-sitting time." I quickly put together an appetizer plate. None of us needed smoked meat tonight, I thought, and instead I made a platter of blueberries, strawberries, and a great artichoke dip and crackers. I poured us each a glass of pinot noir. "I just have to return one more phone call, and your next two weeks are booked," Kathryn said with a smile as we walked outside. "We are doing this thing, big time. You have a closing rate, overall, of about 16 percent. I'd like to see you get that up a bit."

"Yes, I'll work on it. At least I'm getting a lot of practice handling rejections," I said.

"But you need to work on overcoming objections so you get the sale," Kathryn said.

"Fine, fine, but right now, I need you to hurry. The sunset waits for no woman, even the Type-A ones," I said, and placed the appetizers on the table. Patrick had already claimed the rocking chair, so Kathryn and I shared the couch.

"This is wonderful," I said, and stretched. And it was.

The three of us clinked our wine glasses and quietly sat together, each of us lost in our own thoughts.

I thought about Charlotte, soon to be at Jim's funeral service. I thought, as always, about my boys in Maine, who, an hour or two earlier, had probably watched the sunset's vibrant purples and oranges dance across the pristine lake and mountains beyond. On our way to the airport after Drop-Off Day we'd stopped at one of the many antique stores lining the rural roads along our drive. I'd picked up an old tin sign that read: Do one thing every day that scares you. So far this summer, I'd done just that. And I'd grown because of it. I knew, sitting in the dentist's chair earlier in the summer, that something about my life had to change. What I also had discovered was that I was the only one who could do it. Not having that realization was what had held me back for so long. I was ready to rewrite Things to Change rule Number One: My life is up to me to define. I needed to make my own dreams come true. And I smiled as I thought: you know, I'm doing it.

As I looked around at the blue and periwinkle hydrangeas and the pink sunset, I said aloud, "I am happy!" forgetting, of course, Patrick and Kathryn were on the porch, too.

"What?" Kathryn asked, smiling at me.

Patrick was looking at me with sparkly eyes.

"I'm happy. This is a great time of life. This sunset. Your friendship. A business. Great kids. A mostly perfect husband. I am not trying to brag or anything, I'm just feeling so thankful and blessed. I really love my life, myself, right now. And, even turning forty doesn't seem so bad anymore," I said.

"You're lucky to be in that place, feeling so confident," Kathryn said, grabbing a cracker and some dip. "I used to feel like that. Like I was doing what I should be doing: married to the right guy, working at a career that I should be pursuing, where I was valued, and of course, raising a daughter who was confident and happy. Now it all seems like someone else's life."

"Would you have changed anything, though? I mean, you loved Bruce once; Melanie is a brilliant young woman who will get her feet back under her. And your career? Heck, how many women can say they've achieved all you have? You changed an industry. You're a trailblazer," I said.

I looked into Kathryn's deep brown eyes and saw the shiny reflection of tears there. But what were they for? The reality that her life was dramatically different now, or the memory of all of the sacrifices she had made along the way?

"Thanks, Kelly, you've always been there for me, even if I haven't spent enough time cheering you on in return."

"Uh, you've been there whenever I needed you. We all just

get so busy taking care of everyone and everything, we forget the care and feeding of friends. That is one of my Things to Change points—number five on the list, to be exact—and look, it's what we're doing now."

Patrick cleared his throat. "Well, given that this is girls' talk, I think I'll go inside and make some real food for dinner."

"Thanks chef." I said.

"He's a great guy," Kathryn said after Patrick skedaddled.

"I'm lucky," I agreed.

We sat quietly and watched as the sun turned to a magenta pink. Two hummingbirds were busy refueling their tiny bodies at my feeder. It was a beautiful night. I should probably be cleaning or doing something for tomorrow's party, I thought. Then I stopped. Be in the moment now, I reminded myself.

"At the ranch I had a session with a counselor during which we used a mandala as the metaphor for life and renewal," Kathryn said. "It made a huge impact on me." With her calm, reflective tone, she was starting to remind me of Charlotte. I wondered again if she was on drugs, too. Midlife women and antidepressants seemed eerily tied together.

"Uh, what's a mandala?" I asked. I got up to grab the porch candles and lit them as she spoke.

"In the Hindu tradition, mandalas represent the essence of self. They are circles with all different designs in them. The counselor asked me to select the twelve different patterns on transparent cards that spoke to me the most. Then I had to pick one I didn't like. Then I picked colors to place under the transparent cards I liked, and a color that would make the mandala I didn't like feel better. She placed the cards onto a chart that flowed clockwise, starting at the bottom. Picture six o'clock on a watch; that was the first position, where new creations begin. I was actually already on stage seven—think twelve o'clock on the dial—representing renewal and energy, intuition and identity. It was so cool talking about my rebirth, the notion that I was getting reborn. Full-flowered feminine is what the counselor said. I picked all blues, the yin color, the feminine side. Yang is yellow, masculine."

"Let me guess; green is perfect harmony, the yin and yang?" I said, proud of my deductive reasoning.

Kathryn ignored me, lost in thought. "I was proud of that. It meant that I was coming into my own. Finally, as a forty-year-old woman, I was starting to be the real me. At the center of the mandala chart was the central spiritual connection. And I felt it was there. I felt connected to nature, to people, and to God. I need to keep that feeling. And as soon as I completed the session, I felt transformed. That's when I knew I was ready to come home. Ready to settle and forgive and get on with my next chapter."

"That's so great, Kathryn. I want to go there sometime."

"I think you are; you're in the creation phase."

"No, I mean Montana, silly," I said, laughing.

"We will. In fact, let's make it your birthday present. A week together out there, whenever you'd like! It's really a blessing, to let go of grudges, to forgive, and to move on. To allow yourself to get rid of what they called emotional hoarding."

"I'd love to go there with you, but as you may have noticed, I have a business to run. I'm going to be too busy for the next few months, but then, maybe, I'll be able to pay my way out to Montana."

"Okay, but here's the thing. It's such an important part of my next step. I want to work with a friend, control my destiny. I know we'll make an amazing team. Did you know you have ten or so hot referrals you could make today to real estate agents who are dying for business?" she asked.

Well, yeah, I did know, since I had just handed one over to Charlotte. I hoped she remembered. I guess now I actually had nine.

"You think that is a revenue source or a way to get incremental business?" I asked, since she was the businesswoman and, it sounded like, my new partner.

"We need to charge a fee per referral. That will make them more valuable, but we will discount it for agents who refer us business. Make sense?" Kathryn said, swirling the wine in her glass and smiling. "I can set up all of these systems for us. I have some great friends in the IT world who would help and give us a great deal. I called a friend who owns a retail space planning firm I work with—ah, worked with—all the time, and she said she'd be happy to help us find cool furniture for our new office space."

My head was spinning. Kelly Johnson Home Staging was growing into something else before its official launch. "Wow, you are really way ahead of me, Kathryn," I said. "I thought I'd keep overhead low and work from my home, at least for awhile."

"Thing is, another friend of mine is willing to give us lease-free space at his new condo project at the corner of Cambridge and Fifth Avenues. The first floor is retail, but he's having trouble filling it and the units above. We can help him stage the units in exchange for prime space, and you'll be a minute from home," she added.

"Wow."

Kathryn looked at her watch and jumped up. "I have got to go. I'm meeting Bob at Spagio in ten minutes and I should probably freshen up."

"What? You're going on a date with Bob? That was fast."

"Well, Kelly, I have to start now rebuilding my life. He asked, I was free, and gosh, I haven't been on a date in twenty years. The last five years with Bruce, we never went anywhere alone. I'm kind of nervous, actually."

"It's gotta be just like riding a bike," I said, blowing out the candles. "Except, I guess, the seat has changed, and the handle bars, and . . . Oh, it will be fun. Just don't—"

"I know. No rebound relationships. Just friends, right? But maybe friends with benefits? Bye, Kelly. Bye, Patrick!"

She hustled out the front door, leaving me with the rather disturbing image of Bob and Kathryn making out. Ick. Hopefully Patrick could take my mind off of that by joining me in some making out of our own. I was inspired.

Patrick was still making dinner in the kitchen, so I sneaked up the stairs, darted into our bedroom, and rummaged in my pajama drawer. I dug down past my typical long underwear and the Hanna Anderson, striped pants-and-top set and found one of my honeymoon numbers. No kidding—from seventeen years ago. It was light blue silk, long and flowing, with a plunging neckline that made my breasts, although fuller and lower now than they were back then, look good, I thought. I was all about self-confidence tonight.

I ate Patrick's chicken dinner dressed in my plunging lingerie, and he had trouble keeping his eyes off me. I have to say, self-confidence must be sexy, if Patrick's reaction was any indication. We'd finished dinner and were cleaning up the kitchen, eager to head upstairs, when the doorbell rang.

My mom had arrived.

44

THE NEXT MORNING, MOM AND I SAT IN THE KITCHEN together. I was in a panic. I was worried about Kelly Johnson Home Staging. What would it be called if Kathryn became my business partner? Kelly and Kathryn Home Staging? I had just opened the first box of my new business cards. I really liked them. Argh.

I was still pondering the problem when Patrick came downstairs and joined us. Fresh from the shower, he had that dewy look. So in, I thought with my Sephora-influenced mind.

"Hey, Kathryn wants to be my partner in the business, Patrick. What do you think?"

He stopped pouring his tar and gave me a puzzled look. "I thought she already was. I mean, she and Mel seem to be a part of your team, setting up your systems, booking appointments. Aren't they?" He gave his hair a vigorous rub before joining Mom and me at the table.

"They are. Mel is part-time until school starts, but Kathryn, I just . . . well, she's been used to a big business, big staff, and all of that," I said.

"You're afraid she'll overpower you?" he asked softly.

"I guess I am." So much for feeling my power, I thought, wrapping my robe around me tightly.

"Listen, there's only one Kelly Johnson. You know what you have. You have innate sales skills and design talent. Most importantly, people like you. Really like you. Some of us—your sons and me, in particular, and really anyone you meet—fall in love with you. It's up to you whether you should share your new business. I think as long as you keep the name, you're the lead, and you set boundaries, roles, and responsibilities. You'll be the leader of a great team," Patrick said. "It's like at the law firm. We all bring different strengths. Some of us like yours truly are the rainmakers. Without us, the law firm would suffer. That's you. You're the rainmaker. If Kathryn can handle being second fiddle, you're set. If not, it won't work."

My mom was nodding vigorously at everything he said, but she hadn't spoken a peep.

"Mom?"

"I agree with everything Patrick said. Stop being such a worrywart and get moving."

"And you both think Kathryn will be okay with second fiddle?"

"I think, if I were her, it would be a relief, and a lot of fun. Kathryn knows what she's getting into. She asked you if she could help, remember? I've gotta run. I'll be home at noon to help get ready for your big coming-out party! Let's have some fun tonight, okay? No worries, just fun?"

"You know, I'm working on that. Thank goodness Mom is here to help, too," I said, following Patrick out of the kitchen. "Last night was fun," I said quietly, smiling.

"Oh, it was," he said, kissing me on the lips. He stopped and whispered: "I felt like we were back in our honeymoon suite. Well . . . until your mom arrived."

❄

The caterers rang the doorbell just after I walked through the door from my back-to-back appointments. Three home staging meetings, two signed contracts. I was starting to get worried about how I'd keep up with it all. And I hadn't even launched the business. Egads.

I opened the door, and from that moment on, the house was a constant swarm of activity, like a well-orchestrated yet chaotic relay race to the finish line of tonight's party. People dashed by, doing different tasks depending on their role in the production. Mom took charge of the gardens around the house and was a weeding and watering machine.

The cast of characters ebbed and flowed. Blue and periwinkle hydrangeas, carted in by the very efficient florist, were on every table, in every bathroom, on every outdoor café table, and on every coffee table. The overall theme we'd picked was, loosely, *The Great Gatsby*: the Roaring Twenties, Champagne and ragtime, bee lights and candles. Kathryn was the conductor. She'd been in an exceptionally great mood when she showed up this morning as I was leaving for my first appointment.

I figured she'd had a great night with Bob but didn't ask. She was glowing. But maybe it was the party. Mel looked equally happy. They'd both embraced my mom before scurrying to their duties.

"Hey, Kelly, great close rate today," Kathryn said, grabbing the contracts and the checks and handing them to Mel. "Can I talk to you for a couple of minutes? Out on the porch? I wanted to review a few ideas I have for tonight."

"Oh, right, leave me in here, working my fingers to the bone," Mel said, and then we all laughed. "I know, the skin and bones jokes don't work so well right now," she said, "but I'm getting better."

"Yes you are," I said, giving her shoulders a squeeze and then following Kathryn out the door.

"Bruce and I met early this morning to attempt an amicable agreement on our divorce," she said.

"And how'd it go?" I asked, hoping for the best for everyone's sake.

"Really well. The one thing Bruce insisted on was that I tell you the truth. Thing is, I'm the one who had an affair first. It's not important with whom. It's over. What is important, though, is that long before Bruce and Charlotte got together, I left my marriage, both physically and emotionally. I needed more than Bruce could give at the time. Maybe I needed more than Bruce could ever give. But that's the unflattering truth. I promised Bruce I'd let you know."

Not knowing what to say, I simply nodded. I was glad I was sitting down, because I swear the whole backyard had tilted ten degrees to the right. Or maybe it was just the new perspective I was getting used to in my mind. The good news was that it was going to be a beautiful night for a party, and for the world to shift a little.

"Can you say something? Are you mad?" Kathryn asked. "I'm sorry."

"Don't apologize to me, for heaven's sake. Everybody makes mistakes and well, there you have it. Who is, or was, he?"

"You don't know him, and you won't. He's married and he lives on the West Coast. It's over," she said. "Charlotte knows, too, probably has for a long time. And I think she and I might even be able to be friends again one day."

Okay, I thought, I've had enough revelation for one day, but Kathryn seemed to want to explain more fully.

"I guess now, having all of this out in the open, is part of the healing. I wasn't happy; I was looking for love in all the wrong places, as the song goes. But I'm starting over. Life is full of possibilities, and I really believe I deserve happiness, as you would say: real happiness this time around. Thank you, Kelly. You and this business are such an important piece of my new life."

"Well, we had better get going on it then, hadn't we?" I said, finally standing up, executing my need for escape. "I think it's time for me to start getting ready for my debut."

"Oh, no problem. Mel and I will keep everything moving forward," she said, heading to the kitchen as I walked up the stairs.

Upstairs, I thought about what Kathryn had said. I understood her loneliness. Bruce traveled constantly. I didn't know what it would take to make a person vulnerable to an affair, but unhappiness and loneliness had to be the leading causes. I felt bad that I had assumed Bruce was the unfaithful one. How stereotypical of me. Equalish rights, or the quest for them, were creating equal opportunities for all kinds of power plays, I suppose.

I walked into my closet and wondered if I'd be able to fit into an outfit from the medium-sized area. I love my blue and white Tory Burch summer dress. Plus, it would complement the hydrangeas. But could I zip it up? Deciding life was short and it was getting shorter pondering the possibilities, I pulled it out, pulled it on, and miracle of miracles, I could zip it up easily. I did a little dance in front of my full-length mirror and thought again about permanently adopting Mel and inviting Beth and her family to come live with us. I need to keep the people on the road to healthy eating around me. This could be way better than Weight Watchers or Jenny Craig. I could save money and spend it on clothes.

The doorbell rang, but I figured there were enough people downstairs who could answer it. I turned to my makeup and turned on my flat iron. Thomas made me swear I'd flatten for my big event. I wished someone had invented ear guards to protect me from myself and my sizzling appliance.

"Kelly!" Mel called up the stairs. "The door is for you!"

Rats. It was 4:30, so I shouldn't be dressed yet, but I didn't want to change, so I didn't. I ran down the hall and down the steps—impressed myself with the lack of panting involved while doing those two things—and met Charlotte at the front door. She held the bouquet of flowers I'd taken to her house yesterday.

"I wanted you to have these, to help decorate for the party, but I see you have flowers all over the place," Charlotte said. She seemed clear-eyed. "It looks beautiful around here, Kelly."

"Thanks, Charlotte. How are you holding up? Was the funeral okay?" I took the flowers from her and led her into the living room. No one had used the counseling couch today that I knew of. I put the vase of flowers on the mantel and sat down next to Charlotte.

"I'm glad it's over. It would've been nice to be included in some way, but the girls were precious and so brave. Jim and I loved each other. He knew that. Bruce was amazing the whole time."

"Yeah, I'm coming around to Mr. Majors' charms," I said with a smile. "I think I might actually like him."

"I'll alert the media," Charlotte said. "No, really, that's great. He just said the same thing about you. So we're all ready to host the throngs parading through. Do you need me to do anything special or just keep the flow going?"

"Thank you, Charlotte! Are you sure you're up to it?"

"Yes, it's our pleasure to help."

"Well, great, then, just keep them moving through and thank you—for giving me this idea, for telling me I could do it . . ."

"You're the one putting it all together. You're making it happen, Kelly. I just can't believe how fast."

"It's amazing. Ever since I did that television interview, the phone has been ringing off the hook. I know there will be hurdles, but I'm really enjoying the moment. Speaking of that, I did recommend you to that adorable couple I told you about."

"I know, and thank you. I will call them tomorrow. I really appreciate you forgiving me and wanting to move forward. And I'm sorry I let you down, with Bruce and stuff. I was just afraid to lose you if I told you sooner, and I was afraid to lose him, too. It caused a lot of lies. One lie just led to another."

"It must have been hard. And my reaction when you told me probably made you wish you hadn't," I said, remembering the scene I'd made at lunch.

"Yes, well, it was all tangled. But now, Bruce and Kathryn have settled and she seems okay, and you're referring me to your clients so that must mean you're not so mad anymore?" She gave me that beauty pageant smile. "I think, just maybe, everything's going to work out fine."

"I hope so, and I'm not mad anymore. But I do need to go get ready for my big night."

"Yes, you do. And while you're milling around with all of the real estate agents in town tonight, just remember who got you into this business in the first place. Any other referrals for me yet, by the way?" she asked, and her eyes had a knowing look. She'd heard I had more.

"I'm surprised how many of my new clients either don't have an agent yet or are unhappy with who they are using. I'd love to give you the majority of the leads, but how will I get referrals from the other agents if they know I only give business to you?"

"Well, I thought about that, and I agree. I won't be the right agent for all of your clients, but I will be for most. Same with me referring you. Remember, originally you were going to be working with me, on my team. I'm so tired of working alone. The office where I work is catty, people snark each other behind their backs. I couldn't take it anymore, so I'm leaving. I'm opening my own Real Living franchise."

"Oh my goodness, Charlotte, good for you! But isn't that a big step? You've got to get office space, and I'm just learning about all of the accounting nightmares and things like spreadsheets and all."

"Here is my proposition to you and Kathryn," she said. "Kathryn helps me with the business systems of my real estate office, just like she's doing with your home staging business. Bruce says she has a brilliant business mind, and just like you, I'm good at sales. I'll lease space right next to yours at the new Crossroads condo tower. What do you think?"

"What? You and Kathryn are going to work together?" I thought the earth had just tilted a little more.

"Only if you agree that it's okay. We both think it's a great idea! And so does Bruce. I know that sounds weird to you, but we're all in a really good place. It's going to be great for Mel, too. We're all committed to her, and the twins, of course."

Who was I to stand in the way of such miraculous teamwork? I just hoped it would all stay this harmonious. But I'd learned you can't predict the future, no matter what the business or life partnerships or arrangements. This would be a good time to trust my instincts (T2C #22), and so I did.

"Fine with me, as long as I get to help design your office, too," I said, giving her a big hug.

"Of course! Your exquisite taste is in high demand these days. I'd be honored. Go get ready for your coming-out party. Oh, and if you don't mind, I'm going to put out my new business cards at my house. I need to recruit some other agents to join my office."

"You go, girl." I walked her out the door.

The party, everyone told me, was perfect. The crowd didn't dissipate until after midnight. But the best part of the evening was that Patrick kept telling me I looked beautiful, and that he was proud of me. I couldn't remember having spent a more special evening together—more affirming, more loving even than our wedding. I told him that (T2C #20).

Kathryn and Melanie had changed into their party attire at some point before the guests began arriving. Kathryn wore an all-white linen pantsuit, and she was dripping with diamonds: a vision of sophisticated elegance. I noticed Bob Thompson following her as she directed people out the porch door and toward Charlotte's house. Melanie wore a simple white blouse, skinny jeans, and black flats. Her hair was swept up in her signature ponytail, and she looked as if she'd popped out of the J. Crew catalog. Gavin was by her side, helping clean up stray glasses and cocktail napkins when I passed by them.

Every time I spotted my mom, she was talking to a different man. I'd need to talk to her about her flirting, I thought with a smile.

Rachel had appeared sometime during the evening. She'd obviously come under the heading "plus guest." I saw her before she spotted me, and realized I had a choice. I could allow her to raise my blood pressure, stress me out with her very presence, or I could let it go. Move on. She only had power over me if I allowed it. Eventually, she made her way through the crowd and arrived at my side.

"Nice party, Kelly," she said, her beady, bespectacled eyes staring at me.

"Thank you, Rachel," I said. And instead of telling her to beat it, I asked, "Have you tried the grilled beet salad? It's amazing. Oh, and be sure to go next door and see my staging work. I know you're not familiar with my new business or what I can do, but I'd appreciate your support." Or, at the very least, you keeping your mouth shut instead of driving away potential clients, I wanted to add, but didn't.

"Yes, I hope it goes well for you, Kelly, but really, with Amy and all my volunteer activities, I could never take on a job. What about your boys?" she said. "It's not like you have to work, right? You don't, do you?"

"No, Rachel, I don't have to work; I want to work. And that's the point, really. Some women like us are lucky. We have choices. And when we make them—whatever they are—the best thing we can hope for is to have other women, especially women who know us, support our choices," I said. "I'm glad there are women like you who volunteer to make our community and our schools so much better. I value that. Just imagine how great it would be if we could all value each other, no matter what path we choose."

And then I smiled and walked away.

45

THREE MONTHS LATER . . .

After working on top of each other at my house for the past few months, moving into our office would feel great, and today was the day. I was driving the kids to school. Sean had just informed me he had a new girlfriend named Samantha, and David reminded me he needed his football gear dropped off at three o'clock.

"Why couldn't you just have taken it with you?" I asked for the third time this morning.

"Because," he said, sulking. "Can't you just pretend you're a normal mom and drop it all off with a snack, like you used to?"

"You don't think a working mom is a normal mom?"

"Let's not get into this again." Sean, my little peacekeeper, jumped in. "Mom, we're proud of your new business, we're just not quite used to it yet. It's like when your friend gets braces. At first you notice, but then you forget."

"Whatever," David said as we pulled up in front of the middle school.

"I'll have it here by three," I promised. "Have a great day you two!" I swallowed a gulp, and shook my head. I was doing what I wanted to do, putting my passion for decorating and helping people into action. And people were paying me to do it. So why did I feel so guilty? Surely I wasn't the only working mother among David's friends. Surely.

It took Doug and me three minutes to make it from the school to the parking lot of the Crossroads building. As I pulled into the space I admired the signage. The corner windows were dressed with periwinkle blue and white striped awnings. Above the awnings was my logo: Kelly Johnson Home Staging + Design. My name, in huge letters, above my very own storefront. Next door, the look was more contemporary, yet welcoming. The round Real Living logo was screened onto the front windows, and words such as home, dream, believe, live, imagine, find, in various typography covered the rest of the window. Perfect, if I did say so myself.

I turned the key to unlock the back door, and walked inside. Kathryn was already at work. Since she lived above the office and the high school started earlier than the middle school, she could drop off Melanie, drive back, park in her underground private spot, and get to her desk at least twenty minutes before me. It was fun having her here to greet me.

About halfway through the build-out of the space, we had a meeting. I suggested blowing out the shared wall between our business and Charlotte's. The two entities were naturally complementary, and since I was designing both spaces, I knew the look I could achieve.

"Really, you guys would consider that? With me?" Charlotte had said. She'd already recruited ten real estate agents for her office, yet still seemed surprised that people wanted to be around her. The love she showed to others still hadn't sunk through to her own soul. But she was working on it.

"Of course, it'll be great," I answered, and Kathryn agreed. It would be easier for Kathryn to handle both of the operations that way, too. So here we were, three friends, bursting with entrepreneurial spirit, know-how, and a burgeoning client list.

"How did we get so lucky?" I asked Kathryn as I dropped my purse on my desk and looked around at all we'd accomplished so far.

"This isn't luck," Kathryn answered. "This is what we deserve."

Yes, we did, I thought, and added a postscript to my T2C list: "You deserve it!"

THINGS TO CHANGE

1. Capitalize on skills (Put passions into action)

2. Minimize visits to dentist (Find healthy outlets for stress)

3. Read business books, take classes (Keep learning)

4. Don't compare yourself to others (Love who you are)

5. Don't forget the care and feeding of friends (Stay connected)

6. Curtail time spent watching *Law & Order* (Be present)

7. Earn designation (Keep developing)

8. Remember my blessings (Be grateful)

9. Take charge of my hair (Step into your power)

10. Keep self-deprecation to self (Be positive)

11. Take self-defense classes (Be strong)

12. Cardio exercises are good for you (Be healthy)

13. Make my own vacation plans (Take charge)

14. Pursue a job, hobby, or volunteer opportunities (Meet your own needs)

15. Reconnect with old friends (Make time to nurture relationships)

16. Take it one day at a time (Live now)

17. Practice yoga (Breathe)

18. Don't be gullible/clueless (Be aware)

19. Trust your instincts (Listen to your intuition)

20. Yell without crying (Acknowledge all of your feelings)

21. Tell the ones you love that you love them, daily (Share your heart)

22. Avoid insincerity (Be true to yourself)

You deserve it!

❉

Thank you for reading *Here, Home, Hope.* I sincerely hope you enjoyed the story and were inspired by the characters I created. The questions that follow are suggestions for further discussion. If you'd like to read more Q&A and information about the characters in the book, or if you want to find out about my next novel, please visit www.KairaRouda.com.

I am passionate about empowering women in business specifically, and women in life generally. As a wife to a great husband and the mom of four kids, I know what it's like to try to have it all and, in the end, discover that it's really about having what you want. So, here's to a robust discussion. And if you'd like me to join in, send me a Facebook message or find me on Twitter. I'd love to talk with your group.

QUESTIONS AND TOPICS
FOR DISCUSSION

When we first meet Kelly Mills Johnson, she has the perfect suburban life: married to a successful attorney, living in a fabulous house in an upscale neighborhood, mother of two adorable boys, and she has the summer off from parenting while her sons are at camp in Maine. Yet, she's grinding her teeth to a pulp and crying at the drop of a hat. So, why is she unhappy, and what is driving her need to change? Do you think there is anything wrong with her life? Why do you think she's restless, searching? Does the revelation of her cancer scare resonate with you?

Kelly's archrival is Rachel White, a woman she describes as her personal Gladys Kravitz and a militia mom. What is it about Rachel that stirs such animosity in Kelly? And why, as women, do we often work against each other instead of together?

How would you describe the relationship between Charlotte and Kelly? How does the fact that Charlotte was a friend of Kelly's younger sister first affect their relationship?

How does Kelly view her friend, Kathryn, at the beginning of the novel? How does her perception of Kathryn change and how do they help balance each other by the end of the story?

What is it that Kathryn represents in today's society? Does being a powerful corporate woman, by definition, mean disappointment and heartache in a woman's personal life?

In your opinion, are more women today achieving a greater understanding of and discussing the truth of motherhood and the many different ways to be a "good mother"?

Why is Kelly's visceral response to Bruce Majors so negative? Does she have any justification for her feelings?

Knowing that each character in the novel has her own struggles, whose problems do you see as the most severe? As all of the women attempt to assert themselves, each in her own way, who does it the best? Is it true that there is no one way to find balance and happiness in life?

Why does Kelly talk to her car? Do you find yourself personifying anything around you? And what does Oreo mean to her?

Melanie represents the teenager in all of us, yet, she is a tragic figure throughout most of the story. Do you think Melanie helps to propel Kelly's change?

Have you ever known anyone with an eating disorder? What does such a condition reveal about someone's self-esteem and personality type? How, as a culture, have we continued to fuel this problem?

What does Gavin represent in *Here, Home, Hope*? Why wasn't he at Melanie's illegal party? Why is he there for Melanie when all signs point to him leaving?

What do you think of Kelly and Patrick's relationship? How is their family? Do the parents have a close relationship with their sons?

Which of Kelly's Things to Change resonated with you? Why?

Do you think Bruce and Charlotte love each other? Will Bruce be able to be there, fully committed to his family, this time around?

What did Kathryn discover in Montana? Have you ever had a similar retreat or spent time focusing on yourself?

How did Kelly grow and change throughout the story? What did she find? Is life balance something you find externally, through roles, or internally, through your heart?

Which characters best represent each of the words in the title, *Here, Home, Hope*?

ACKNOWLEDGMENTS

THERE ARE SO MANY PEOPLE WHO HAD A PART IN MAKING MY dream of this book come true.

First—*you.* Thank you for choosing *Here, Home, Hope.* As a debut novelist, I experience no greater joy than seeing someone reading the book I wrote and, I hope, enjoying it.

To the supportive circle of talented and generous women novelists, thank you for welcoming me with such open arms.

To all my social media friends, thank you for your encouragement during the creation of this novel and through the process of bringing it to life. I have met some amazing, supportive, and light-filled people online, and my life is better with you and your tweets and Facebook messages in it.

To my lifetime friends, who are like family—those I grew up with in Columbus, I met in Nashville, and have embraced me in Malibu. Thank you for giving me the blessing of roots. And particularly for supporting this book, thank you to: Elizabeth Paulsen, Beth Dinsmore, Lynnie Biglow, Meg Melvin, Lonnie Galate, Connie Ballenger, Sarah Bacha, Trish Cadwallader, Kathleen Cottingham, Catherine Cassone, Laura Rosenthal,

Mary Beth Thomas, Nell Ivy Prince, Joellyn Helman, Kathleen Murphy, Cathy Walker, Karen Kasich, Maureen Miller, Sheila Elsbrock, Valerie Baker, Dianette Wells, Penelope Stockinger, Jerri Churchill, Allen Young, Bonny Fowler, Lisa Bishoff, Jane Roslovic, Lynne Damer, Leslie Welsh, Julie Trotter, Cheryl Macey, Marie Wexler, Lori Webster, Susan Berg, Kristen Kieffer, Melanie Brown, Melissa Wallace, Linda Little, Arthur Joseph, Jackie Cassara, Kelly Meyer, Kathy Adams, Karen Rich, Elizabeth Lamont, Nora Wendell, Angie Ball, Ellen Schneider, Merlin Clark, Susan Meeder, Axelinta Martin, Lisa Farriss, and Allen Young. (I know I forgot someone important, so I will thank you first in the next book.)

To my family. You are my heart, my inspiration. My sons, Trace, Shea, and Dylan, and my daughter, Avery—I'm so proud to be your mom. To my husband, Harley. And to my mutt, Oreo, who is very much a part of my life and this book. To Lisha and Halsey Wise, Colleen and Brian Sturdivant, and all of my nieces and nephews, thank you. To my parents, Frederick Sturdivant and Patricia Robinson Sturdivant, and my great aunts Ilse Kelso and Edie Hauk, and to Harley Rouda Sr.

To my writing teachers: Dr. Vereen Bell and the Vanderbilt University English department, Doral Chenoweth, Adrienne Bosworth, Michael Chevy Castranova, Lenore Brown, Ben Cason, Linda Kast, Anne Collette. And to Virginia Gardier, my first librarian at Burbank Elementary School, for instilling her love of books in me. Thank you.

And finally, to my book team for keeping hope alive and turning my dreams into reality: thanks to book publicist extraordinaire Crystal Patriarche and the amazing team at Greenleaf, especially Tanya Hall, Kristen Sears, Sheila Parr, Carrie Winsett, Bryan Carroll, and my wonderful editor, Linda W. O'Doughda.

ABOUT THE AUTHOR

KAIRA STURDIVANT ROUDA IS ALL ABOUT EMPOWERING women like those in this, her debut novel. An award-winning entrepreneur, marketer, speaker, and author, she has founded numerous companies, including Real You, and she was the brand creator of Real Living Real Estate, the nation's first women-focused real estate brand. Her business book, *Real You Incorporated: 8 Essentials for Women Entrepreneurs* (Wiley, 2008), was an Amazon.com bestseller and USA Book Awards winner.

As an authority on entrepreneurship, branding, marketing to women, and work-life balance, Kaira has been a speaker at conferences across the country. She has been featured in *Entrepreneur* magazine, on Fox Business, ABC, NBC, WomenEntrepreneur. com, and on the ABC Radio Network, among others. She is a favorite interviewee and contributor to online women's communities and was recently named to the *Forbes* list of the Top 30 Women Entrepreneurs to Follow on Twitter and as one of TwitterGrader's Most Powerful Women on Twitter.

Named 2008 Best Entrepreneur by the Stevie Awards for Women in Business, Kaira has also been listed as one of the 2008 top ten real estate newsmakers and top fifty most influential women in real estate by the industry's trends report. For her marketing work and influence, she's received multiple Addy, Webby, Telly, Communicator, Prism, WebAward, and W3 awards.

Also active in her community, Kaira created Central Ohio's first homeless shelter for families, served two terms on the board of the Mid-Ohio Food Bank, and served on the boards of the YWCA, March of Dimes, and The Wexner Center for the Arts, among others. She is an underwriter of The Women's Fund. She has received numerous awards for her civic service, and she also volunteers countless hours at her kids' schools.

Kaira is a magna cum laude graduate of Vanderbilt University with a BA in English, and she has taken numerous graduate-level writing courses. She has studied with The Writer's Studio in New York and has attended writer's conferences, including Antioch Writer's Workshop and the Maui Writer's Conference.

Kaira and her husband, Harley, have four children. After spending most of their married life in Columbus, Ohio, they recently relocated to the beach in Southern California. Visit Kaira on her website at www.KairaRouda.com and follow Kaira on Twitter.com/KairaRouda and Facebook.